A Robot W
Of Its Own...

Jeff said, "Look here, I'm asking a question. You've got to answer. That's an order, and you've got to obey an order."

From under the hat came a small and muffled, "Do I have to? Can't we be partners?"

"Partners! Well, Norby, I see now why your other owners had trouble with you. You spent too much time with an old spacer who was so alone that he forgot you were a robot and treated you like another human being. You're not one, you know. You're my teaching robot, and you're not going to be able to do much teaching if you act insubordinate."

The hat elevated slightly, and Norby's eyes peeked over the rim of the barrel. Only part of them could be seen. "That's not why the other owners had trouble with me. I just didn't want them. I was wrong about them, so I made them take me back."

"Next you'll say you made a mistake with me, and make *me* take you back."

"I might—if you act the way you did just then..."

JANET AND ISAAC ASIMOV

THE NORBY CHRONICLES

ACE SCIENCE FICTION BOOKS
NEW YORK

The Norby Chronicles has been
previously published as two titles,
Norby the Mixed-Up Robot, and
Norby's Other Secret.

All the characters and events portrayed
in this book are fictitious.

This Ace Science Fiction book contains
the complete text of the two original
hardcover editions. It has been reset
in a typeface designed for easy
reading and was printed from
new film.

THE NORBY CHRONICLES

An Ace Science Fiction Book/published by arrangement with
Walker and Company

PRINTING HISTORY
Walker and Company editions published 1983, 1984
Ace Science Fiction edition/April 1986

ISBN: 0-441-58633-3

Ace Science Fiction Books are published by
The Berkley Publishing Group,
200 Madison Avenue, New York, New York 10016.
PRINTED IN THE UNITED STATES OF AMERICA

NORBY
THE MIXED-UP ROBOT

To all who like our robot stories,
especially to
H. Read Evans and Robert E. Warnick

1

Into Trouble and
Out of School

"Trouble?" asked Jeff, a little shakily. "Why am I in trouble?" He was only fourteen, for all his height, and it seemed to him that he had been asking that question for at least twelve of those years.

At first he had had to ask it of his parents, then his older brother, his teacher, and his computer control. It hadn't been too bad then, but having to ask it now of the head of the Space Command was setting a new record. He didn't exactly feel good about it.

Standing right next to Jeff was Agent Two Gidlow, who was no help at all. He was dressed entirely in gray, and his angry red eyes glared at Jeff with contempt. Even his skin seemed sallow and off-color.

"You're not only *in* trouble," Gidlow said to Jeff. "You *are* trouble." He turned to Admiral Yobo and cut the air horizontally with a sweep of his hand, as if that were Jeff's neck it was passing through. "Admiral, when a troublemaker muddles the computers. . . ."

The admiral stayed calm. The Space Academy, which was under Space Command, had serious problems to face and he was at the cutting edge of it all. The matter of a misbehaving cadet was not something he had to twist his insides over.

Besides, he liked Jeff, who was the kind of tall and clumsy teenager he himself had once been some years ago (though that was beside the point), and he found himself wearied now and then by Gidlow's strenuous disciplinarianism (though that was beside the point, too).

"See here, Gidlow," said Admiral Yobo with a mild frown corrugating his wide, black forehead, "why all the fuss? Remember that you are not part of the academy and have no authority here. If you're going to follow up every prank by hauling the cadet in question into my office to be grilled by

Federation Security Control, I'm going to have no time for anything else. All I've gotten so far is that he was trying to sleep-learn, and there's nothing in the rules against that."

"If you do it right, there isn't, Admiral," said Gidlow. "Doing it wrong is another thing. He tied into the main computer network—he says by accident—"

"Of *course* by accident, Agent Gidlow," said Jeff earnestly. He pushed his curly brown hair out of his eyes and stood as straight as he could so he'd be taller than the agent. "I mean why should I do it on purpose?"

Gidlow smiled unpleasantly. His rather pointed teeth seemed as gray as his clothing and his sallow skin. "If you prefer, Cadet, you did it out of stupidity, which is no better. Admiral, I bring this to you because it is a security expulsion matter, and that's for you to handle."

"Security?"

"The way this cadet tied himself into the main computer network—by accident, he says—has resulted in the kitchen computer getting the wrong set of data."

"Data? What data?"

Gidlow pursed his lips, "It would not be proper to discuss it before a cadet."

"Don't be a fool, Gidlow. If this is an expulsion matter, the young man has a right to know what he's done."

"One thing is—and it may be enough all by itself—as a result of his idiotic link-up, *everything* is being filtered through the kitchen computer. And this means, among other things, that all the recipes are now in Martian Colony Swahili."

The admiral, who had been playing with the buttons on his desk, began to chuckle as he stared into his private viewer. "I see that one Jefferson Wells, age fourteen, failed to pass Martian Colony Swahili last semester."

"Yes, sir," said Jeff, trying not to fidget. "I didn't seem to get the hang of it. I'm doing makeup now, sir, and I was trying to sleep-learn before the final exam next week. I'm terribly sorry about the computer. I thought I was following the directions correctly, and I can't think where I went wrong."

"You can't think, period," said Gidlow. "What it amounts to, of course, Admiral, is that until the recipes are reconverted into Terran Basic, or until the kitchen computer is reprogrammed to handle Martian Swahili, there's no way of running the kitchen. No one in Space Command is going to be able to eat. We won't even be able to have canned food released. I think," he added glumly, "we might be able to get a supply of stalk celery that hasn't yet been indexed."

"What!" roared Yobo.

Jeff stirred uneasily. He remembered with a sinking sensation that Admiral Yobo was famous for his thorough knowledge of Martian Swahili, including its colorful expletives— and also for his prodigious appetite.

"Yes, sir," said Gidlow stiffly.

"But that's ridiculous," said Admiral Yobo through clenched teeth. "The computer should *know* Martian."

Gidlow looked sidewise at Jeff, who was trying to stiffen his stand at attention even further. He said, almost in a whisper, "Very important secrets have been shoved into the kitchen computer, along with everything else, and Computer Control now says that everything in the kitchen computer is classified. That means the cook-robots won't work, and it will be a long haul before we can get into the kitchen computer to do anything about it."

"Which means," said the admiral, "it will be a long haul before I—before any of us can get anything to eat."

"Yes, sir, which is why this is expulsion material. In fact, we're going to have to take this cadet mentally apart before we expel him, in order to find out if he's learned any classified material."

"But Mr. Gidlow," said Jeff a little hoarsely, for his mouth had gone dry with fright—he had heard stories about what could happen to people under mental invasion—"I don't know any Swahili, not even now. The sleep-learning didn't do any good, so I didn't get any classified material. I didn't get *anything* except some strange Martian recipes—"

"Strange?" said the admiral, glowering. "You think Martian food is strange?"

"No, sir, that's not what I meant—"

"Admiral," Gidlow said, "he clearly got classified information he thinks are recipes. He *must* be taken apart."

Jeff felt desperate. "There's nothing classified in me. Just recipes. What makes them strange is that they're in Martian Colony Swahili, which I keep telling you I don't understand."

"Then how do you know they're recipes? Eh? Eh? Admiral, this little troublemaker is convicting himself with his own mouth."

"I know the Martian names for some of their dishes," said Jeff. "That's how I know. I like to go to Martian restaurants. My brother used to take me to them all the time. He always says there's nothing like Martian cooking."

"Quite right." Admiral Yobo stopped glowering and nodded. "Quite right. Your brother has good sense."

"That has nothing to do with anything, Admiral," said Gidlow. "The cadet will have to leave school and come with me. I'll find out what he knows."

"I can't leave school," said Jeff. "The semester is almost over, and I've signed up for summer school so I can learn advanced robotics and invent a hyperdrive."

Gidlow sniggered. "With your record, you'll probably use the hyperdrive to send Space Command into the Sun. No one's invented a hyperdrive, and no one ever will. And if anyone ever does, it won't be a numbskull like you. You're not going back to school, because you're suspended—permanently, I hope."

Yobo said very quietly, "Am I not the one to make that decision?"

"Yes, Admiral," said Gidlow. "But under the circumstances, you'll find you can't make any other decision. Where matters of security are concerned—"

"Please," Jeff said faintly, "it was all an accident." The dark, paneled walls of the admiral's private office seemed to be closing in on him, and Gidlow seemed to be getting bigger and grayer.

"Accident? Hah! You're a danger to the Solar Federation," said Gidlow. "And even if you weren't, your stay at the academy is over. It so happens, Admiral, that Cadet Jefferson Wells's tuition payments are long overdue. I have investigated the matter and found that there is no money with which to make the payment. The Wells family corporation is bankrupt. Farley Gordon Wells—the so-called Fargo Wells—has seen to that."

"No! That's a l— That's not true!" Jeff shouted in outrage.

Admiral Yobo bent forward in his enormous chair. "Fargo Wells is the head of the family?"

"Yes, sir," said Gidlow. "Do you know him?"

"Only slightly, only slightly," said Yobo without any expression in his face. "He used to be in the fleet."

"Forced to resign—because of general incompetence, I suspect. It clearly runs in the family. And he's just as incompetent in handling the family finances."

"It's not so! It's not so!" Jeff said.

"If it's not incompetence, then it's general sabotage. It's the only alternative. He could be in the pay of Ing's League for Power. One of Ing's spies."

"You're wrong!" shouted Jeff. "My brother is no traitor. He wasn't forced to resign. He *had* to resign when our parents were killed in an accident and there was no one else to run the family shipping business. And I'm sure he did a good job."

"Such a good job," said Gidlow, "that he didn't even leave you enough money to pay your tuition. Which doesn't matter, because even if you had a million credits, you would have to leave—and that should be a consolation to you. You will come with me to Security Control for prolonged probing. And if you know where your brother is, I'll send you to him when we're quite through with you." Gidlow looked up at the admiral. "I tried to locate Fargo Wells and failed."

"I don't know why," said Admiral Yobo calmly. "I've consulted Computer Central, and there seems to have been no trouble." His fingers stabbed quickly at the control buttons on his desk, and the screen on the wall lit up.

Jeff's heart leaped as his older brother's image appeared. He needed Fargo's strength and cheer—but that was only an initial feeling, followed by sudden dismay. There was no familiar twinkle in Fargo's sharp blue eyes, and his rumpled black hair was neatly combed.

I really am in trouble, Jeff thought. Even Fargo isn't letting himself be himself on my account.

Fargo's holographic image nodded gravely. "I see that you have company, Admiral, and I can guess the reason. Does our Mr. Gidlow believe that Jeff is in Ing's pay? I admit that my kid brother is big for his age, but no Space Cadet should be forced to undergo one of Gidlow's famous probings. Even the matter of Ing the Ingrate should not justify that."

"Your guesses miss the mark, *Mister* Wells," Gidlow said stiffly. "It is not that we suspect your brother of being in league with Ing—though there are few we can completely trust these sad days. We merely want to find out what classified material he learned from the computer in Martian Swahili, and I assure you we will. You will not stop me, Mr. Wells."

"Gidlow, I admire your firm and absolute assurance, but Space Academy is part of Space Command," said Yobo, "and when probing is in question, I somehow suspect that *I* am the final authority."

"When matters of security are concerned, we cannot have divided responsibility, Admiral. With respect, I make the decisions there."

"With respect, Gidlow, you don't." Yobo rose majestically, looming up like Mons Olympus on his native Mars. "I will decide what's to be done with the boy."

Suddenly Fargo laughed and began to speak in rapid Martian Colony Swahili.

Gidlow gasped, while Admiral Yobo clenched his huge fists and frowned.

Jeff felt bewildered. "Fargo, what are you doing?"

"Mentioning a few state secrets, little brother."

The Admiral looked down at Jeff. "You didn't understand a word of that, did you?"

"No, sir."

"He's lying," Gidlow said.

"I don't think he is," said Yobo. "It would have taken a polished actor to remain blank-faced, considering what Fargo Wells said. It is quite safe to accept the fact that Wells has just proved, in his little charade, that the boy's attempt to sleep-learn failed, as he said it did. He may return to the academy."

"I must protest, Admiral," said Gidlow. "The director of the academy has admitted to me that the boy's tuition is so far overdue that only his excellent—his *previously* excellent—record has kept him in school. She said she thought the boy could get a scholarship, but in view of his damage to the computers, that is not in the range of possibility now."

As Admiral Yobo began to glower again, Fargo Wells intervened smoothly. "There is something in what Gidlow says, Admiral. We don't have much money, and we can't pay any tuition. It's almost summer and my brother can probably use a vacation, and—well, we may be able to begin to restore our fortunes in the interval." He winked at Jeff.

But Jeff drew back at the suggestion. "I don't want a vacation, Admiral. I like it at the academy. I want to join the fleet some day."

"Not this summer," said Fargo flatly. "And it will be worthwhile for you, Jeff. We're not completely penniless. We have a scoutship, and we can get spacer jobs, which will be useful experience. There's even enough to get you back to Earth by transmit so that we can celebrate summer solstice together."

At any other time, Jeff's heart would have bounded at the thought. Summer solstice was tomorrow, and the entire system would be at one in its celebration. All the giant space homes, or "spomes," each with their tens of thousands of inhabitants— the Lunar State, the Martian Colony—all kept the conventions of the calendar of the Earth's Northern Hemisphere. (Even Australia had finally given in.) It was in deference to the original Solar Federation headquarters in the old UN on the Northern Hemisphere island of what was now the Manhattan International Territory, which had agreed to consider itself, rather reluctantly, part of the Solar Federation.

Jeff turned pleadingly to the admiral. "If I can be allowed to stay at the academy, sir, for my summer courses—"

Fargo intervened. "Kids that mix up computers need to get away from them and stay awhile in a nice primitive spot like Manhattan. Under my care, of course. Don't you agree, Admiral?" Fargo and Yobo exchanged a long look.

Jeff felt resentful. He hated it when grown-ups talked over his head as if he were not there. Fargo hardly ever did that. What was the matter?

"Yes," said Yobo. "Go and pack, Jefferson Wells."

"But I—" began Gidlow.

"The boy goes home," said Yobo. "He's of no interest to you."

"Come on, Jeff," said Fargo. "The faster you hurry, the sooner you'll be deprived of Gidlow's fascinating company. Come on, and I'll tell you interesting stories about the misdeeds and ambitions of Ing the Ingrate. Remember the motto TGAF, eh? See you tonight." His image faded out.

"What does that motto mean?" demanded Gidlow.

Jeff thought quickly. "That's just Fargo's way. He means all difficulties can be overcome."

"TGAF? All difficulties can be overcome? Admiral, there is some sort of conspiracy—"

"No," said Jeff. "It's just the way he thinks of difficulties. He's so handsome that...well, TGAF means 'the girls are findable.'"

The admiral burst into a loud roar of laughter. "That's authentic Fargo," he said, and Jeff tried to stifle his sigh of relief.

"In any case," said Gidlow, "this boy will not be coming back to the academy. Be sure of that, boy!" He swirled out, the very lines of his back showing his anger.

Why does he hate me so? Jeff wondered.

But Admiral Yobo, looking down kindly at him, said, "Things will be better after a while, Jefferson. I once knew your parents, you know. They were good friends of mine—and good seismologists, too, till Io got them. Not good businesspeople, though, any more than Fargo is." He held out a slip of paper to Jeff.

"What is this, sir?"

"A credit voucher. Use it to buy a teaching robot, one that can tie in to the Solar Educational System. Learn enough to get back into the academy on a scholarship."

Jeff put his hands behind his back. "Sir, I won't be able to pay you back."

"I think you will. I don't think Fargo would ever be able to, but somehow I suspect you have a firmer hold on common sense than he has. Anyway, it isn't that much money, because I'm not all that rich—or all that generous. You'll have to buy a *used* robot. Here, take it! That's an order."

"Yes, sir," said Jeff, saluting automatically. He hurried out, confused and worried. TGAF? Was Fargo right?

2

Choosing a Robot

Packing did not take much time. Cadets owned very little besides clothes and notes, although Jeff did have one valuable item, thanks to Fargo—a book. It was a genuine antique, a leather-bound volume with yellow-edged pages that had never been restored. It contained all of Shakespeare's plays in the original, in the very language from which Terran Basic was derived.

Jeff hoped nobody from Security Control would stop him, open the Shakespeare, and see Fargo's underlining in "Henry the Fifth." Or that, if they did, they wouldn't understand the old language.

"The game's afoot," Henry had cried out, but what game was Fargo after with his TGAF? Was it Ing?

Jeff told his closer friends among his classmates about the bankruptcy and the kitchen computer, but he went no farther than that. He put the book into his duffel bag with a fine air of indifference, even though he was alone in his quarters. One should always practice caution.

He took the shuttle to Mars.

Once on Mars, he made a quick meal of spicy eggplant slices on cheese, as only Martian cooks could make it; then he lined up at the Mars City matter transmitter. Through the dome he could see the distant vastness of Mons Olympus, the largest heap of matter on any world occupied by human beings. It made him feel very small.

And very poor.

Maybe I should give the credit voucher to Fargo, Jeff thought. He needs it more than I need a teaching robot. But I've always wanted a teaching robot, came the immediately rebellious afterthought.

"Wells next!"

For a second, Jeff almost decided to turn on his heel. Why

9

should he take the transmit? It was so expensive.

Matter transmitters had been in use for years, but they still required enormous power and very complex equipment, and the cost of using them reflected that. Most people took the space ferry from Mars to Luna and then to Earth. Why shouldn't Jeff be one of them? Especially now with the family near bankruptcy?

Still, the ferry took over a week, and with the transmit he would be home today. And Fargo clearly wanted him there in a hurry.

All this went through Jeff's head in the time it took for the most momentary of hesitations. He went into the room. It was packed with people, luggage, and freight boxes. The people all looked rich or official, and Jeff slumped in his seat hoping no one would notice him.

As he waited for the power to go on, he wished again that he could invent a hyperdrive. Everyone knew there actually was a thing called hyperspace, because that's what hycoms used for the instantaneous voice and visual communication that was now so common. It was by hycom that Fargo's image had appeared in the admiral's office, for instance. That's what "hycom" meant, after all: "hyperspatial communication."

Well then, if they could force radiation through hyperspace, why couldn't they force matter through it? Surely there should be some way of devising a motor that would let a spaceship go through hyperspace, bypassing the speed of light limit that existed in normal space. It probably meant that matter would have to be converted into radiation first, and then the radiation would have to be reconverted into matter. Or else....

Fifty years ago, an antigrav device had been invented, and before then everyone had said *that* was impossible. Now antigravs could be manufactured small enough to fit into a car.

Maybe the two impossibles had a connection. If you used antigravs in connection with matter transmitters (that operated only at sub-light speeds), you could—

He blacked out. One always did that in transmit.

There was no sensation of time passage, but the room was different. It held the same contents, but it was a different room. He could see the clock in the cavernous chamber outside. Not quite ten minutes had passed, so the transmission had been carried through at—he calculated rapidly in his head, allowing for the present positions of Mars and Earth in their orbits—not quite half light-speed.

Jeff adjusted his watch, walked out of the transmitter room, and was on Earth. He wondered if his molecules had survived the transmission properly. Now wasn't this a case of conversion into radiation and back, after a fashion? Surely it could be improved to the point where—oh well!

The matter-transmission people always insisted that it was impossible for molecules to be messed up in transit, and no one had ever claimed damage. Still. . . .

Nothing I can do about it anyway, Jeff decided.

But if you were going to take the risk, he thought, why not do the thing right? Hyperdrive would be much the better deal. It might still mean conversion to radiation and back, but at least you could go *anywhere,* and that would give you much more in return for the risk.

Right now, by transmit, you could only go to another transmit station. If you wanted to go somewhere that didn't have a transmit, you would have to go by ferry or freighter to the nearest transmit, and that could take anywhere from weeks to years. No wonder the Federation was stuck in the Solar System.

And that's why Ing's rebellion was so dangerous.

Jeff called the family apartment from Grand Central Station, Manhattan's public transmit terminal, to let the housekeeping computer have enough time to send cleaning robots out to make a last-minute cleanup of the dust.

The apartment, when he got there, looked as always. Old, of course, but that was as it should be. All the Wellses had been proud to own an apartment on Fifth Avenue in a building that had been kept going, apparently with glue and wishes, for centuries. It had disadvantages, but it was homier.

"Welcome, Master Jeff," said the housekeeper computer from the wall.

"Hi," Jeff grinned. It was nice to be scanned and recognized.

"There is a message for you from your brother Fargo, Master Jeff," said the computer, and a cellostrip pushed out of the message slot with a faint buzz.

It was the address of a used-robot shop, which meant that Fargo and Admiral Yobo had talked again after Jeff had left the office.

Why? Jeff wondered. For old time's sake? Did Gidlow know?

It was still afternoon in Manhattan. There was time to go to the shop.

Jeff felt faintly uneasy about buying the robot now that he was about to make a purchase. Should he argue with Fargo and try to make him take the admiral's money for himself?

But the admiral had to have talked with Fargo on the subject. There had to be something behind all this, but what?

Before leaving, Jeff dialed a hamburger from the kitchen computer, which was always in perfect order, thanks to Fargo. He said, "First things first," and hunger came first, even for him, let alone for a growing boy. (How much more will I grow? thought Jeff.) It was a good hamburger.

The self-important fat little man who ran the used-robot shop considered the sum Jeff announced he had at his disposal and didn't seem at all impressed. "If you use that for a down payment," he said, "you can have an almost-new model like this. A *very* good buy."

What he referred to as "this" was one of the new, vaguely humanoid cylindrical robots in use as teachers at all the expensive schools. They could tie in to main computer systems in any city and have access to any library or information outlet. They were smooth, calm, respectful, good teachers.

Jeff studied the almost-new model, wishing that manufacturers had not decided years ago to make intelligent robots look only *slightly* like human beings. The theory was that people wouldn't want robots that could be mistaken for real people.

Maybe they were right, but Jeff would much rather have one that could be mistaken for a real person than one that could be mistaken only for a cartoon of a real person.

The almost-new model had a head like a bowling ball, with a sensostrip halfway up like a slipped halo. It was the sensostrip that served as eyes, ears, and so on, keeping the robot in general touch with the universe.

He stepped closer to look at the serial number above the senostrip. A low one would mean it was fairly old and not as almost-new as the manager of the store made it sound. The number was quite low. What's more, Jeff didn't like the color combination of the sensostrip. Each one was different, for easier differentiation of individual robots, and this one was clashing and unesthetic.

But it didn't matter whether Jeff liked or didn't like any part of that robot. If he used his money for a down payment, where would the rest come from? He just couldn't commit himself to monthly payments for a year or two.

He looked about vaguely at the transparent stasis boxes, each of which held a robot with a brain that was not in operation. Was there something he could afford here? Something he could buy in full? An older model that worked?

He noticed a stasis box in a corner, all but obscured by others in front of it. He wriggled between two boxes and moved one of them in order to look into it. Half-hidden like that, it had to be a not-so-good robot, but that was exactly what he could afford.

Actually, what was inside didn't look like a robot at all. Of course, it had to be one because that was what stasis boxes were for. Any intelligent robot had to be kept in stasis until sold. If the positronic brain were activated and then kept waiting to be sold, it would get addled.

Just standing around doing nothing, thought Jeff, that would addle *me*. "What's in that box?" said Jeff abruptly.

The manager craned his neck to see which box Jeff was referring to, and a look of displeasure crossed his face. "Hasn't that thing been disposed of yet? You don't want that, young man."

"It must be an awfully old robot," said Jeff. The thing in the box looked like a metal barrel about sixty centimeters high, with a metal hat on top of it. It didn't seem to have legs or arms or even a head. Just a barrel and a hat. The hat had a circular brim and a dome on top.

Jeff continued to push the other boxes out of the way. He bent down to see the object more clearly.

It really was a metal barrel, dented and battered, with a label on it. It was an old paper label that was peeling off. It said, "Norb's nails." Jeff could now distinguish places in the barrel where arms might come out if circular plates were dilated.

"Don't bother with that," said the manager, shaking his head violently. "It's a museum piece, if any museum would take it. It's not for sale."

"But what is it? Is it really a robot?"

"It's a robot all right. One of the very ancient R2 models. There's a story to it if anyone is interested. It was falling apart, and an old spacer bought it, fixed it up—"

"What old spacer?" Jeff had heard stories about the old explorers of the Solar System, the human beings who went off alone to find whatever might be strange or profitable or both. Fargo knew all the stories and complained that independent spacers were getting rare now that Ing's spies were everywhere, and now that Ing's pirates stole from anyone who dared travel to little-known parts of the system without official Federation escort.

"The story is that it was someone named McGillicuddy, but I never met anyone who ever heard of him. Did *you* ever hear of him?"

"No, sir."

"He's supposed to have died half a century ago, and his robot was knocked down to my father at an auction. I inherited him, but I certainly don't want him."

"Why isn't it for sale, then?"

"Because I've tried selling it. It doesn't work right, and it's always returned. I've got to scrap it."

"How much to you want for it, sir?"

The manager looked at him thoughtfully. "Didn't you just hear me tell you that it doesn't work right?"

"Yes, sir. I understand that."

"Would you be willing to sign a paper saying you understand that, and that you cannot return it even if it doesn't work right?"

Jeff felt a cold hand clutching at his chest as he thought of the admiral's money being thrown away, but he *wanted* that robot with its spacer heritage and its odd appearance. Certainly it would be a robot such as no one else had. He said, with teeth that had begun to chatter a bit, ". . . sure, I'll sign if you take the money I have in full payment and give me a receipt saying 'paid in full.' I also want a certificate of ownership entered into the city computer records."

"Huh!" the manager said. "You're underage."

"I look eighteen. Don't ask to see my papers, and you can say you thought I was of age."

"All right. I'll get the papers filled out."

He turned away, and Jeff squatted. He leaned forward and peered into the stasis box. This McGillicuddy must have put the workings of a robot into an empty barrel used for Norb's Nails.

Jeff looked more closely, putting his face against the dusty plastic and lifting one hand to block off light reflections. He decided that the hat was not all the way down. A band of darkness underneath showed that the robot had been put in stasis with its head not completely inside the barrel.

And there was a strange thin wire stretching from inside the darkness to the side of the stasis box.

"Don't touch that!" shouted the manager, who had happened to look up from his records.

It was too late. Jeff's outstretched finger touched the stasis box.

The manager had hopped over, mopping his forehead with a large handkerchief. "I said don't touch it. Are you all right?"

"Of course," said Jeff, stepping back.

"You didn't get a shock or anything?"

"I didn't feel a thing." But I did feel an emotion, thought Jeff. Awful loneliness. Not mine.

The manager looked at him suspiciously. "I warned you. You can't claim damage or anything like that."

"I don't want to," said Jeff. "What I want is for you to open that stasis box so I can have my robot."

"First you'll sign this paper, which says you're eighteen. I don't want you *ever* bringing it back." He kept grumbling to himself as he put it through the computoprint device that scanned the writing and turned it into neat print in triplicate.

Jeff read the paper rapidly. "You look eighteen," the manager said. "Anyone would say so. Now let me see your identification."

"It will tell you my birthdate."

"Well, cover it with your thumb. I'm not bright and won't notice you've done that. I just want to check your name and signature." He looked at the signature on the card Jeff presented. "All right," he said, "there's your copy. Now, credit voucher, please."

He looked at it, placed it in his credit slot, and returned it to Jeff, who winced, for it meant that virtually everything the admiral had given him had been transferred, quite permanently, from his account into the store's. It left him with practically nothing.

The manager waddled through the mess of boxes and touched the raised number on the dial box of the one that held the robot in the barrel. The top opened. With that, the thin wire slowly withdrew into the barrel, and the hatlike lid seemed to settle down firmly so that the band of darkness disappeared. The manager didn't seem to notice. He was too busy trying to shift the stasis box into better position.

"Careful! Careful!" said Jeff. "Don't hurt the robot."

With its hat up and its wire out, Jeff wondered if the robot had really been in a position to *think*. He felt again a stab of sympathy. If that had been so, it must have been awful to be trapped inside a box, able to think but unable to get out. How long had it been there? It must have felt so helpless.

"Please," he said to the manager. "You're being too rough. Let me help you lift it out."

"Too rough?" said the manager with a sneer. "Nothing can hurt it. For one thing, it's too far gone."

He looked up at Jeff with an unpleasant expression on his face. "You signed that paper, you know. I told you it doesn't work right, so you can't back out. I don't think you can use it for teaching purposes because it doesn't have the attachments that will allow it to tie into the Education System. It doesn't even talk. It just make sounds that I can't make sense of."

Now, for the first time, something happened inside the barrel. The hatlike lid shot up and hit the shopkeeper in the shoulder as he was leaning over the box.

Underneath the lid was half a face. At least that's what it looked like. There were two big eyes—no! Jeff leaned across and saw that there were also two big eyes at the back—or maybe that was the front.

"Ouch," said the manager. He lifted a fist.

Jeff said. "You'll just hurt yourself if you try to hit it, sir. Besides, it's my robot now, and I'll have the law on you if you damage it."

The robot said in a perfectly clear voice that was a high and almost musical tenor. "That vicious man insulted me. He's been insulting me a *lot*. Every time he mentions me, he insults me. I can speak perfectly well, as you can hear. I can speak better than he can. Just because I have no desire to speak to my inferiors, such as that co-called manager, doesn't mean I can't speak."

The manager kept puffing out his cheeks and seemed to be trying to say something, but nothing came out.

Jeff said, quite reasonably, "That robot can certainly speak better than you can right now."

"What's more," said the robot, "I am a perfectly adequate teaching robot, as I will now demonstrate. What is your name, young man?"

"Jeff Wells."

"And what is it you would care to learn?"

"Swahili. The Martian Colony dialect—uh—sir." It suddenly occurred to Jeff that he ought to show a decent respect to a robot that clearly displayed a certain tendency to irascibility and shortness of temper.

"Good. Take my hand and concentrate. Don't let anything distract you."

The little robot's left—or possibly right—side dilated to a small opening, out of which shot an arm with a swivel elbow and two-way palms, so that it was still impossible to tell which was its front and which its back. Jeff took the hand, which had a pleasantly smooth, but not slippery, metallic texture.

"You will now learn how to say 'Good morning, how are you?' in Martian Swahili," said the robot.

Jeff concentrated. His eyebrows shot up, and he said something that clearly made no sense to the manager.

"That's just gibberish," said the manager, shrugging.

"No, it isn't," said Jeff. "I know a *little* Swahili, and what I said was Martian Swahili for 'Good morning, how are you?'; only this is the first time I've been able to pronounce it correctly."

"In that case," said the manager hastily, "you can't expect to get a teaching robot that's in working order for a miserable eighty-five-credits."

"No, I can't," said Jeff, "but that's what I got it for. I have the paper and you have the money, and that ends it, unless you want me to tell the police you tried to sell an inoperable robot to a fourteen-year-old. I'm sure this robot can act inoperable if I ask him to."

The manager was puffing again.

The robot seemed to be getting taller. In fact, it *was* getting taller. Telescoping legs were pushing out of the bottom of the barrel, with feet that faced in both directions. The robot's eyes were now closer to the level of the little shopkeeper, who was a good head shorter than Jeff.

The robot said, "I would suggest, inferior person, that you return the eighty-five credits to this young man, and let him have me for nothing. An inoperable robot is worth nothing."

The manager shrieked and stepped back, falling over a stasis box containing a set of robot weeders. "That thing is dangerous! It doesn't obey the laws of robotics! It threatened me!" He began to shout. "Help! Help!"

"Don't be silly, mister," Jeff said. "He was just making a suggestion. And you can keep the eighty-five credits. I don't want them."

The manager mopped his brow again. "All right, then. Get it out of here. It's your responsibility. I don't ever want to see that robot again. Or you, either."

Jeff walked out, holding the hand of a barrel that had once contained Norb's Nails and had now sprouted two legs, two arms, and half a head.

"You've got a big mouth," said Jeff.

"How can you tell?" said the robot. "I talk through my hat."

"You sure do. What's your name?"

"Well, Mac—that was McGillicuddy—called me Macko, but I didn't like that. Mac and Macko sounds like a hyperwave comedy team. But at least he referred to me as 'he' instead of 'it.' That was something, anyway. It showed respect. What would you like to call me, Jeff?"

Jeff should have corrected the robot. All robots were supposed to put a title before a human name, but it was clear that the robot he had didn't follow customs too well, and Jeff decided he didn't mind that. Besides, he would get tired of being called Master Jeff.

He said, "Have you always been inside a barrel of Norb's Nails?"

"No, only since McGillicuddy found me; that is, since he *repaired* me. He was a genius at robotics, you know." Then, with obvious pride, the robot added, "The barrel is part of me, and I won't wear out. Not ever!"

"Oh, I don't know," said Jeff coolly. "Your label just fell off."

"That's because I don't need a label. This old but serviceable barrel doesn't contain nails any longer. It contains me. I like this barrel. It's good, strong stainless steel."

"All right," said Jeff. "In that case, since this wonderful barrel once held Norb's Nails why don't I call you Norby?"

The robot blinked and said, "Norby . . . Norby . . . ," as though

he were rolling the sound round on his tongue and tasting it—
except that he didn't have a tongue and probably couldn't taste.
Then he said, "I like it. I like it very much."

"Good," said Jeff. And he and Norby walked off, still hand
in hand.

3

In Central Park

The housekeeping computer, not having feelings or much intelligence, didn't disapprove of Norby. That relieved Jeff, who realized that he should have known that the housekeeper would not give him anything to worry about, and would, in fact, be incapable of doing so. Of course, the housekeeper didn't *approve* of Norby, either, but that didn't matter.

Now that he was home and could relax, Jeff surveyed his purchase critically. "Does your head come out of the barrel any further, Norby?"

"No. This is all there is of my head. It's all I need. It's all anyone needs. Does it matter?"

Jeff studied Norby's large, oddly expressive eyes. "I guess it doesn't, but how do you get repaired? Do you come out of the barrel?"

"Certainly not. There's no me to come out of the barrel. it's part of me now. Mac welded me in so tightly, this barrel is my armor, my skeleton. Do you get out of your bones when you see the doctor? Come out of the barrel indeed!"

"Don't get mad about it. I'm just asking. How *do* you get repaired? Let's face it, Norby, I can't afford much in the way of maintenance, so I hope you're not planning on breaking down."

"If you're worrying about cost, Jeff, forget it. I will *never* need repairs. I am good at repairing *other* machines, but as you see me, I will always be." Norby whirled rapidly around on two quickly moving feet, but his eyes kept staring firmly at Jeff. Or the front two did—or was it the back two? "As you see, I work perfectly. Mac was a genius."

"McGillicuddy?"

"Of course. Why use five syllables when one will do? Besides, that's what Mac wanted to be called. Mac. I said to him, "If you want Mac, Mac, Mac you'll get.""

"That's three Macs in a row."

"As many as he wanted for the way he worked me out. Of course, he had help."

"Oh? What kind of help?"

Norby, who had been jiggling happily, came to a dead halt. He stared at Jeff solemnly, then sucked in his head.

"I said, what kind of help?"

Norby said nothing.

Jeff said, "Look here, I'm asking a question. You've got to answer. That's an order, and you've got to obey an order."

From under the hat came a small and muffled, "Do I have to? Can't we be partners?"

"Partners! Well, Norby, I see now why your other owners had trouble with you. You spent too much time with an old spacer who was so alone that he forgot you were a robot and treated you like another human being. You're not one, you know. You're my teaching robot, and you're not going to be able to do much teaching if you act insubordinate."

The hat elevated slightly, and Norby's eyes peeked over the rim of the barrel. Only part of them could be seen. "That's not why the other owners had trouble with me. I just didn't want them. I was wrong about them, so I made them take me back."

"Next you'll say you made a mistake with me, and make *me* take you back."

"I might—if you act the way you did just then. And why should you expect me to obey orders? Would you have bought me if I were just another teaching robot?"

Jeff laughed. "If you put it like that, no. I suppose you'd say it was a weird impulse. I think I liked your looks. You're the funniest-looking thing I ever saw."

"Funny? There's a certain dignity about me. Very gracefully proportioned is what I am."

"All right. Don't get offended again. I guess it was your graceful proportions. It made me buy you on a strange impulse."

"No impulse, either."

"No?"

"No! After the last time I was returned, I managed to keep my head just a little elevated, and I even put out my feeler and grounded it. The manager was entirely too inferior to notice. Anyway, it meant I wasn't going to be sold to just anyone who walked in. I could watch customers and feel them—"

"Feel them?"

"Feel their minds. That's why I knew right away that I liked you and—"

"Thank you, Norby."

"Well, you seemed reasonable and not too uppity. You felt like the kind of person who wouldn't come over all superior to a poor robot. I think maybe I was wrong."

"I apologize, Norby."

"All right. Apology accepted. Anyway, I did my best to appeal to you so you would want to buy me, and I tried to get the manager to say nasty things about me—that wasn't hard—because that would get you to want me more. It worked."

"Okay, then, Norby, we're partners." Jeff realized that Norby had not mentioned the loneliness, so Jeff didn't either. "Could you have fixed that rattletrap taxi we took home from the robot shop?"

"If I had the parts—which would have to be enough to build an entirely new taxi, I think. The taxi's antigrav was so bad we skimmed two feet off the ground most of the way. And the robot brain of the taxi was so old and deteriorated that it should have been scrapped two years ago." Norby sounded distinctly superior.

"Most of the taxis in Manhattan are like that," said Jeff. "Are you going to tell me about Mac and what he did to you and what kind of help he had? I only ask as a friend and partner."

"Oh, sure. No problem. Absolutely. But not now. What I'm going to do right now is plug myself into the house current and enjoy a refreshing electronic bath. I hope you have enough money to pay your electric bill, Jeff."

"So far," said Jeff. "If you don't take baths every hour, that is."

"I am not that gluttonous," said Norby haughtily. He scuttled over to a corner and plugged himself in, his barrel body over the carpet with his legs out just far enough to balance him as he rocked back and forth humming to himself.

Jeff grinned. Whatever this McGillicuddy had done to manufacture Norby, it must have been unique. Jeff had never encountered a robot like Norby, or heard of one either. Wait till Fargo came home and met the thing!

Come to think of it, why wasn't Fargo already home?

•   •   •

Midnight came and went. The summer solstice should be celebrated at dawn. That's what Fargo had said. And he took the celebration seriously, so where was he?

Jeff finally slept, uneasily, because he was worried and because he could hear Norby exploring the apartment, opening books and fiddling with equipment—and he couldn't help wondering if Norby were doing any damage.

But mostly he was worried about Fargo. Fargo was a good brother. He'd been almost like a parent, reliable and responsible, except for his habit of getting into trouble unintentionally and upsetting schedules.

"Wake up! It's almost dawn!"

"Fargo?" said Jeff, rubbing his eyes.

"It's Norby. If you want to celebrate the solstice at dawn in the park, you'd better go."

"But Fargo isn't here, and the park's not all that safe—"

Norby's head popped up to full extent. "Not safe! What are you worrying about? You have me, don't you? I'll protect you."

"You're too little. I need Fargo. He's an expert in martial arts. He's been teaching me, but I'm not as good as he is, and he made me promise I wouldn't go into the park at night without him."

"What are martial arts? Show me."

"All right," said Jeff, getting out of bed and shaking his head woozily, "if you'll let me wash up first."

Fifteen minutes later he was in his pants and shirt. He struck a pose in front of Norby and yelled.

"Well?" said Norby, after waiting a little. "What happens next?"

"You're supposed to attack me."

Norby promptly rushed at Jeff, who leaned back, grabbed one of Norby's arms in passing, and heaved.

The barrel hit the opposite wall and bounced to the floor. All the limbs had been reeled in and all the openings shut as soon as Jeff had let go. The barrel rolled across the room.

"Norby? Are you all right? I didn't mean to throw you so hard. It was just reflex."

No sound came from the barrel.

"Hey, are you damaged, Norby?"

The sound came, muffled and sulky, "I can't be damaged—physically. But my feelings are hurt."

"You're not supposed to have feelings."

"But I do, just the same. Just because you're human doesn't mean you have the right to decide I don't have feelings."

"I'm really sorry. I'll be more careful." Jeff picked up Norby and started toward the door. Norby's barrel was awkward and heavy, and Jeff realized he had a hard task on his hands.

Norby's hat elevated, and his eyes looked at Jeff. "What are you doing, Jeff?"

"I'm carrying you to the park. I thought maybe you wouldn't want to walk on those short legs."

"What you mean is that with your long legs it would be painful for you to shorten your stride to match mine, right?"

"Well, yes."

Norby made a small grinding noise. "You mean well, Jeff, but there's a great deal you don't know."

"I never denied that," said Jeff.

"And well you shouldn't. I'll let you in on a secret."

"What secret?"

"This one," said Norby, extruding a hand that grabbed Jeff's. He then floated upward and forward, pulling a surprised Jeff toward the window.

"You've got antigrav!" shouted Jeff. "Miniaturized anti—"

"Not so loud," said Norby. "We don't need to have everyone hear about it."

"Ouch!" said Jeff, his head grazing the bottom of the lifted windowpane. He had time to be glad that their apartment was so old that it had windows that could open, and then he was sailing across Fifth Avenue toward Central Park. He wasn't dangling downward with an arm being pulled out of its socket, as he would have been if he were holding onto a passive rope. Instead it was as though Norby's antigrav were spread out over him, holding him up, lifing him. . . .

Norby said, "I *thought* I had antigrav, but you can never tell. I suppose I can remember how to work it."

Central Park was beneath them now. Behind them, low in the east, the sky showed a diffuse light behind the skyscrapers even though the sun was not yet up. Beneath them the park was still in the deep shadow of night.

"I've always wondered what personal antigrav would be like," said Jeff, excited and breathless. The wind whipped his curly brown hair back from his forehead.

"It's hard work, if you want to know, and I don't know when my next electric bath will come."

"It seems easy to me. Easy and delightful, like swimming in an ocean of water you can't feel, like swooping through—"

"That's because you're not the one who's producing the antigrav field, so it's no work to you," grumbled Norby. "Don't get so stuck up about how it feels that you forget to hang on. Hold more tightly! Also, tell me where I'm supposed to go for this solstice celebration of yours."

"It's in the Ramble—that wooded section beyond the boathouse, with the boating pond circling 'round to the other side. Go down—now."

"Not so fast. I've got to figure out how. We can't just drop. You'll dent a bone or something. Besides, it's dark, and I can't make my internal light bright enough to show the ground without running out of power. I can't do antigrav and bright light both. What do you think I am? A nuclear powerhouse?" Norby circled, and they sank downward, then up again with a jerk.

"Hey," shouted Jeff, "watch out!"

"Look, I've got to get this right, don't I?" said Norby. "It's not easy to ease into the gravitational field and let yourself sink just right." He grunted. "Okay—now—now. I wish I breathed so I could hold my breath."

"I'll hold mine," said Jeff.

"Good! That helps psychologically. It's hard to make out the ground from the shadow in this dark."

With a thump that rattled his teeth, Jeff found himself on his knees and elbows, which were dug well into moist dirt. His head stuck out over a pool of goldfish in the center of the small grassy clearing. They were lucky—it was the very place Jeff would have had Norby aim for if it had been light enough to see.

Jeff could see the goldfish despite the dark. The pool seemed to be lighted from within, which was odd, because Manhattan was usually too broke for fancy lighting in public parks.

"Norby! Where are you?" Jeff called, trying to shout in a whisper.

The light in the pool brightened, and slowly a shape rose up and out of the water. It was a barrel shape, draped in water lilies. It continued to rise until it was suspended a foot over the water, and then it spun rapidly in the air, scattering drops, as a dog shaking itself would do.

Jeff received some of the spray and shouted, "Hey!"

The barrel slowly stopped spinning. Two legs emerged from the bottom and started a good try at a dignified walk—in the air—down to Jeff.

Norby's hat popped up. "I didn't judge it quite right. I turned on illumination just a little too late. Still, that was an excellent landing, if I do say so myself."

"You'll have to say so yourself," said Jeff, brushing at himself without much effect. "I've got mud all over me, and you've managed to make me good and wet, too."

"You'll dry," said Norby. "The mud will dry, too, and then you can shake it off."

"How about you?" said Jeff. "Are you waterlogged? You won't turn rusty, will you?"

"Nothing damages me," said Norby. "Stainless steel outside; and better than that inside." He carefully untwined a water-lily frond from around his middle and dropped it in the pond with a finicky gesture.

Norby put out his illumination, but it was getting light enough for Jeff to be able to see him even in its absence. "Now I know why a simple judo throw landed you on the dome of your hat," he said.

"You charged before I was ready," Norby said.

"I did no such thing. *You* charged," Jeff said.

"I mean you defended yourself before I was ready."

"No such thing, either. You just can't manage your own technology. You said so yourself when we were antigravving."

"It was hard, I admit, but I managed," Norby said. "Look at that landing."

"You managed imperfectly," Jeff insisted. "That landing nearly drove us through to China."

"Well, I try," said Norby in an aggrieved voice. "You couldn't get any other robot to do this for what you paid for me. Besides, it's not my fault. I was damaged in a spaceship crash, and then Mac fixed me so that I would be undamageable, you see. He used salvaged equipment for that and—"

"What salvaged equipment?" demanded Jeff.

"Oh, well, if you're going to disbelieve everything I tell you, I've got nothing more to say."

"*What* salvaged equipment? Darn it, you've got to answer my questions *sometimes*. You're a robot, aren't you?"

"Yes, I'm a robot, so why don't you understand I've got to tell the truth?"

Jeff took a deep breath. "You're right. If I sounded incredulous, I apologize. What salvaged equipment, Norby?"

"Salvaged equipment from an old spaceship we found on an asteroid."

"That's impossible—I believe you, Norby, I believe you. I know you wouldn't lie, but that's impossible. Nobody's ever found a ship on an asteroid just lying around. Wrecks are always salvaged at once by Space Command. In this computerized age, Space Command always knows when a wreck takes place, and exactly where, too."

"Well, this one wasn't salvaged by Space Command. It was just lying there, and it was salvaged by *us*. And how can I tell you which asteroid it was? There are a hundred thousand of them. It was a small asteroid that looked exactly like all the other small asteroids."

"What happened when he repaired you?"

"He just kept chuckling all the time. He seemed very pleased with himself and kept saying, 'Oh boy, oh boy, wait till they see this.' He was a genius, you know. I asked him what it was all about, but he wouldn't tell me. He said he wanted me to be surprised. And then he died, and I never found out."

"Never found out what?"

"About the things I could do. Like antigrav. And how to do it. Sometimes I can't get things sorted out in time, and that's why you could throw me. And then I don't land right because I don't have enough time to make the judgments I need. Please don't tell anyone about this."

"Are you kidding? Of course not."

"The scientists would take me apart, or try to, in order to find out how I do the things I do, and I don't want them to . . . to try to take me apart, I mean. I'd be glad to tell them if I only knew myself."

Jeff sat back, his arms wrapped around his muddy knees. He looked up at the sky, which was reddening now in the onrush of morning. "You know, I'll bet it was an *alien* spaceship. It would be the first real proof that there is alien intelligence out beyond our Solar System. In fact, Norby, if that were so, *you* would be the first real proof of that."

"But you won't tell. You promised." Norby's voice sounded panicky.

"Never! I won't tell—Friend." Jeff reached out and shook Norby's hand. "But we've got to get on with the solstice celebration."

"All right," said Norby, "but that might not be easy. It seems to me that there's a herd of elephants somewhere."

Footsteps were indeed approaching. Lots of them.

Jeff seized Norby and scuttled behind a bush. Down the path between the trees came a group of people. Each person was holding binoculars.

"Bird-watchers," whispered Jeff.

"What are those?" Norby asked. "A new species of human being? I haven't seen anything like that before."

"That's because you spent too much time in space with McGillicuddy watching asteroids. Human beings like to observe the activities of other animals. These people watch birds, not asteroids."

"You mean they pry into the privacy of birds?"

"Birds don't care."

"But don't these human beings have anything better to do?"

"Watching birds is a good action. Would you rather they stood about and littered?"

"Birds litter. They—"

"Shut up, Norby."

The leading human, an elderly lady in tweeds, stopped beside the fishpond. "Here," she said, "is a good place to watch for owls. We've had them in Central Park for the last century. Before that, they would stop here occasionally, but wouldn't stay. There were always enough rats and mice for them to eat, but either the air was too polluted or the city was too noisy. Either way, they would decide that the price of a good meal was too high. Now they seem to like Manhattan, as all of us good Manhattan patriots do. At least the little screech owls do. I've been told they nest in the trees around here, and since it is not yet sunrise, there's hope we may see an owl on the move."

"I don't want to see an owl on the move," said Norby.

"What's that?" said the tweedy woman sharply. "Who said that? If there's anyone here who doesn't want to see owls, why did you come?"

"I don't like owls. They're probably scary," said Norby.

"Only if you look like a rat," whispered Jeff, "and you don't—though I wouldn't put it past you to act like one. Now keep quiet!"

"There's something behind that bush," said a boy. "Right there!"

"Muggers!" screamed a girl, waving her binoculars. "They'll knock us down and take our binoculars!"

"I don't need your binoculars," said Norby. "I have telescopic vision when I want it."

"Really?" said Jeff, fascinated. "That could be convenient."

"Maybe they're Ing terrorists," said a man, "and they're holding a secret conference here in the park."

The group of bird-watchers was suddenly very still.

Jeff held his breath, and even Norby was quiet for a change.

At that moment, a shape detached itself from a dark tree and swooped down over the heads of the bird-watchers.

"We're being attacked by the terrorists," yelled the same man who had mentioned them before.

The woman in tweeds stood transfixed, clasping her hands. She didn't seem the least bit frightened—only excited. "Look! Look! It's a great gray owl! A Canadian! It's rarely seen this far south! My first Central Park sighting!"

The other bird-watchers paid no attention. They were scrambling back up the path, clutching their binoculars. "Let's go back," one of them shouted. "What's the use of watching birds when terrorists are watching *us*."

Jeff couldn't bear to ruin the bird-watching. He didn't particularly want to get involved, but he had no choice. He stood up, facing the bird-watching leader. "I'm not a terrorist, ma'am, or a mugger, either. I'm here to celebrate the summer solstice. A family tradition."

"Oh my," said the woman. "The owl is gone."

"I hope so," said Norby. "It was big enough to decide I was a mouse."

Jeff pushed Norby with his elbow. "I'd be ashamed to be afraid of a little bird."

"A little bird? Its wings were twelve feet across!"

"Quiet!" said Jeff, and Norby subsided, muttering.

"Perhaps you'll see it again, ma'am," Jeff said.

"I certainly hope so. Seeing it even once was the thrill of my life—but what is that behind the bush?"

"That's—uh—sort of my baby brother. He scares easily."

"I do not," said Norby. "I'm as brave as a spacer."

"As a what?" asked the woman.

"He said he's brave. He's not afraid of anything as long as he knows he can run away."

"I'm as brave as a lion," shouted Norby.

"He's never even seen a lion."

"I've seen lions in pictures," Norby said. "Mac had an old encyclopedia on his ship. I know how to be brave. I don't run from danger."

"Your baby brother talks quite well for someone so small," said the woman, edging toward the bush.

"He's a prodigy," Jeff said, blocking her off, "but he's very shy. You'll embarrass him very much if you come too close. Of course, he does talk a lot, but that's only because he has a big hat—mouth, I mean. Now I really have to start celebrating the solstice."

The woman said timidly, "I don't suppose I could watch?"

"No, you can't. You're supposed to be bird-watching, not me-watching," shouted Norby.

"He means it's just a private family ceremony," Jeff said apologetically. "It's not traditional for anyone to watch."

There came a shout from the woods. "Are you all right, Miss Higgins?"

The woman smiled. "See that. They were very afraid, but they came back to rescue me. That's very touching isn't it?" She raised her voice. "I'm perfectly all right, good friends. I will be right with you." Then, again to Jeff, "Would you like to join our group some other morning?"

"Oh, certainly," said Jeff, "but hadn't you better go back to them? They must be dying with worry for you."

"I'm sure they are. We meet every Wednesday morning and on special occasions. I'll send you a notice. What is your name and address?"

Jeff told her, and she wrote it down in a small black notebook.

Off in the distance, the owl hooted.

"This way!" called Miss Higgins to her group. "We may get another glimpse of it."

She plunged back into the darkness of the wood, and Jeff could hear that she had found her group and was leading them off on another path. Finally the park seemed deserted again, except for the small sounds of animals and the predawn twittering of birds.

"That was horrible!" Norby said.

"Not at all," Jeff said. "It was just a little delay, and a harmless one. Far worse things used to happen in good old Central Park."

"Muggers and terrorists?" Norby asked. "Tell me about them."

"They're violent people from long ago. Central Park is perfectly civilized today."

"Then why did you say you weren't supposed to go into the park at night?"

Jeff blushed. "Fargo worries about me too much. Sometimes he thinks I'm a little kid. Still, the park is civilized now. You'll see."

"I'd better see," said Norby. "I'm a very civilized object, and I prefer to avoid anything uncivilized."

4

Out of Central Park

Jeff stretched. He hadn't had enough sleep, but daylight was on its way, and it was the solstice. "Come on, Norby. Let's go our civilized way to the special place of the Wells brothers."

"Special place? It's yours? You own it?"

"Not really. Not *legally*. It sure feels ours, though. It feels deep-down ours."

"But not legally? If we're going to have trouble with policemen, I don't want to go."

"We won't have trouble with policemen," said Jeff irritably. "What do you think this is? The asteroids? Just follow me." He started to walk down another path on the other side of the fishpond, but stopped and looked back at Norby, who hadn't budged.

Jeff said, "Well then, go on your antigrav if you want to, Norby. I know walking is difficult for you."

"I can walk perfectly well when I want to," Norby said. "I like to walk. I've won walking races. I can walk higher and deeper than anyone; just not faster. Human beings think that fast is everything when it comes to walking, and they're not so fast anyway. Ostriches and kangaroos go on two legs, and they're much faster than human beings. I read about them—"

"In Mac's encyclopedia, I know. Kangaroos don't walk, they hop."

"Human beings hop, and they can't go as fast as kangaroos. Besides, they look undignified when they hop. If they had bodies like barrels, like *mine,* they wouldn't. Watch me when *I* hop."

"Okay, hop if you want to, but watch where—"

It was too late. Norby tripped over a tree root and went over headfirst. His head didn't move downward, however; his legs moved upward. His body rose in the air, upside down, legs waggling out of the upper end, eyes upside down at the lower end.

Jeff tried to be serious about it, and managed for about fifteen seconds. Then he burst out laughing.

"There's nothing to laugh at. I just decided to turn on my antigrav," said Norby, outraged.

"Upside down?"

"I'm just showing you I can do it every which way. It's a poor antigrav that only works rightside up. Anyone can do that. I've won upside-down races. I can be more upside down than anyone else."

"And can you also be rightside up?"

"Certainly, but it's not as dignified, and I wanted to show you the dignified way. Since you insist, however, we'll do it *your* silly way." Norby righted himself with what certainly looked like an effort, then sank down slowly until his feet were on the ground again. He teetered a little, but he said, "Ta *ta*," and stood on one foot as though he were trying to look like a ballet dancer.

"Well," he said, "how do you want me to go? Forward or backward? I can go any possible way. Do you want diagonal?"

"What you really mean," said Jeff, "is that you don't know which way you'll go until you actually try it. Right?"

"Wrong! said Norby in a loud voice. "And let me tell you one thing, if you're so smart."

"Yes."

In a much milder voice, Norby said, "The one thing I want to tell you is that I think we should walk to your solstice place, Jeff, before the sun comes up on us and it's too late."

He held out his hand. Jeff took it and, hand in hand, the robot and the boy walked on the woodland path into the more deeply wooded part of the Ramble. The sky was sufficiently light now to make it easy to see the shapes of trees and stones.

They walked happily down the path into a deep glade with a little stream running through it, a stream that ran from a spring that seemed to come from a cleft in the enormous rock face at the end. On top of the miniature cliff of the rock face was a railing. There another path crossed the rock, became a tiny bridge, and circled down to join their path.

A willow tree, small but graceful, bent over the stream, and around its roots grew lilies-of-the-valley, their white cups clear in the dim light. The light wind caused them to nod and send out their delicate perfume.

"I like this," whispered Norby. "It's beautiful."

"I didn't know robots could understand beauty," Jeff said.

"Sure. An inflow of nice electricity is beautiful when your potential is down. I thought everyone knew *that*. Besides, I'm not just an ordinary robot," Norby said.

"I can see that. The alien bits in you were from another robot, a wholly different kind, or from an alien computer or something."

"That has nothing to do with it, Jeff. The trouble with you protein creatures is that you think you invented beauty. I can appreciate it, too. I can appreciate anything you can appreciate, and I can do anything you can do. I'm strong and I'm super-brave, and I'm a good companion in adventure. Let's have adventures, and I'll show you. Then you'll be glad you have me."

"I'm sure of it, Norby. Honest."

"Mac always wanted adventures, but he kept waiting, and the result was that he ended up never having any—except finding the alien ship. And then nothing happened."

"Except to you."

"You're right! I got fixed up."

"Mixed up, you mean. You're certainly one mixed-up robot."

"Why do you make fun of me? Just to show me that human beings are cruel?"

"I'm not cruel. I'm glad you're mixed up and have the alien parts in you. That's what makes you strong and brave and—"

At that moment Norby, who was standing with his legs stretched to their full length, widened his eyes to their fullest. "Yow!" he yelled.

"What is it?" Jeff asked. He tried to let go of Norby's hand, but the robot held on with painful tightness, while pointing backward with his other hand. Jeff remembered that Norby had eyes in the back of his head.

"Danger!" said Norby. "Enemy! Alien! Death and destruction!"

"Where? What? Who?" Jeff looked here and there and, finally, up, just in time to see motion across the little bridge.

Two figures were advancing quickly, too quickly to be made out in the half light.

There were three men; two men chasing one man.

"Norby!" Jeff cried out. "It's Fargo, and he's being attacked!"

5

Spies and Cops

"Let's go," shouted Jeff as Norby lifted them with his antigrav. "Bombs away!" And they came down directly on the head of the larger of the two attackers. Jeff was ready for the most desperate fight of his life, but the man wasn't. He crumpled to the ground under Jeff's weight, hit his head against the paving, and passed out.

"Get the other one, Fargo," Jeff yelled. He was panting because most of the wind had been knocked out of him.

"I don't have to," Fargo said. He was panting, too. "Your barrel did."

There was Norby, closed up and on his side, next to the other attacker, who seemed to be groaning in his sleep.

"That's no barrel, Fargo," said Jeff, scrambling to his feet. "That's—"

Fargo wasn't paying attention to him. His eyes were shining with excitement. He liked fights and running and risks and danger, while Jeff did not especially like them. He wouldn't avoid them, but he didn't *like* them. In fact, he *would* avoid them if he could, whereas Fargo usually went out of his way to get into trouble. Jeff wondered again, as he often had, whether it was worth being related to Fargo. All in all, though, he always decided it was.

"Now what's this all about, Fargo?" he asked, feeling like the older brother instead of the younger.

"I might ask you the same question. How did you get here? You weren't here a minute ago. Where did you come from? The sky? And how did you knock out that bruiser, and what are you doing carrying a barrel about with you?"

"Never mind all that. Who are these guys, and why are they after you? I thought the city administration was going to get rid of the muggers."

"They're not muggers, Jeff. Anyway, not ordinary ones.

They've been following me ever since I talked to Admiral Yobo about you and—uh—other things. I thought I'd lost them in the station at Luna City, but that was dumb of me. They just went on ahead and waited at the apartment. Fortunately, I've this sixth sense...."

"Like me," came Norby's muffled voice. "I've got a sixth sense, too."

"What?" said Fargo. "Did you speak, Jeff? Or is there someone else here?" He looked about.

"Never mind. Go on, tell me. You were coming to the apartment with that famous sixth sense of yours—"

"Yes. Something told me not to go in without questioning the computer outlet I stuck under the doormat, and it told me that the apartment had been broken into and that two men were inside. I questioned it further, and it told me you had gone out before the break-in, so I knew you were safe. Well, there was nothing in the apartment I was worried about except you, and I wasn't going to fall into their trap. I had to find you first. Then we could take care of them together. As we did, kid, right?"

"Don't forget I helped out," said Norby in a loud whisper.

"What?" said Fargo.

"Pay no attention," said Jeff. "So you came to the park?"

"Certainly; I knew you'd be here solsticing. But they came after me, and I had to lose them. I almost did. But just before I got here, there they were when I was practically on you, so to speak, and then you were on *them.*"

"Me, too," came the whisper.

"There it is again," said Fargo. "I'm not insane, and I'm not hearing things, and you wouldn't be just sitting there, Jeff, if you didn't know who was talking. You better tell me." He walked over to Norby, still on his side, and looked down at the barrel. "What is this? Don't tell me you brought a libation for the solstice and then spilled it."

"No," said Jeff. "That barrel is my robot."

"Are you kidding? What kind of robot is a barrel?" He put out his foot and pushed it gently.

"That's extremely impolite," Norby said. "Why do you let him do that, Jeff?" The robot extruded his legs and arms and struggled upright. His hat lifted, and two eyes glared furiously at Fargo. "If I kicked *you,*" he said, "I'm sure you would object."

"What do you know?" said Fargo, sounding dumbfounded. "It *is* a robot. Where did you get it, Jeff?"

"At a secondhand robot store. You told me to get a teaching robot, and that's what it is. And he's my friend, mostly. Are you all right, Norby?"

"Yes," said Norby, "and I'm glad you think I'm your friend, even though you don't treat me like one. Surely you don't expect me to stay all right when you persist in putting us into these dangerous situations with muggers—"

"That's a teaching robot?" said Fargo.

"He sure is. He's teaching me that life is complicated and dangerous," said Jeff. "But you still haven't told me who these muggers are. Or don't you know?"

"Well, I don't know them by name, but I suppose they're a pair of Ing's henchmen." With his foot he prodded the smaller one, who was still groaning. "They don't seem to be badly damaged, unfortunately."

Suddenly the larger one grunted, opened his eyes, and rolled over, reaching for a short stick that lay in the grass.

Norby extended an arm farther than Jeff knew he could, grabbed the stick, and touched the henchman with it. The henchman yowled and seemed to collapse.

Norby threw the stick to Jeff. "Take it," he cried. "*My* sixth sense tells me you may find it useful."

Fargo walked over, took the stick from Jeff, and examined it closely. "Hey, what we've got here is an illegal truth wand, with a built-in stunner. That's an expensive item and a beautiful job, too. This shouldn't be available outside the Space Fleet."

"That shows how inefficient the fleet is," Norby said. "Anyone can rifle its stores."

"Don't tell *me* the fleet is—" began Fargo. He broke off and said, "What kind of robot have you got here, Jeff? Robots have a built-in prohibition about harming human beings. It's called the First Law of Robotics."

"There's another sample of gratitude for you," Norby said. "I suppose you would have been happy if that mugger had used the stunner on *you*. You didn't even recognize what it was when it was lying on the grass. Come to think of it, he probably couldn't have managed to stun you with it. If you don't have a brain, there's nothing to stun."

"Listen here," said Fargo, "a robot shouldn't be insulting!" He strode toward the robot, who galloped toward Jeff.

"Leave him alone, Fargo," Jeff said. "He doesn't really hurt human beings."

"Of course not," said Norby. "It's not my fault I fell on one of them. It was Jeff who said 'Bombs away.' And I was just trying to protect human beings—meaning you, Fargo, using the word loosely—by seizing the truth wand before the mugger did. How did I know it was set to the stun intensity? And I didn't mean to touch him *accidentally*. Listen, Jeff, I don't trust that dumb brother of yours. Is he on our side?"

"Yes, he is," said Jeff. "And he's not dumb."

"Well, he worries about my hurting muggers, and he doesn't worry about the fact that he's hurting my feelings, and I call that dumb."

"He doesn't know you yet. And he doesn't know how sensitive your feelings are."

Fargo asked, "Why is your robot talking to you, Jeff, while he's facing me with his eyes closed?"

"His eyes are open on this side," Jeff said. "He has a double-ended head with a pair of eyes on each side. I bought him at the store you recommended."

"Which has a proprietor," said Norby, "who is seriously dishonest—and stupid. He tried to cheat Jeff."

"You mean that the proprietor stuck you with that barrel, Jeff?"

"No," said Jeff. "I insisted on having Norby. He sort of . . . appealed to me. Actually, the proprietor tried to keep me from taking him."

"Really? It appealed to you? And this robot calls *me* dumb?"

"Listen, Fargo. Don't call the robot 'it.' This robot's name is Norby, and he's a very unusual robot. He's just a little mixed up."

"You weren't going to tell anyone about me," wailed Norby.

"Fargo isn't just anyone. He's my brother. He's part of us. Besides, saying you're mixed up isn't *telling*. Fargo is going to find that out after he's been with you for five minutes. With you around, it's got to be the worst-kept secret in the world."

"There you go hurting my feelings again," said Norby. "Just because I'm a poor, put-upon robot, you think you can say anything at all to me."

"Let's stop this love feast," Fargo said drily. "We have more important things to do. For instance, our captives are about to wake up. You'd better use the stunner, Jeff."

"We've got to get them to talk, Fargo, and we can't do that if they're stunned. Norby, tie them up before they're completely awake."

"With what?" asked Norby. "I may be a mixed-up robot, but I'm not so mixed up that I can tie up people without rope. Do I look as though I'm carrying rope on my person?"

"Use this," Fargo said, tossing Norby a coiled wire. "This was going to be a fancy solstice celebration in keeping with family tradition, but what with one thing and another we won't have any at all."

"What has the wire got to do with the solstice?" Jeff asked.

"Never mind," said Fargo loftily. "I'll surprise you next year. That is," he added with a sigh, "if we get to next year—what with one thing and another."

Norby, meanwhile, with surprising efficiency, tied the hands of the captured pursuers tightly behind their backs with the single length of wire so that they were tied to each other as well. He then closed up again and appeared to be just a barrel resting on the grass beside Jeff.

"Give me the wand," said Fargo.

Jeff hesitated. "Don't you think we'd better get the police? Even in Manhattan, civilians are not supposed to take the law into their own hands."

"This is my affair," said Fargo, "And I'll handle the police if it comes to that."He took the wand from his younger brother, who gave it up with obvious reluctance, and waved it in front of the two men. "Welcome to the world, gentlemen. First, your names."

The two men clamped their mouths shut, but at the first touch of the wand, the big, burly one yelped. Then, with a growl, he said, "I'm Fister. That's Sligh."

"Ah," said Fargo. "A sly spy?"

"Spelled S-L-I-G-H," said Sligh. "And you can't keep us, Wells. The longer you do, the worse it will be for you in the end—and for your brother, too. I warn you."

"Warning noted," Fargo said. "But before I cower in terror and let you go, let's find out a few things." He adjusted the wand. "You won't get hurt now unless you lie. Telling the truth pleases a wand like this—and do keep in mind that this is *your* wand I'm using. Any illegality in this respect is on your side." He prodded Sligh. "First, I'd like to know who Ing is, and what he looks like. Is he by any chance a beautiful woman? That might make things a little better."

"I don't know," said Sligh. He was—or had been—neatly dressed in brown, with slicked-back hair and a long, sharp face.

Fargo continued prodding, but when Sligh didn't flicker an eyelash, Fargo said a little discontentedly. "Odd! You must be telling the truth, unless the wand is malfunctioning. Are you fully determined to tell me the truth, then?"

"Sure," said Sligh, and almost immediately cried out, "Yipe!" and writhed a bit.

"No, I guess the wand is not malfunctioning, so you'd better tell the truth unless you like the sensation you just felt. That goes for you, too, Fister. Very well, then, Sligh, you don't know what Ing looks like. Does that mean you've seen him only in disguise or that you've never seen him at all?"

"No one's ever seen him," said Fister hoarsely.

"Shut up," said Sligh.

"What's Ing's ultimate goal?"

There was a pause, and Sligh's face contorted itself.

"The truth, Sligh Fox," said Fargo. "Even trying to lie hurts when the wand nudges you."

"There is actually no need to lie," said Sligh with a growl. "You know what Ing is after. He wants to head the Solar System—for its own good."

"Of course, for its own good," said Fargo. "I wouldn't think for a moment that he's thinking of *his* own good, or that you're thinking of *your* own good. You're all just a noble bunch of patriots thinking only of others. I suppose you want to replace the more-or-less democratic Federation with a more autocratic type of government."

"A more efficient one with more determined leadership. Yes, it will do Ing good, and me good, too, but it will do everyone good. I'm telling the truth; the wand isn't touching me."

"That just means you believe what you say to be the truth. I'll give you credit for kidding yourself into thinking you're noble. Maybe Ing feels that way, too, though I doubt it, and wish I had *him* under the wand. What will you call Ing when he's won out? King Ing? Queen Ing? Boss Ing? Leader? Lord? Emperor?"

"Whatever Ing chooses."

"And how is Ing planning to accomplish all this? Where do I come in?"

Sligh squirmed. "Anyone opposing Ing would have to be negated or converted. You would be an ideal convert."

"You hoped to do it by applying this wand long and hard."

"That would just keep you quiet and cooperative till we took you away. We have other methods for the actual conversion."

"No doubt, but there's more to it," said Fargo. "You weren't after me until quite recently. I wonder why?"

"It would not be advisable for me to tell you."

"I'm sure you believe that, so it's not a lie, is it? Yes, you can avoid pain by telling truths that reveal nothing. On the other hand, perhaps I don't need your revelation. I suspect that Ing's plan is to take over Space Command, first of all. Once that is in his control, he can maneuver easily to take over the Federation itself. And it has recently occurred to him that I would be an ideal person to infiltrate the command and betray Admiral Yobo. After all, the admiral is my friend and trusts me, and I am badly in need of money, and that need will make it easier for me to be converted. In fact, there's your 'other method' for conversion. Plain, old-fashioned bribery. Am I right?"

Sligh hesitated only briefly. "All I can say is that Ing has plenty of money, and he is generous with those he considers his friends."

Jeff broke in suddenly. "Fargo, that's not all—"

"Shut up, Jeff. Now, Mister Sligh, I am turning the truth wand on myself. See, I haven't changed the setting."

"Yes. So what?"

"I'm going to tell you something, and if it isn't the truth, I'll feel what you felt when you tried to lie. Do you think I can hide it? Do you think I'm tougher than you are?"

"No," snarled Sligh.

"Very well. I'm telling you that there is no chance of converting me. I'm out of the fleet and I don't care, because I've got other things to do, but my brother's only ambition is to be in the fleet and serve Space Command someday. He's not like me. He's only fourteen, though he's tall for his age, but he's already shown that he's dead serious and reliable. Nothing will make *him* side with Ing, and nothing will make *me* do anything to spoil his plans. So give up on both of us."

"Is that wand still turned on?" said Sligh.

"Jeff, ask me a question I can lie to."

"Are you interested in women, Fargo?"

"Not at all," said Fargo, who then let out a wild cry and dropped the wand. "Did you have to ask me for that *big* a lie?" he said, holding both sides. His eyes were watering.

Then, as the pain abated, he said to Sligh, "Now let's get back to you and Ing. Tell me—"

Jeff interrupted. "Something's coming."

The soft whirring noise of an antigrav motor sounded not too far away, and in a moment there was a blue-and-white police car hovering overhead. Its searchlight was aimed down at the shaded clearing where the sun, still low on the horizon, had not yet penetrated.

A directed and magnified sound beam came down sharply, its loudness carrying all the overtones of authority: "We are answering a general distress call, giving these coordinates. No one move. We are the police."

Fargo at once stepped away from the two bound figures, dropped the truth wand, and raised his arms. Jeff raised his arms as well. Norby remained a barrel. After a moment's hesitation, Sligh and Fister began to call out, "Help! Help!"

"What in blazes is going on down there?" said the amplified police voice. A figure in blue leaned out, surrounded by the faint glow of a personal shield.

"Hey, Fargo," said Jeff. "Personal shields are finally on the market. Can we afford a couple?"

"Not on your life," said the policeman. "They cost a fortune, and civilians aren't allowed to have them."

"Is that why you don't have one, Sligh?" asked Fargo. "Or is Ing too cheap to get you one?"

"Mine is out of order," said Sligh. "The manufacturer guaranteed it, but—"

Fargo laughed. "I guess Ing tried the bargain basement."

The policeman leaned out further. The personal shield glittered on all sides but did not hide the very efficient stunner that the policeman was holding.

Fargo said, "If it's that expensive, officer, how come City Hall can afford them?"

"They can't," said the policeman. "Very few of us are equipped with them. Fortunately, for me, the mayor is my father. Now just what is all this?"

"As you can see—" began Fargo.

"Don't tell me what I can see, because I can see what I can see. I see two helpless men tied up, and two others standing near and in possession of what looks like an illegal truth wand. Which in turn makes it look very much like a mugging, and makes me sense, somehow, that I have the honor of speaking to the muggers."

"Hey," said Jeff. "You're not a policeman."

The policeman said sharply, "Do you wish to see my identification?"

"I mean, you're a *woman*."

Fargo said, "Better late than never, Jeff. There's hope for you if, at the tender age of fourteen, you've finally learned to tell the sexes apart."

The policeman said, "A policeman is a policeman, regardless of gender. Now, have you anything to say before I arrest you on the perfectly obvious evidence that—"

"Hey!" said Jeff. "You've got it wrong. We're the *victims*."

"Indeed. Victims are usually the ones that are tied up."

"That's right," called out Fister. "Get us loose. They jumped us when my friend and I were here in the park for a religious observance of the solstice."

"Are you Solarists?" asked the policeman with interest.

"Brought up Solarists by very pious parents," said Sligh. "Both of us. My friend and I. And these two hoodlums violated our religious rights by—"

"Madame Cop," said Fargo. "I suggest you take these two men—and my humble self—to the nearest police station for questioning. Using their truth wand, or a police version if you'd rather, you will soon find out that these men are followers of Ing the Ingrate, and that they were pursuing me in order to force me to join them in their nefarious business. With great skill, I turned the tables on them and—"

"Okay. Stop talking, if you know how. In the first place, untie those two men. When that's done, I will have you grabble-meshed individually to the police car, and my partner and I will loft you to the station. Any objections?"

"I sure haven't," Fargo said. "Jeff, untie those villains, but don't get between them and this stunning woman's stunner."

"Your manner," said the policeman, "is somehow familiar."

"Women usually find it so."

"To an obnoxious extent, I am sure. What's your name?"

"Fargo Wells."

"Farley Gordon Wells, by any chance?"

"That's the full version. Yes."

"You're the kid who put fabric dissolver into the air-conditioning system of Neil Armstrong High School?"

"The same. I *knew* that would never be forgotten. And, jumping Jupiter, you must be the first girl who got it—full-strength. Albany Jones, right? If you weren't wearing that uniform, I'd have recognized you at once, except you probably look even better now."

"You'll never know," said Albany Jones. "And I think my father, the mayor, still has a strong desire to meet you."

Fargo swallowed. "Well, maybe later—when all this is over."

Sligh, who was now standing upright and rubbing his wrists, said, "This is an immoral person, you see. You can't believe anything he says."

"The truth wand will tell us," said Jones. "All four of you take hold of the grabble—"

"Wait," said Fargo. "Not my brother. He's here for the solstice celebration, and he's only fourteen. Please let him go with our keg of nails—that barrel there. You have me."

Jeff said, "Just because I'm fourteen doesn't mean I—"

"Shut up, Jeff. Our parents are dead, Albany. I've had to bring him up, and it's hard being an only parent to a headstrong youth."

"Stop," said Jones, "or I'll dissolve in floods of tears. You'll do; he can go."

"Go home, Jeff," Fargo said. "Sligh and Fister no longer infest the apartment, obviously; but check the door computer first anyway."

As the three men were grabble-meshed upward, Fargo waved and called out, "I'll be back as soon as possible."

Jeff watched them sail out of sight. The park was in full daylight now.

He picked up Norby and tried to balance him on his right shoulder. The barrel seemed to weigh a ton, as though it were full of scrap iron—which, in a way, it was.

"You could at least turn on your antigrav," he whispered into Norby's hat.

Slowly, Jeff began to rise.

"Only a *little* antigrav, idiot!"

Just as slowly, he sank back to the grass, holding what now seemed like an empty barrel.

He began to walk in the direction of home, swinging along briskly, when Norby's eyes suddenly peered out from under his hat. "Are you going home right away? Don't I even get to see the solstice celebration?"

"You can't. We missed it. The sun's well above the horizon."

"Can't we pretend it hasn't come up yet? Who'll know?"

"*We'll* know. You can't make fun of things like that. . . . Well, I'll tell you what. I can do the Oneness; that doesn't have to be exactly at sunrise. It's supposed to be done each solstice and each equinox. That's four times a year."

"I know elementary astronomy, Jeff!"

Jeff walked back to where they had been interrupted by Fister and Sligh in pursuit of Fargo. It was still in shadow, still fairly cool, and if the brilliance of day was distracting, it at least added a touch of friendliness to the surroundings.

Jeff put Norby down and sat cross-legged on the grass beside the tiny stream. He rested his hands, palms up, on his thighs, and half-closed his eyes.

After a minute, Norby said, "You're not doing anything. What's happening?"

Jeff opened his eyes. He sighed and said, "Don't interrupt me. I'm meditating. I am trying to sense the Oneness of the universe, and you have to quiet your nervous system to be able to do that."

"My nervous system doesn't need quieting."

"How do you know? It's never been quiet. If you don't sit still without making silly sounds, we're going straight home. Just let me tune into the Oneness."

Norby pulled in his arms and legs with an annoyed snap, but he let his eyes peer out from under his head.

Jeff resumed his position. It felt good, as always.

After a while, he said softly, "I am part of the universe, part of its life. I am a Terran creature, from the life that evolved here on Earth. Wherever I go and whatever I do, I will remember Earth. I will respect all life. I will remember that we are all part of the Oneness."

After another silence, Jeff stood up. He bent to pick up Norby, who extended his legs suddenly and moved away.

"What's the matter?" asked Jeff.

"Does all that apply to me, Jeff?"

"Of course it does. You're as much a part of the Solar System as I am, and everything that lives in it is ultimately of earthly origin."

"But am I alive?"

"You have consciousness, so you must be." Jeff started to smile, but Norby had seemed so serious. "Look, Norby, even if you're not alive in a human sense, you are part of the Oneness."

"What about the part of me that is alien and isn't part of the Solar System?"

"It doesn't matter. The Oneness includes every star in every galaxy, and everything that *isn't* a star or a galaxy, too. Terrans or aliens, *everything* is part of the Oneness. Besides, I sure feel part of you and Fargo and everyone I care about. Don't you feel part of me?"

"I guess I do," said Norby, shooting out his left arm so that he could take Jeff's right hand in his. "Maybe we're *both* important."

He jiggled happily on his backwards and forwards feet for a second and then said, "Jeff, we'd better walk home. That will look better than using antigrav. I feel better. I'm funny-looking, but nobody should mind that. I've got consciousness and I'm alive and I'm at one with the universe. Isn't that right, Jeff?"

"Yes, Norby."

"And what's more, the universe is at one with me, isn't it, Jeff?"

"I think it's more fitting for you to be at one with the universe."

"I think it would be nice to consider the universe's feelings, too, Jeff. I think the universe would be pleased to be at one with me."

"Well . . . maybe."

It was an exceedingly pleasant day. There were joggers moving along the roads now, and Norby waved to each as they passed, crying out, "I am at one with you."

Jeff pulled at his hand. Don't disturb them, Norby. Jogging is hard work."

"You know," Norby said, "when you were meditating, Jeff, I tried to do the same. I think I had a dream."

"You're not supposed to sleep. Come to think of it, I don't

think robots know how to sleep."

"I had to learn while I was in the stasis box. It protected my mind. Anyway, I half-thought I was in a strange land. I was aware of the park, but I was also aware of the strange land. I was aware of both at the same time. Doesn't that make it a dream, Jeff?"

"I don't know, Norby. I don't think that's the way *I* dream."

Norby ignored that. "I dreamed about this strange land that seemed to be something I had never actually seen, but I can't be sure. How do I know where all of me has been, come to think of it? Maybe I was remembering instead of dreaming."

"If you go to this strange land, Norby, don't go there without me."

"I won't go anywhere without you, Jeff, except I think I don't know how to *go* anywhere, really. I only know how to get back."

"Back where?"

"Back *here* from wherever I've been."

"But how can you get back if you don't know how to get there in the first place?"

"I can *go*. I just don't know how *how* to go."

"You mean whenever you travel anywhere, it isn't really controlled."

"I guess that's it."

"That's inconvenient, Norby."

"But I'll always get you home. After all, my function is to protect and teach, so you can't blame me if I'm not perfect at taking you places. You'll keep me, won't you, Jeff, even so? You won't sell me to someone else? I will try to be a good robot."

"I know you'll *try*," Jeff said, but he did wonder just a little bit what good it would do for a robot as mixed up as Norby to try.

6

MANHATTAN FALLS

"Here's Fifth Avenue," Jeff said, rounding the corner of a wall, "and pretty soon we'll be home and ready for a nice breakfast."

"And a plug into the socket for me," said Norby. "Don't forget *my* needs."

They started out across the sidewalk, hand in hand. They had nearly reached the curb when Jeff said in a tense, low voice, "Oh, *no!*"

"What? What?" said Norby.

"Get back!" whispered Jeff, turning and taking sudden long strides.

Norby went over backwards, and his barrel body made ominous scraping noises on the sidewalk until Jeff shook the robot's arm. "Turn on your antigrav a little!" he whispered.

They melted back into the nearest bush.

"I don't suppose you care to tell me what's happening," Norby said in an aggrieved tone. "I'm just a robot, I suppose. You think I'm just a hunk of steel, I suppose. I don't have any—"

Jeff caught his breath. "Shut up," he said, still panting a little. "Why don't you use your eyes instead of that noisy rattle you call a voice? Can't you see there are men in uniform around the apartment house?"

"Cops?" said Norby.

"Those aren't police uniforms."

"Sanitation men? Park Security? Hotel doormen?"

"Is this a time to be funny? I think they're Ing's men. And if they're strong enough and bold enough to conduct a raid—"

Jeff was talking to himself rather than to Norby, but Norby interrupted. "Maybe they've taken over the city."

"I don't see how they can have done *that*. Manhattan Island runs itself—sort of—and insists on having no outside armed

49

force on its acres, but even so—"

"If it's just a raid," Norby said, "they're taking a big chance and they have to be after something important. I guess they must be after me."

"You?"

"Who else? It's our apartment house, isn't it? And you and I live there, and we've just had a fight with two of Ing's men and it can't be *you* they're after, so it's got to be me. That's logic. I'm very good at logic."

"Why does it have to be you? Why can't it be me?"

Norby made a sound like a snort and didn't answer. "They can't have taken the whole city," he said. "Albany Jones approaches."

A police hover-car was circling above, moving slowly as though searching for something. The uniformed men guarding the entrance to the building shot at the car without effect.

"How do you know it's Albany?" Jeff asked.

"It's her car. I don't know if she's in it, of course, but it's her car. I tune into motors. It's very simple to recognize one from another. That's one of the things I could teach you besides languages. Don't forget I'm a teaching robot. Languages are my specialty, but I'm sure I could manage a few other things."

The hovering police car dropped a spine-cluster into the midst of the men below. Understandably, the result was panic. Some of the men dived for the doorway and the others for the two ends of the block. When a spine-cluster explodes, the results are felt only in the immediate vicinity and are not fatal, but those at the receiving end feel as if they've tangled with twenty porcupines. And removing the spines is neither easy nor painless.

Street traffic diverted quickly as drivers recognized that a fight was going on.

"Why don't you signal the hover-car?" Norby said. "It has to know where we are."

"I was about to," said Jeff, waving energetically from behind the bush. The police car sank downward slightly, and something fell out. Jeff tried to catch it, misjudged, and received it roughly on his right shoulder.

"Ouch!" he groaned. "Ever since I met you, Norby, things have been falling on me, or I have been falling on things. I feel black and blue all over. Why didn't *you* catch it? You can't be hurt."

"My feelings can. And with you lurching around trying to catch it, what could I do? You nearly stepped on me as it was."

Jeff was still rubbing his shoulder. "What is this?"

"It's the same belt device that Albany was wearing in Central Park—a personal shield. If you use it, Ing's men won't be able to touch you."

"But how am I going to use it? I don't know how it works."

"That's why you have *me*. I know how it works. I've already deciphered its simple mechanism. Put it on, then turn this switch here when you need protection. Your arms go in these places. No, no, that metal part goes in front. Can't you see?"

"That metal part," grumbled Jeff, "is what hit my shoulder. Is it on right now?"

"Yes," said Norby, "though actually I'm plenty of protection for you anytime."

"Anytime there's no danger." Jeff turned the switch on the belt and was instantly aware of the faint radiance that surrounded him. The street, the sky, and the buildings all took on a slightly yellow tinge that made everything look particularly bright and cheerful.

Norby didn't sound cheerful, however. "Jeff! I can't get through to you."

"Sure you can, Norby. I hear you perfectly."

"I don't mean that. I mean I'm outside the field."

Jeff turned off the field, picked up Norby, and turned the field back on. The personal shield enveloped them both.

"What's the difference?" Jeff said. "You can't be hurt, and if you can protect me, you can surely protect yourself."

"I get lonely," said Norby.

The police car had descended nearly to surface level. Albany leaned out and shouted, "Get in! Hurry! Those Ingrates are coming up with a full-sized blaster."

Jeff tried to climb aboard with Norby desperately hanging onto him. Norby activated his antigrav and it came on so strongly that Jeff found himself turning upside down. Albany pulled him in. "Goodness," she said, "you and that barrel are light. Don't you have any insides?"

Jeff could hear shouting and heavy footsteps behind him. There was the sound of an unpleasant explosion as the car zoomed upward. It shook in the air vibrations but remained untouched.

"Ing's men seized the police station," Albany said. "They

came right behind me. They may have seized all the police stations in Manhattan." She bit her lip and shook her head. "I'm afraid we've underestimated the Ingrates. They always seemed a minor nuisance, a bunch of inept terrorists. But it's clear now that that was just a screen. They've set up a formidable force, and they're prepared to take over the system."

"How did you get away?" Jeff asked anxiously.

"My personal shield, of course. I must tell my father to get the City Council to equip *all* the cops with shields. But I suppose it's too late now, at least for Manhattan. It's Space Command that—"

"But what about Fargo?" Jeff said anxiously.

Albany swallowed. Her brows contracted unhappily over her large eyes. "The truth is I don't know. They grabbed him when they came out of the police transmit, and I was so busy getting away I had no chance to see what became of him. He had given me his address when I was taking him to the station." She looked a little guilty. "We always get the names and addresses of those we take into custody," she added. "Purely routine."

"Yes, yes," said Jeff, who wanted her to get to the point. What had happened to Fargo?

"I drifted by the apartment house, just in case he had gotten away and gone there. I had no idea where else he might go. When I saw the house guarded by the Ingrates, I thought he might have been trapped in the vicinity. Then, of course, I found *you.*" She said that with a certain note of disappointment.

Jeff disregarded that. "Then you don't know where Fargo is?"

"No. I'm afraid I don't. What we've got to do now is to find a transmit in Manhattan that hasn't been taken over by the Ingrates. We've *got* to notify Space Command, or the Ingrates may be able to take over all Earth. They wouldn't attack Manhattan unless they've already seized the key communications network. That's what worries me." She paused and looked solemnly at Jeff. "If we can't notify Space Command—"

"Put me down, Miss Jones," Jeff demanded. "I have to find Fargo!"

"I can't put you down. You'd be taken instantly. And there's no need to worry about Fargo. Your brother is quite attractive. . . . What I mean is, he's quite intelligent, and I'm sure he can take care of himself. We have bigger worries. Space Command itself may be infected by Ing's people."

"Fargo had some kind of private conversation with Admiral Yobo," Jeff said. "That may have been the problem they were concerned with. And maybe *that's* why Fister and Sligh were after him. They didn't want to convert him. They wanted to finish him. Miss Jones, *please* let me look for him. They'll kill him."

"If I may make a suggestion," Norby said.

Albany jumped at his voice, and the hover-car lurched as she inadvertently yanked at the controls. "That's not a barrel," she said. "It's a robot. Don't let that silly thing get in our way."

"That silly thing!" shouted Norby. "*You're* the silly thing, or you wouldn't be so busy talking you can't see the danger right ahead. There are cars approaching, shield-protected hover-cars that probably belong to this Ing person you're so worried about. If I were you, I'd go somewhere else quickly, but, of course, I'm just a silly thing, so don't listen to me."

"Ing's cars?" Albany looked about in horror. It was clear that the trouble was even worse than Norby had thought. They were surrounded.

Albany's mouth tightened. "Ing must have been planning this a long time. He's taking over Manhattan as though it were a meatball and he were a wolf. Well, we've got shields. Shall we fight it out?"

"With what?" said Jeff.

"I've got a long-range stun gun and a hand-blaster."

"Will they work on shielded cars?"

"No," admitted Albany.

"Does this car have shielding?"

"Are you kidding? With the Manhattan fiscal situation? No, only our personal shields, courtesy of Daddy."

"Then they'll destroy our hover-car in fifteen seconds, and we fall"—Jeff looked down for a quick estimate—"thirty stories, I think."

"You might as well surrender, then," Norby said. "That will give us time, and I'll be able to think of some way of saving the situation. I'm terribly ingenious."

"Is surrendering a sample of your ingenuity?" Albany asked. "Anyone can surrender—"

"There's nothing else to do right now," Jeff said, "and it

may be the only way of finding Fargo. We'd better do it right away. One of Ing's cars looks as though it's bringing a blaster to bear on us." He turned off his shield and handed the device to Norby. "Can you hide this in your—uh—inside?"

"I suppose I can," Norby said, "but it will make me feel as though I have indigestion. Why don't *you* swallow it? You have a sort of hollow inside, too."

"Funny, funny. Here, take Miss Jones's."

Carefully, while making little noises of displeasure, Norby put away both shield devices as Albany took the hover-car down to the ground. They were followed, of course, and when the Ingrates swarmed out of their cars, Albany and Jeff surrendered.

They were careful to look scornful and superior when they gave themselves up. At least they tried, and it was especially hard for Jeff, who kept Norby under his arm. Norby made no attempt to look either scornful or superior. He merely concentrated on looking like a barrel.

The Central Park Precinct Station was inside an old brick building and had the aura of centuries of use and occasional slipshod repairs.

Sligh and Fister hustled Albany and Jeff toward the station's transmit. Despite the chronic shortage of municipal funds and the best efforts of every city councilman, there seemed no way of economizing on those transmits. Each police station simply had to have one for any necessary travel through space.

Jeff was still holding Norby. Sligh scowled. "You're not dragging that barrel around everywhere, Wells," he growled. "It made a lump on my head once, and you're not going to use it as a weapon again. Hand it over and I'll melt it down for scrap. Or we'll use it as ballast. Maybe we'll just smash it with a sledgehammer."

Jeff clutched Norby tightly. "I need this barrel," he said. "It's a device that's necessary to—to my health."

"Are you going to tell me you've hidden a kidney filter in that old barrel?"

"I didn't *want* to tell you."

"And I suppose you'll die without it?"

"I, ah. . . ." Jeff hated to lie, but Sligh seemed to be doing it for him.

"You're not fooling me, you dumb kid," said Sligh. "You look too big and healthy to need any machine for your health. I bet that's got Wells money in it. Maybe gold. Give it over!"

Norby whispered through his hat, "Don't stand there, Jeff. Step back into the transmit."

Jeff paused to wonder what Norby had in mind, and suddenly he felt a pinch.

"Hurry up!"

Albany was already in the transmit. Fister and Sligh, facing it, were on either side of Jeff, who had his back to it. The pinch made Jeff jump backwards, and as he did, Norby's hands extended full length, pushing Fister and Sligh in the other direction, out of the transmit doorway.

Albany, reacting at once, slammed the door shut. "Now what? The transmit mechanism works from outside."

"Maybe so," said Norby, leaning against the door, "but I'm managing to work it through the metal—didn't I tell you I'm ingenious?"

"They're going to force their way in—" began Albany.

"I'm almost finished," Norby said.

"But we have to get to where they've taken Fargo," Jeff said.

"I'm sensing his presence," Norby said, "and I'm adjusting the controls so we'll go there directly. I hope."

A queasy sensation hit Jeff in the pit of his stomach, and he blacked out dizzily. When he came to, he saw that they were in a different transmit. He scrambled to his feet and helped Albany to hers. She brushed at her clothing and seemed pretty annoyed.

"You didn't exactly handle that in a smooth way, Norby," Jeff said.

"Well," said Albany, "I don't suppose we can blame your robot. The transmit is old and not working well. I don't think any of the city transmits have had repairs for five years."

"Norby, are you going to be able to get the doors open?" Jeff asked.

"In a minute. In a minute. And—on the other side—we will find your brother." The doors opened, and they stepped out into a huge, gray room. Overhead there was a section of glassite dome and beyond that a dim, rolling fog.

"Or maybe we won't," Norby said in a small voice.

"Where on earth—" said Albany.

"I don't think *anywhere* on Earth," said Jeff. "Norby! Where are we?"

"Is there a city named Titan anywhere on Earth?" Norby asked.

"A city named what?"

Jeff said blankly, "What does it say?"

"It's in Colonial German. That's another language I can teach you. It would come in handy anywhere beyond the asteroids."

"*Beyond the asteroids?*" said Jeff in a shout. "What does it *say?* I don't care if it's Sanskrit. What does it say?"

"It says 'Property of Titan outpost.' I figure Titan is a city in the German sector of the European Region and I just may have miscalculated a small bit."

"Titan," said Jeff in an exasperated tone, "is a satellite of Saturn, and you have miscalculated *a whole lot.*"

"Are you sure?" Norby asked. "It could happen to anyone."

"Of course I'm sure. Where on Earth would we be under a dome? Look up there. You realize Titan has a thick atmosphere that is mostly nitrogen at a temperature near its liquefying point. You might have gotten us *outside* the dome, and then Miss Jones and I would have died a horrible death."

"How could I have gotten you outside the dome?" Norby shouted. "I sensed human beings, and I thought it was Fargo. There are no human beings outside the Titan dome, so I wouldn't have brought you there. There are human beings *inside* the dome, and it's not my fault one of them isn't Fargo."

He turned back to the transmit controls. Jeff blacked out again.

"We're here!" said Albany. "Space Command! Thank goodness! We're safe. Norby, you rate a medal."

"No, he doesn't," said Jeff angrily. "He rates a blaster shot in the bottom of his barrel. Those are not Space Command uniforms."

"Are you sure?" said Albany.

"Well, look at them again."

Two men approached them as if ready to attack. "Down with the enemies of Ing the Incomparable!" they shouted as they rushed at them.

"Oh, *no,*" said Albany. "They've even taken over out here."

One of the men reached Albany, but seemed to trip and went flying over her shoulder.

She looked pleased. "Did you see that?" she asked. "It works. They taught me judo and combat techniques during training, but I didn't think I could really—oof—"

The other man reacher her and threw an arm about her neck.

Jeff rushed toward her. In a strangled voice, Albany said, "No, let me handle him. Get the other one."

The first man was getting groggily to his feet. Jeff stepped back to let him rise, but Norby kicked him in his rear end and he went down on his face. Norby then rose in the air, turned off his antigrav, and came down hard on the back of the Ingrate, knocking his breath completely out of him.

Albany, meanwhile, was swaying back and forth with the second Ingrate, who was trying to tighten his grip on her. In rapid succession, she dug her elbow into his solar plexus with a hard jab and stomped fiercely on his toes with her heavy police boot while smashing into his nose with the back of her head. He let out a screech and let go. Albany seized his wrist, spun on her toe, and twisted his arm. When he bent, she placed her hip under him, twisted harder, and sent him flying. He hit his shoulder hard when he landed and lay groaning.

"Let's get into the transmit before any others come," Albany said.

As soon as they were safely inside the transmit with the door closed, Norby extruded from within his barrel body a thin, flat metallic tape that spread out horizontally. He pressed the tape against the wall.

"Ah," he said, "I should have done this the first time. It greatly intensifies my sensitivity and my powers of concentration. It takes a great deal out of me, however, and I never know when I'll get my next gulp of electricity. If ever."

"Have you got Fargo this time?" asked Jeff anxiously.

"Yes. Definitely. No mistake."

Again Jeff felt that queasy sensation, but he managed to retain consciousness this time.

"This transmit is in better condition," Norby said. "And now I think we'll find Fargo."

The doors opened, and Norby said, "In fact, I'm sure you'll find Fargo, because there he is!"

Jeff could see an enormous room draped with banners and

lined on either side with armed men. In the center was a platform, upon which rested what could only be a throne. Fargo,
his arms folded across his chest, was sitting on the edge of the
platform, and someone else—someone clothed in metal to such
an extent that he looked very nearly a robot—sat on the throne.

"Here's company, anyway," Fargo said. "The beautiful Albany Jones, my resourceful brother, and his graceful barrel.
How did you find me anyway? And why haven't you brought
an army with you?"

"Silence!" roared the figure on the throne in a voice as
metallic and rasping as a defective machine.

"Ing speaks!" said Fargo sarcastically. "Let all be silence,
while I welcome the newcomers to the court of Ing the Innocent.
Note the distortion of his voice, which is uneuphonious even
when undistorted. Note the graceful aluminum of his costume,
designed to cover an unattractive body, and the facial mask
which serves to spare his audience a view of his face, which
is deformed, or his feelings, which are disgraceful, and
the—"

The man on the throne gestured, and a guard stepped up to
Fargo and lifted a weapon threateningly.

"Since Ing fears words but is brave enough to attack an
enemy when the odds are a hundred to one, I shall be quiet,"
said Fargo.

Albany and Jeff marched up to Fargo, Jeff holding Norby—
who was, of course, tightly shut.

Ing's voice sounded again, harsh and repugnant. "We have
here two brothers who, between them, know a great deal about
the Space Academy and the fleet. And what they know, I will
know!" His voice took on the sound of contempt. "In addition,"
he rasped, "we have a lady cop with a rich father who will
help me take over Earth, if he wants his little girl back in her
present shape and form. And I see something that looks like a
barrel. Give it to me, Jeff Wells."

Jeff held Norby tighter and said nothing.

"It won't do you any good to hold it," said Ing. "I am told
it is a curious barrel with arms—when it wishes to have arms.
And legs too. It is something I wish to examine. Hand it over,
boy, or I'll have it separated from you at your shoulders."

Norby whispered through his hat, "Move closer to Miss
Jones."

Jeff cautiously stepped sideways until his elbow was against Albany's shoulder.

"Now both of us move toward Fargo," Norby whispered. "We've all got to be touching."

"I'll touch Fargo," whispered Albany. "But why?"

"I have an ingenious idea," said Norby in his ordinary voice.

"It talks!" said Ing. "It is a robot and I want it. I am emperor here, and I must be obeyed."

"The history of emperors on Earth has been a sad one," Fargo said. (Albany was leaning against Fargo's shoulder, and Jeff against Albany's.) "Let me tell you about Napoleon Bon—"

"Keep quiet!" Ing barked. "Sergeant! Get me that robot. Kill the woman if any of them resist!"

Norby suddenly cried out. "The personal shields!" He tossed one to Albany and one to Fargo. Then he clung tightly to Jeff and hummed a strange sound.

7

HYPERSPACE

"Comet tails!" said Norby.

"Where are we?" Jeff asked as he stared at the strange castle on the hill facing them. Terraced gardens spilled down the hill, and directly ahead was an elegant marble castle in miniature.

"What I did," Norby said hurriedly, "was to transfer Fargo and Albany outside the building. That would give them a head start. With their personal shields and Albany's knowledge of judo and Fargo's quick wit—you're always telling me how bright he is—they ought to rally a counterattack—"

"Yes, yes," said Jeff impatiently, "but where are *we?*"

"Well," said Norby, his hat swiveling as he looked about, "what I was trying to do was to get us to Space Command. I memorized the coordinates Mac gave me long ago, but maybe they weren't right."

"Yes, yes," said Jeff, still more impatiently. "Where *are* we?"

"Well," said Norby, "that's the one little thing I don't know."

"You don't know!" Jeff looked about, despairing. The surroundings were beautiful. The sunlight was bright and warm. There was a soothing rustle all about, but where on Earth—or off Earth—were they? "Can't you do *anything* right, Norby? You're a poor excuse for a robot."

"I *try*. It isn't always easy." Then Norby said in a small voice, "I wanted you to own me. I see now that it was a great wrong. You're all mixed up with a robot that's all mixed up. I'll try to get you home, Jeff, and I'll stay here, and you'll be rid of me. I'm sorry."

"No," Jeff said. "I don't *ever* want to be rid of you. It doesn't matter how mixed up you are; I'll just be mixed up along with you." He reached for Norby. "I wish you weren't so hard," he said. "It's difficult to hug you."

60

"I don't care," said Norby. "Hug me anyway. I'm so glad you want to keep me."

"Just the same," said Jeff, "I wish we knew where we were."

At that moment something came out of the small castle. It looked distinctly dinosaurish, except for its size.

"A miniature allosaurus?" said Jeff uncertainly. He stepped back.

The creature came up to his knee; it wasn't even as tall as Norby. It was wearing what seemed to be a gold collar and, as it swished its tail, it emitted a series of variegated sounds.

"Is it talking or just making noises?" Jeff asked, feeling an extreme urge to reach out and pat its reptilian head.

"Don't you understand it?" Norby asked. "I keep forgetting that you're not a linguist. It—or rather, she—says you're cute."

"I think she's cute, too, but what's a miniature dinosaur doing anywhere on Earth? And how is it that she talks?"

"I don't think this is Earth," Norby said.

"But you understand the language. Doesn't that mean you ought to know where this is?"

"To tell the truth, Jeff, I don't know how I come to understand the language. I didn't know it was in my memory banks until I heard it. And I don't remember ever having been here before—unless—unless this is the place I dreamed about."

"But what did you do to get here?" Jeff was scarcely aware that the dinosaur was nuzzling his hand. Automatically, he began stroking her head.

"I just shifted through hyperspace. That's why it's so hard to get back. I could always get you back through normal space, but. . . ."

"You went through hyperspace without a transmit?" asked Jeff in a half-shout.

Norby retreated a step. "Is that illegal?"

"It's impossible. No one can do it."

"I did it."

"But that's true hyperspatial travel. How did you come to know how to do that?"

"I thought everyone knew how."

"Well, then, how do you do it?"

Norby thought awhile. Then he said, "I know *how* to do it, but I don't *know* how to do it."

"That doesn't make sense." Jeff was sitting on the grass, and the creature had her forepaws in his lap and her head resting on his shoulder. She was making a sound like a soft "Gruffle, gruffle, gruffle." Jeff was running his hand down her long neck, which had pointed projections all the way to the tip of her tail.

"Do you know how to raise your arm?" Norby asked.

"Certainly."

"Do you *know* how to raise it? Can you explain exactly what it is you do to raise your arm? What happens inside your arm that makes it go up?"

"I just decide to have my arm go up, and it does."

"Well, I just decide to jump through hyperspace, and I just do. I can go anywhere in an instant. But I don't *know* how I do it."

"But, Norby, that makes you the most valuable creature in the Solar System—"

"Oh, I know that."

"I mean, you *really* are. No one else knows how to go through hyperspace without transmits. It would be the greatest discovery of the age if any human being could make it." Jeff began stroking the dinosaur faster and faster. "It was my ambition to make the discovery myself. That's why I wanted to go through the academy and learn all I could about hyperspatial theory. It's my dream to invent hypertravel some day. Now, with you to help me—"

"I said I only know *how* to do it, nothing else. Is that why you want to be with me, Jeff? Because I know how to hypertravel?"

"*No.* I told you I was glad I was with you *before* you told me about it. But now I'm twice as glad." Jeff was pulling the creature toward himself, yet he still wasn't aware of it. "Well then, if you came here, where are we?"

"But that's the other thing, Jeff. I know how to do it, but I guess I don't know how to aim right. I intended to go to Space Command, and I miscalculated. I don't know where we are—and yet I know that creature's language."

Jeff looked down at the dinosaur and suddenly realized that she was softly licking his left ear with her warm, dry tongue. He went over backward, and she tumbled out of his lap. She got to her feet and unfurled the leathery ridges on each side of her back spines.

"Wings!" Jeff choked. "She's got wings! She's a pterodactyl or something."

"Nonsense," said Norby. "Any fool can see that she's a dragon."

"Dragons are mythical beasts."

"Not here."

"What makes you so sure? You don't even know where 'here' is."

"I think part of me knows, but I can't tune in to it. I'm sorry, Jeff. I'm so mixed up, I think I ought to be destroyed."

"Not before you get us back. And even then, I won't let anyone destroy you. But get us back, Norby. It's important."

"Don't get mad, Jeff, but I'm having a little trouble figuring out how. I may have moved far out of the Terran Solar System. If only I could remember where this was! Part of me seems to have been here before, or why would I dream of it?"

"You know... I'll bet it's the alien mechanisms Mc-Gillicuddy used in you. The alien thing, whatever it was, was once here, whenever *that* was, and you just snapped back to that place without really thinking."

"In that case—Hey!" Norby went over sideways as the little dragon broke into a sudden run and pushed past him. She ran into the small castle.

Jeff helped Norby up.

"Baby dragons *never* have manners," Norby said. "I remember when—" He paused. Then in a discouraged voice he said, "No, I don't remember. For a minute, I was sure I had remembered remembering dragons, but I don't."

"You're getting me confused again."

"I can't help it. Maybe we'll be stuck here too long to be able to help Fargo and Albany defeat Ing."

"I'm hungry, Norby. Maybe we can find some forms of life to eat. But what about you? You'll never be able to plug into an electric socket here. You'll starve. Maybe *that* will inspire you to remember how to get back."

"Actually, I can't starve. Electric sockets give me between-meal snacks. For the real thing I dip into hyperspace, and I can do that anywhere, anytime. There's unlimited energy in hyperspace. You ought to try it."

"I would, if I were able to," Jeff said. "What's hyperspace like?"

"It's nothing."

"That's very helpful."

"I mean it. Hyperspace is nothingness. It isn't space or time, so it has no up or down or when or where. When I'm in it, I can sense a . . . well, sort of . . . I guess it's a pattern that isn't really there but is potentially there because that's what the actual universe is, the pattern that's sort of potentially there in hyperspace. . . ."

"Norby!"

"Well, I didn't say I could explain it. I can't. All I know is that hyperspace is definitely potential—I mean, it's potentially something, as if it's got reserve energy that comes into use for creating a universe, that of course is actually part of itself. . . ."

"You're losing me again. How is a universe created?"

"I think that a spot in hyperspace suddenly gains a where and a when. How it's done or happens is beyond even me, so of course it's beyond everyone in the Solar System, and even if I could explain it to you, you wouldn't know how to understand it."

"Thanks for your high estimate of my intelligence. All *I* really want to know is if you can figure out how to get back to *our* Solar System."

"Certainly. I just have to tune into the pattern in hyperspace and find out where to go."

"Then you'd better do it soon. There's a bigger dragon coming."

"Perhaps," Norby said, as he backed closer to Jeff, "the little dragon's mother wants to thank us for being nice to her baby."

"Don't count on it," Jeff said, snatching up Norby. There was no use running. The dragon had long, strong legs, and wings as well. She was only as high as Jeff's chin, but she had gleaming, pointed teeth in double rows, top and bottom.

She made the same kind of sounds the little dragon had made, only much louder.

"What's she saying?" whispered Jeff.

"She says we are aliens and we might have to be taken to the Grand Dragonship unless she can teach us to talk."

"Well, what are you waiting for, Norby? Tell her you can talk."

Norby delivered a rapid patter of sounds, and the dragon responded with similar sounds.

"Jeff," Norby squawked, "let's leave right now. That foul reptile insulted me."

"What did she say?"

"She said I was simply a barrel and that I smelled of nails."

"I suppose she's right. The barrel did once—"

"Don't finish that sentence. We're going."

"No, we're not. If we dash off somewhere, we'll be lost twice as bad. Let's listen to what she has to say."

But she said nothing more. Instead she plunged toward them, plucked Norby out of Jeff's arms, and then bit Jeff on the neck. She licked her chops and wrinkled her snout as if she had tasted something bad. Then she placed Norby carefully on the ground and went back to the castle.

"Help, Norby! I've been bitten by the dragon. She's probably rabid! I've been bitten by a rabid dragon vampire!"

"Not very deeply," Norby said, examining Jeff's neck. "It's just a scratch. Barely enough to draw blood. I have a feeling there's a reason for it."

"*I* have a feeling I hurt. And *her* reason is that she wanted to taste me. Next time she'll make a meal of me. Do you want me to be eaten up by a dragon? *Think,* you dumb barrel! Get us back home. Get us anywhere! I don't care how lost we get."

My dear sir! There is no need to agitate yourself. Whoever you are, there must be communication in order for there to be a meeting of minds.

Jeff's mouth fell open. He swallowed noisily. "Norby, I just heard a voice—in my mind!"

In order to communicate with you, I had to taste your pattern since you do not understand vocal speech.

"I tell you someone's talking, Norby!"

"It's that abominably rude dragon-mother, Jeff. Do not condescend to answer her."

Just wait until I disinfect myself and my child, for we touched you, and since you are an alien you are probably full of germs.

"I am not full of germs," yelled Jeff. "You are. I'm sure I'll get tetanus from your bite. With all those teeth, you probably never use toothpaste."

No gentleman would say such a thing! I use toothpaste and mouthwash, and so does my dear little daughter, Zargl. I think you had better leave. No respectable Jamyn would want you on this world. I will place the hyperspatial coordinates of this world in the memory bank of your storage barrel—

"Storage barrel!" cried Norby.

And I will thank you to leave.

"Do you have the coordinates, Norby?"

"Yes, but I won't use them. Not if they come from her. Not—"

"Norby, use them, or I will take you apart with my bare hands and mix you up so that you never get unmixed!"

The mother dragon appeared in the doorway of the castle, holding the baby in her arms. She made shooing gestures with her wings.

Away! Away! You crude monster!

"Come on, Norby!"

"All right, I'm trying. But I think you *are* a crude monster to make such vicious threats against me when it was only half an hour ago you were saying you loved me."

"I *do* love you, but that's beside the point. Get going!"

"Give me a chance. If you start shouting and hurrying, I'll just get mixed up."

"Must I tell you that you're always mixed up?"

"All right. I have the coordinates, and I know Earth's co-ordinates, and I'll concentrate on your brother. And now . . . one . . . two—I hope it works—three. . . ."

They were skimming over Manhattan Island, and Central Park was a patch of green far below.

Jeff held Norby firmly under his arm and shouted, "You're too high up, Norby. Farther down and not too fast."

"You've got your hand over two of my eyes. All I can see are clouds and blue sky. Okay, that's better. Down we go!"

"There's a crowd in the park," Jeff said, "and they're surrounding the Central Park Precinct house. Get down so we can see what's happening."

"What if we get within blaster range?" Norby asked.

"Try not to."

"That's easy for you to say. You're not the one who's flying."

"Come on, Norby. Lower!"

The crowd was milling about as if it didn't know its own mind. They had spilled over into the traverse, along which there was no traffic.

A group of Ing's men were outside the precinct house, blasters ready. Their leader was crying out, "Disperse, you rebels, disperse, or we'll fill the park with your dead bodies."

"Do you suppose he'll really do that?" Norby asked.

"I don't know," Jeff said. "If Ing wins the day with too much bloodshed, he'll create hatred for himself, and he must know that, so I think he'd like to take over painlessly. Still, if his men get desperate—"

"Well, they're liable to, Jeff, because there's your brother and that woman policeman friend of his, and they've got personal shields on."

They could hear Fargo's voice shouting, "Forward, citizens, save our beloved island from Ing's Ignominies. Follow me!"

They didn't follow. They remained irresolute. One man shouted, "It's easy for you to say, 'Follow me'; you've got a personal shield. We don't."

"All right, then," shouted Fargo. "Watch us, and then join in. Come on, Albany. Get their blasters!"

The leading Ingman shouted, "Take them alive. Ing will pay a heavy reward for those two!"

They spread out. Fargo charged in, blocking an arm that was bringing down a blaster butt-first, and then landed a heavy blow in his assailant's solar plexus. The Ingman doubled up and lost interest in the fight for a while.

Albany Jones circled another Ingman, making little "come on" gestures with her hands. He charged, and she turned and bent, blocking the charge with her hip, seizing his wrist, and tumbling him over into another henchman. Both Ingmen went sprawling.

Norby cheered loudly. "That's it," he shouted. "Knock them all out."

"There are too many of them," said Jeff. "Fargo and Albany will be smothered after a while if the crowd doesn't help them. Norby, take me over the park. Maybe the bird-watchers are still around."

"What good will they do?"

"I want their leader, Miss Higgins. She struck me as a stalwart woman without fear, and that's the combination we want. Come on, Norby. If we can't find her, we'll have to join Fargo ourselves, and we won't be enough, either."

They were flying over Central Park in zigzags, looking for the small group with a tweed-clad woman in the lead. "What's one crazy woman going to do, Jeff?"

"I'm not sure, but I have a feeling she can help. And she's not crazy. She's enthusiastic."

"Is that they?"

"Maybe. Get down lower, and let's land on the other side of those trees. I don't want to panic them."

Jeff and Norby moved cautiously through the trees. "That's the woman," said Jeff. "Miss Higgins! Miss Higgins!"

Miss Higgins stopped and looked about. "Yes, what is it? Has anyone seen the grackle?"

"It's I, Miss Higgins."

Miss Higgins stared at Jeff for a moment. "Oh, yes," she said. "It's the young man and his little brother. We saw you at dawn, and here you are wanting to join our afternoon expedition. How enthusiastic of you."

"Not quite, Miss Higgins," said Jeff. "It's Ing and his In-grates. They are trying to take over the park."

"*Our* park? Is that the noise we've been hearing? It scared the birds and just about ruined the afternoon watching."

"That's the noise, I'm afraid."

"Well, how dare they?"

"Perhaps you can stop them, Miss Higgins. There's a crowd of angry patriots, but they need a leader."

"Where are they?" cried Miss Higgins, waving her umbrella. "Lead me to them. Bird-watchers, wait here, and make note of any cardinals and blue jays you might see. Remember that cardinals are red and blue jays are blue!"

"We're in a hurry, Miss Higgins," said Jeff. "Would you just hold my hand?"

Miss Higgins blushed. "I suppose it would be all right. You're quite young."

Jeff seized it, pulled her closer, put his arm about her waist, and said, "All right, Norby, full power upward. You're carrying two."

Miss Higgins let out a muffled scream. "Really, young man." And then she just gasped as she rose into the air.

"Back to the precinct," shouted Jeff. "There's still fighting going on."

"It's a *beautiful* view," said Miss Higgins. "This is really the way to do bird-watching. We can follow them as they fly."

Jeff and Albany were hemmed in, and the Ingmen were very wary in their approach, but it seemed just a matter of time. A few of the Ingmen faced the crowd, holding them off with blasters.

"Get down, Norby," said Jeff. "And you, Miss Higgins, lead the crowd against those Ingmen."

"Indeed I will," said Miss Higgins. "Barbarians!"

"We're coming, Fargo," shouted Jeff.

They landed. Miss Higgins broke away quickly, and Norby rolled toward the nearest Ingman who promptly fell over him. One of Norby's arms shot outward and seized the Ingman's blaster. He flipped it to Jeff, who seized it.

Meanwhile Miss Higgins marched up to the crowd, brandishing her umbrella and shouting in a surprisingly loud voice, "Come on, you cowards. Are you going to stand there and let those villains seize your park? Central Park was made for bird-watchers and for good people, and not for villains. Save your park if you have an ounce of manhood and womanhood in you! Are you going to let me do it all alone? I'm one weak, nearly middle-aged woman, and here I go. Who'll follow me? Onward, Higgins's soldiers, marching for the right!"

She charged forward, umbrella high, and Norby suddenly shouted. "Hurrah for Miss Higgins!"

The crowd took it up, and soon there was a confused roar "Hurrah for Miss Higgins! Hurrah for Miss Higgins!"

The mass of people moved forward, and the Ingmen instantly turned and made for the relative safety of the precinct house itself. The crowd, wild with fury, followed.

Jeff held back Norby and kept him from following. "No, no. Things are all right without us now. What we've got to do is get to Space Command. Can you do that if I give you the correct space coordinates?"

"Sure. Right through hyperspace."

"Do you have the energy?"

"You bet. I filled up on hyperspatial charge when we came through it from dragon-land."

"Good. And I must say that going through hyperspace is very pleasant. I didn't feel a thing. It was like blinking, or like a hiccup all over your insides."

"That's because I have a built-in hyperspatial shield," said Norby. "Didn't I tell you old Mac was a genius? I guess that's why I don't need a transmit. *I* am a transmit myself, and if you hold me tight, you come with me."

"How did you know I'd come with you?"

"I just guessed you would."

"What would have happened if you had guessed wrong?"

"It would have been pretty horrible for you, Jeff, but you know I'm never wrong."

"I know no such thing."

"Well, there's no use talking to you when you're *that* unreasonable. Give me the coordinates of Space Command. Okay, here we go!"

8

Showdown!

"Ouch!" said Jeff. This time he had landed on one side, still holding Norby. His right elbow hurt like mad.

"Where are we?" whispered Norby, his eyes peering from between the barrel and the hat. "Have I gotten us to the right place?"

"You have," said Jeff, sitting up with a groan.

"Never-fail Norby, they call me."

Jeff looked about and found himself in the midst of the highest officers in the Space Command, including Admiral Yobo, who looked as if he had been glaring and swearing for some time.

In back of Jeff was the open door of Space Command's transit station.

"It's working!" one of the officers cried, rushing past Jeff into the transmit.

"This boy must have come by transmit and rolled out just now," said another. "Didn't anyone see him? With this kind of security, we could expect Ing himself to appear among us."

"I saw him arrive," said Yobo in his rolling bass voice. "I think you'll find that however Cadet Wells arrived, the transmit is again out of order."

Again out of order, not *still*. The Admiral was careful not to describe exactly what he had seen or hint that arrival had not been by transmit. A good man, thought Jeff. Quick-thinking and on the side of all decent cadets.

"May I speak to you alone, Admiral?" Jeff asked.

Yobo stroked his chin thoughtfully, then nodded at the others—an offhand gesture that had the clear force of a command. The officers left.

"My robot—" Jeff began.

"You bought *that* robot with the money I gave you? *That* was all you could get?" said the admiral.

Norby stirred, but Jeff punched the barrel from behind to

keep him quiet. "It is a very good robot," Jeff said, "with a number of good and also exasperating abilities. And he will teach me Martian Swahili in no time. He is also a clever engineer and can fix the transmit. Ing and his Ingrates have control of Manhattan and—"

"We know about that, Cadet Wells. He's issuing orders for total surrender and insists on being called 'Emperor.' My own feeling is that the transmit isn't broken, but is under control from the other end." Yobo looked calmly at Jeff. Then he said, "And what do you say about that?"

"Aren't you going to do anything?" Jeff asked.

"I'm certainly not going to surrender," Yobo said, "but I have to be careful. All of Manhattan is hostage to Ing, and other places on Earth may fall to him, too, unless—"

"Unless what, sir?"

"Unless your brother can do something. He has been my close adviser in all this. He suspected that Ing would strike at Manhattan first, and he has taken measures."

"What measures?"

"We'll have to see," said Yobo calmly. "Meanwhile, what is it you want to do? Anything besides fixing the unfixable transmit?"

"I guess my robot can't really fix the transmit if Ing's blocked it. May I consult Norby—that's my robot's name—sir?"

"Go ahead, Cadet."

Jeff bent over Norby's hat and asked in a whisper, "What now?"

Norby's answer was so soft that Jeff couldn't hear, so he bent closer until his nose touched Norby's hat. His nose tingled and he stood up. "Ow!"

Norby's hand reached over to Jeff's leg and grabbed it hard.

I don't want the admiral to hear! I think I could gimmick a small ship (if he'll give us one) and hyperjump us to Earth.

Jeff gulped. "Norby?" he said faintly, feeling the tingle through his leg this time.

I think the dragon made you responsive to telepathy if I touch you. Get me a ship!

"Cadet Wells!" said Yobo. "Are you sane?"

"Most of the time, sir. And Norby is, too, some of the time. What we want is a small ship, just large enough to hold me and Norby."

"Why?"

"The idea is to move it past any security network Ing may have, and then fit it into his headquarters. I've been there, and I recognized it. He had it all draped in flags, but I could tell it was the main waiting room of the Old Grand Central Station. It had a museum smell about it, and I learned every inch of it when I used to visit it as a youngster. I know the transmit coordinates of the station, or at least Norby does because he memorizes transmit coordinates whenever he's been any-where. . . ."

"Cadet, you mean well," said Yobo, "but without a transmit it will take days to get to Earth, and with a transmit you wouldn't need a ship. You don't need a ship to make a trip to Earth. I've got the fleet itself ready to do it, but Ing threatens to blow up Manhattan if I as much as move a ship."

"That's just bluff."

"You're sure of that? You'd risk Earth's most renowned relic of ancient days, its most famous center of population, on your certainty?"

"The fleet would be noticed if it made a move, but one ship—one small ship—"

"Nonsense! It would be noticed, too. You should understand the efficiency of space detection, Cadet. You've been in the academy long enough for that."

"Please, Admiral," said Jeff. "Trust me. My robot is very good with machinery, and perhaps he can speed up one of your small ships and arrange to have it deflect the spy beams and move it right into the Grand Central waiting room."

"You're suggesting an impossibility," said Yobo, "un-less. . . ." He stared hard at Norby. Then he added, "Unless this—uh—barrel you clutch so tightly is by way of being a sorcerer. What about my private cruiser? Would that be small enough?"

"How small is it?"

"Small enough to hold just me, although you and your robot-barrel can squeeze in if you don't mind sleeping on the floor."

"Why would we have to sleep on the floor, sir?"

"Because you can't have my private cruiser without me on it, and I sleep in the one bed. That's the privilege of rank, Cadet."

"Take you, sir?" Jeff leaned over Norby's hat and whispered, "Can you move the admiral along with the ship and us?"

Norby squeaked, "No! Look at the size of him!"

Yobo heard that and smiled. "I'm not exactly stunted, but I am not going to sit here helpless. I've had enough of this whole thing. If you can get a ship into Grand Central Station, Cadet, I want to be with it. If anything happens to me, there are several good men—in their own estimation, if in no one else's—any one of whom could succeed me at once."

Jeff said promptly, "Norby, you can do it. Don't let me hear any negatives. Admiral, you can come, but let me be in temporary command."

"Cadet Wells," said Yobo with a grim smile, "you are more like your brother than I would have imagined. But before we make a move, you're going to tell me exactly how you expect to move the ship to Earth. Any ordinary movement and we'll be lost—and you know it."

Jeff thought awhile. "Admiral," he said, "will you give me your word that what I am about to say will be held in strictest confidence?"

"That's an impertinent request," Yobo said. "Any information you have that is of importance to system security should be delivered at once and without restrictions. What do you mean 'strictest confidence'?"

Jeff said miserably, "Well, sir, Norby can move us through hyperspace without a transmit."

"Indeed? I rather suspected you had something like that in mind, since nothing else would accomplish what you plan to do. And how does Norby bring about this impossibility?"

"I don't know. And he doesn't, either."

"After this is over, shouldn't he be taken apart so that we can find out the secret of hyperspatial travel?"

Norby squawked. "Jeff, have nothing to do with this oversize monster. He's as bad as that dragon."

"What dragon?" asked Yobo.

"Just a mythical monster, sir. But that's why I want the information held confidential. If it's found out, all the scientists would want to take him apart, and they still might not find out, and then we might not be able to put him together again, and we would end up with nothing."

"We would kill the goose that lays the golden eggs," whispered Norby angrily. "Tell him that, Jeff. Only make it a more intelligent bird."

Jeff nudged Norby into silence. "As it is, Admiral, Norby would make an important secret weapon for the Federation.

He has all sorts of powers that he can handle with perfect ease—almost."

"Very well, but why aren't we taking a squadron of armed men and a battle cruiser, then?"

"Well, Admiral, Norby's powers are, for the moment, somewhat limited."

The admiral laughed. "You mean he's a small robot and can only handle small things."

"You are not a small thing, you overgrown human, you!" shouted Norby.

The admiral laughed again. "I suppose I'm not. But let's go ahead, you undergrown barrel, you. I'll have my personal cruiser made ready."

An hour later they were on the cruiser, and Norby had plugged himself into the ship's engine. "I don't promise I can make this work," he grumbled. "Getting an entire ship with me through hyperspace is no small task."

"You can do it, Norby," Jeff said.

"Me? An undergrown barrel?"

"Yes, you. An ancient, intelligent, very brave, and powerful robot," said Jeff. "And if you don't, I will take out your works and fill your barrel with peanut butter—rancid peanut butter, so that the dragon-mother won't notice the nail smell anymore."

The jump through hyperspace was not *quite* perfect.

"We're not inside Grand Central," said Jeff.

"Well, there it is, right ahead," Norby said indignantly. "You have to allow for a little slippage. Ask any engineer."

"This will do fine," said the admiral. "We just require a tiny normal space correction."

Two seconds later, the admiral's personal cruiser was hovering on an antigrav beam in the air above Ing's throne. The ship was draped in flags, and a window behind it was smashed.

"Brilliant, Admiral," said Jeff. "Brilliant."

Norby groaned. "It was my hyperspatial jump, and it's my antigrav beam. *I'm* the one who's brilliant, only I don't know how long I can hold the ship up. My insides feel as if they're caving in."

Let the admiral get some credit, Norby, Jeff said telepathically. *Rank has its privileges.*

"Now hear this!" The admiral's bass voice rolled out across the vastness of the room. Ing himself, his mask still in place, was standing next to his throne looking up at the ship. He made no sound. His soldiers stood as if in a trance, stunned by the appearance of the ship.

"We have all of you under our guns," said Admiral Yobo, touching a button so that at least one gun extruded from the hull and aimed itself directly at Ing. "Put down your weapons and surrender. There will be no Solar Empire and no Emperor."

The ship settled slowly upon the throne, smashing it. Jeff heaved a sigh of relief.

Ing ran for the transmit.

"Stop him!" Jeff cried.

"We don't want to kill him," the admiral said, "or they'll make a heroic martyr out of him. Let's see, now, I might be able to destroy the transmit, but that might—"

"Let me out, Jeff," said Norby. "I'll do it."

The admiral, coming to an instant decision, touched another button, and a panel opened. "Get him, little robot!" he cried.

Norby hurtled out and aimed himself at Ing, but the transmit doors were opening and Ing was almost there.

Out of the transmit stepped Fargo, Albany, and a band of armed Manhattan policemen. "Greetings, Emperor," Fargo said with composure. "We were about to depose you, but I see from Norby here that my younger brother must have arrived with the same notion in mind. You can't beat the Wells brothers."

"Fargo," came the booming and unmistakable voice of Admiral Yobo, "what happened? Report!"

"Admiral? You're here, too? Well, it was simple. We were imprisoned here, but Albany and I got out, thanks to Norby, and after that things worked out exactly as I had hoped. The population of Manhattan was rising in revolt. It may be small, but the people of this island are very patriotic. I attacked the Central Park Precinct house and took it, aided by some clever martial arts on the part of this beautiful policewoman, Albany Jones, whom I expect will be promoted as a result."

"We were also helped by a woman who said she was a bird-watcher," Albany said. "The woman, a Miss Higgins, said she didn't care what happened to the rest of the universe, but that Central Park belonged to the people. She led the crowd against Ing's Ignominies and personally incapacitated at least seven Ingrates before I lost count."

"We liberated and armed a number of policemen and then

proceeded to take over other areas," Fargo continued. "At this moment any part of Manhattan not under our control is rapidly coming under it. And as for you, Ing the Inglorious, I suspect you will shortly have a large headache."

Ing had been standing in stunned and helpless silence, while his men were raising their arms in surrender. Norby, who had been circling him, now lunged for his head, which he struck with a metallic clang. Ing went down hard and, as Norby sat on him, the mask came off his face.

The admiral's voice rang out in disgust. "I might have known," he bellowed. "Ing the Intriguer is fussbudget Two Gidlow. I suspected it might be someone in Security! How else could a takeover be carried through with such precision?"

"Gidlow knew you would suspect that," Fargo said. "I think he tried to sell you the notion that _I_ might be the traitor to turn you off the scent."

"He almost succeeded," Yobo admitted. "My apologies, Mr. Wells. I will make it up to you. The contributions of you and Cadet Jefferson Wells will not be forgotten."

"How about Norby?" shrieked Norby, pounding his feet on Gidlow-Ing's chest.

"Nor will Cadet Norby be forgotten."

"I'll be a cadet?" Norby cried out in delight.

"Honorary," the admiral said.

"Take this demon off me!" Gidlow-Ing yelled. "You can't kill me like this. I demand a fair trial."

"Let's give him a fair trial right now," Norby said.

Using his antigrav to lift him in the air, Norby clamped his legs about Ing's neck and dragged the would-be emperor to his feet. Norby swayed from side to side, forcing Ing to waltz about on his skinny, silver-covered legs.

The waiting room rocked with laughter. Even Ing's erstwhile henchmen joined in. The police photographer eagerly ran his holographic camera, filming it all in moving three-dimensional image.

"Ing's revolution is over," the admiral said. "The men of the Manhattan police force have done nobly."

"If you'll notice," Albany said, sweetly but firmly, "half the police force are women."

"True, my dear," the admiral said, and bowed to her with admiring gallantry. "And so are half of the soldiers in my Space

Command. I was merely using an old-fashioned figure of speech. Which reminds me that your uniform seems to be strategically torn, and I must compliment you on *your* figure."

"Admiral," said Fargo, "it is as nothing compared with what textile dissolvers can do, but all such compliments are reserved for me."

"Then I congratulate *you*, Mr. Wells," said the admiral, "on your good taste—in cops as well as brothers."

9

Full Circle

After the revolt had been settled, there was a victory dinner in the admiral's private quarters on the great revolving wheel of Space Command.

The admiral had been given a new decoration for his broad chest. Fargo had been rewarded with a grant of money that made him thoroughly safe from bankruptcy. Albany, who sat close beside him—very close—had been promoted to Police Lieutenant Jones. And Jeff had been given a scholarship and a commendation, too, so that he could continue his studies as a Space Cadet.

Norby sat in the seat next to Jeff's, with a large portfolio under his arm. Within the portfolio was the official piece of pseudo-parchment that proclaimed to "all and sundry to whom this citation shall come to notice" that Norby Wells was hereby appointed to the rank of Honorary Cadet in the Space Command "with all the privileges and honors inseparable from that position." Norby had not yet found out what those privileges and honors were, but he was still asking.

Jeff noted with satisfaction, for he was still a growing boy, that the food at the admiral's table was considerably better than the food at the cadets' table. Norby had an extension cord leading into the nearest electric plug, and he was gorging himself to repletion, though, as he remarked later, the admiral's electricity tasted no better than anyone else's.

"I guess the kitchen computer is working now, eh, Admiral?" Jeff said.

"Perfectly," said the Admiral with great satisfaction.

"You can thank Norby for that," Jeff said. "He's very good with computers."

"When I fix them," Norby said, "they work like poetry in motion."

"Good," said the admiral. "But, Fargo, what was that remark you made to your brother the day he ruined the computer—TGAF?"

"It stood for 'The Game's A-Foot.' It was my way of telling him that he and I were going to try to find Ing. I didn't know he was right there with you. One thing, though, Admiral. . . ."

"Yes?"

"Confining Ing to an asteroid prison doesn't seem enough. Security is notoriously lax in the asteroids, and he may get out."

"What if he does?" the admiral said indifferently. "Everyone's laughing at him. The quickness with which his attempted revolt collapsed and the holographic images of his final dance with Norby on top of him have reduced him to a figure of fun. The film has been shown throughout the Solar System. He could do nothing at all now, even if he were released."

"I don't know about that," Jeff said darkly.

A junior officer, looking uneasy, rushed into the room. "Admiral!"

"Yes, Ensign?"

"The main computer of Space Command has just started reciting poetry. All the messages come out in verse, including the recipes from your private kitchen computer, which is now too addled to get the robot cooks to perform properly."

The admiral rose from his chair. Putting his napkin gently beside his place, he asked, *"My* kitchen computer?"

"Yes, sir. The remainder of this meal will be delayed."

The admiral roared, "Norby!"

There was no response.

"Norby!" Jeff shouted, banging on Norby's head.

Norby said in a low, snuffling voice, "I told the computers to work like poetry in motion. Maybe they took me literally. Computers are *very* stupid."

The admiral roared, "I demand that this barrel—"

"Cadet barrel," said Norby in a whisper.

". . . be thrown in irons."

"Please, Admiral," said Jeff, "he'll fix it in a jiffy."

"I give him fifteen minutes."

"Norby, get rid of the extension and get to work."

"Oh, all right, but it's the fault of the computers."

"And of a very mixed-up robot," Jeff said. He looked up defiantly at the rest of the company. "But *my* very mixed-up robot, and no one else can touch him. Not even you, Admiral."

NORBY'S
OTHER
SECRET

to the beautiful younger generation
Patti
Leslie
Nanette
Robyn

1

DANGER

Jefferson Wells sat in front of the main computer screen, trying to keep his mind on Earth history.

"Hey, Norby," he called out, "I hope you're fixing the kitchen computer without making things worse. Albany Jones and my brother, Fargo, will be here soon and I don't want to leave the Roman republic again just because the chicken has to be basted."

No one answered.

"Norby?" Jeff made it to the kitchen in a fast stride—his legs were long for a fourteen-year-old—and found no one fixing the computer *or* attending to the cooking.

Jeff shook his head. He knew lots of people with personal robots, but he was the only one blessed with a *mixed-up* robot. He basted the chicken in a hurry, muttering to himself. Then he hastened back through the living room and into the bedroom.

There, in front of the other terminal of the main computer was Norby, his back eyes firmly shut. Jeff could tell from the dim reflection in the computer screen that Norby's second pair of eyes were open on the other side of his head. Those eyes were staring at words that moved down the screen almost rapidly enough to blur, for Norby could read faster than most people could think. This was especially true when he closed one pair of eyes in order to concentrate entirely with the other pair.

Norby's body—a metal barrel about sixty centimeters high—teetered back and forth on his fully extended legs, the feet of which were symmetrical fore and back. His multi-joined arms, just as fully extended, had hands that also faced both ways. One of those hands remained pressed dramatically to his barrel torso. The other flung itself away suddenly, in a gesture common among politicians and actors.

"Friends, Romans, countrymen," intoned Norby in a voice a little too deep to be natural to him, the words sounding through a hidden speaker in his unremovable domed hat. Norby always talked through his hat, which lifted only far enough to show his four remarkably human eyes. He proceeded to raise his outstretched arm and point at the computer terminal as if it were an audience.

"Lend me your ears, I come to bury Caesar, not to praise him. . . ."

"I'll bury *you*," Jeff said, "if you don't fix the kitchen computer in a hurry."

Norby opened his back eyelids and blinked at Jeff. "It's such a boring machine, Jeff. It doesn't know any Shakespeare."

"I think that means you haven't figured out how to repair it yet."

"And it doesn't like me. It thinks I'm alien."

"The kitchen computer has no feelings and practically no brains. There's no use bragging to it about how your first owner put alien parts in you."

"Oh," said Norby. "Then don't you think I should avoid associating with inferior machines? Don't you think I should improve the quality of my mental data bank by studying?"

Jeff groaned. "You could at least study real history. All you do is indulge yourself in Shakespeare or try to remember how to get to whatever alien planet your alien parts came from."

"Well, *you* won't find it. You humans haven't even settled beyond your own solar system, and you haven't developed telepathy. . . ."

"Great galaxy! What's the use of you being able to communicate with me telepathically if you're not going to use it to help me learn history quicker?" Jeff stomped back to the kitchen and set about mashing the potatoes, a job the kitchen computer was supposed to do.

Norby pattered after Jeff, his telescopic legs almost completely withdrawn so that he seemed very small and humble. "You don't seem grateful that I succeeded in helping you pass the Martian Swahili exam."

"Right now I need help with history," said Jeff, thumping the bowl so hard that a bit of unmashed potato flew up and hit him on the nose. Exasperated, Jeff rolled his eyes upward and saw that more potato was stuck on the ceiling. "For a supposed teaching robot, you probably haven't learned one bit of history yourself."

"I have too. I'll prove it to you."

Jeff never had a chance to ask Norby what he meant, because at that moment the door speaker buzzed to attract attention. Then it announced, "Cadet Wells—Admiral Yobo is here to see you."

"He's *here,* on Earth? To see—*me?* Let him in!"

Jeff dashed into the living room, forgetting the large plastic apron he had tied around his waist. Norby, retracting his legs all the way inside his barrel, made use of his personal anti-grav to sail through the air beside him.

Jeff's legs tangled with a scatter rug and he sat down abruptly, while Norby hovered over his head and made an odd sound.

"Are you laughing at me?" Jeff asked through clenched teeth.

"That's an interesting question," said Norby. "Let me see if the facts correlate. Number one, I do have emotive circuits, and number two, you do look rather funny . . ."

"That's enough," said Jeff, scrambling to his feet. "Robots manufactured in *this* solar system do *not* have emotive circuits or a perverted sense of humor. I order you to go into the bedroom, and don't come out until you've learned history— or how to cook."

Norby shut his back eyes at Jeff, went into the bedroom, and slammed the door shut.

"Hello, Admiral," Jeff said as he opened the door to the hall. "Welcome to my apartment."

Boris Yobo was big and his enormous black hand engulfed Jeff's in a hearty shake that seemed to loosen Jeff's shoulder from his body.

"Cadet," he rumbled, "where's that brother of yours? I haven't been able to reach him." Yobo took off a plain civilian coat to reveal a splendid uniform, weighed down with solid rows of medals, most of which could be worn only by the head of the Federation's Space Command.

Jeff was sure that Admiral Yobo was not in the habit of paying calls on Space Academy cadets—not even orphaned ones—nor even on their older brothers who happened to work as agents for the Space Command. Especially unannounced calls. "Fargo should be here soon for dinner, Admiral."

Yobo sniffed. "Whatever it is, it smells good after the synthomeals they've been feeding me at the meetings I've been attending. If we continue to eat those meals we'll never work out ways of controlling this new batch of pirates plundering the solar system. In fact, I'd be tempted to join them myself."

He sniffed again. "Your Earth food doesn't have quite the tang of the stuff we grow under domes in the Mars Colony. Personally, I don't think you Earth people know how to season properly. Shall I demonstrate?"

"It's almost done, sir," Jeff said, "so it's too late for improvements." Admiral Yobo was known for his exotic gourmet taste in food, and once a dish suited his fancy, it was inedible to anyone else. "Would it be all right for me to know why you are here?"

"Smells like roast chicken."

"And left-over meatloaf. Albany Jones is coming, too."

"You can have the meatloaf, but the chicken would suit me well. I suppose, Cadet, you want to know why I didn't phone first."

Yobo sat on the couch heavily and didn't wait for Jeff to reply. "For all I know," he said, "your phone is tapped by spies from the Inventors Union. They're a difficult, proud and powerful group, and they're determined to get the secret of miniaturized-antigravity devices like Norby's. That's why I've come here secretly to warn you that the Inventors Union may try to kidnap your robot. Maybe soon."

"No!" said Jeff. "They'll want to take Norby apart. I'm not going to let them."

Yobo said, "The Inventors Union is working around the clock to discover how to make miniantigrav units, and they're getting impatient. So are some others. Everyone's tired of antigrav units so big that only a six-person vehicle can accommodate them. Even *I'm* tired of them. Now either that old, mad spacer, McGillicuddy, *invented* miniantigrav, or he *found* it on an alien spaceship that nobody else can find and used it when he constructed Norby. Since McGillicuddy's been dead for years, there's only Norby left to work with. You know, Jeff, I'm fond of Norby, but surely you understand that the needs of the Federation. . . ."

"Norby doesn't know how he does it, Admiral, and he doesn't remember an alien ship."

"He doesn't have to know or remember. My scientists at the Space Command could analyze his workings down to subatomic levels. . . ."

"No!" said Jeff. "No—sir! I won't allow it. Norby is my property." He shoved both hands through his curly brown hair.

The phone rang with the family call signal.

Relieved at the interruption, Jeff said, "Wells answering."

The screen lit up to show Farley Gordon Wells—twenty-four-years-old, athletically wiry, a little taller than Jeff, his eyes blue, his hair wavy and dark. Behind Fargo was a strikingly attractive girl in a Manhattan police uniform. She was beautiful, and she looked happy in a way (it seemed to Jeff) that most women looked when they were around Fargo.

"Hello, kid monster," said Fargo. "I'm still at the precinct. I'm afraid I'll be late."

"Hello, geriatrics case," said Jeff. "You always are."

"Albany's fault. Her professional responsibilities required her to foil a holdup with some high-powered karate, which made it necessary for her to change uniforms and. . . ." Fargo's eyebrows suddenly elevated. "Is that Admiral Yobo behind you? What have I done?"

"Probably a great deal," said Yobo, "but nothing I'm aware of at the moment. This is a social call. Space home life gets boring, even in a spome as big as Space Command. Don't you remember my suggesting dinner when I was in New York for meetings?"

Fargo's eyebrows came down and closed together, "Is this the week you're having meetings in Manhattan? When I'm in love?"

"Just for this week?" asked Albany, her beautiful eyes crinkling.

"Bring some TGAF candy with you when you come, Fargo," said Jeff.

"Sure," said Fargo, with a grin. "You'd better start dinner without us, though I won't be expecting too much left over with the Admiral there."

The phone shut off.

"TGAF," said Jeff, "is our private family code. It stands for 'The Game's A-Foot'. It means trouble so Fargo understands that you're here on business, not a social call."

Yobo sighed, and sat down at the table. "I know that private family code of yours. I wish you had one that indicates *big* trouble, because your romantic brother believes he can always talk himself out of danger, and we may need more than talk this time."

"Are we going to need weapons?" asked Jeff.

"I'm not sure, but we had better be ready. I don't know

when or where—or even, if—the Inventors Union is likely to strike, but we've got to prepare for the worst." The admiral stopped talking and sniffed. "You're letting the chicken dry out," he said.

"Norby," called Jeff, "serve the chicken!"

There was no answer and Jeff flung open the bedroom door. "That crazy barrel has gone again!"

"Taken off into hyperspace?" asked Yobo.

"He must have. I hurt his feelings—or maybe he needed to refuel. That's where he does it. What are we going to do?"

"About Norby? Nothing. The chicken comes first," said Yobo, heading for the kitchen.

During dinner, Jeff managed to make his way through half a drumstick with an almost total lack of appetite as he waited for Norby to return. Finally he said, "Sir, I'm afraid that Norby may have overheard you. He's a pretty brave robot, but he does have this prejudice against being taken apart, and he may have gone into hyperspace to save himself. I can't communicate with him when he's there, and he's supposed to tell me when he's going."

"Indeed?" said Yobo, who had already demolished his drumstick and a mountain of mashed potatoes and was slicing himself a helping of white meat. "Since there's nothing we can do about it, let's finish dinner. I'm sure he'll come back because it will get lonely out there after a while." Admiral Yobo attacked the chicken again. Between bites he said, "But see here. Everyone knows about Norby's personal antigrav. But only you and your brother and I know about Norby's secret ability to enter hyperspace with his built-in hyperdrive mechanism. If the greedy Inventors Union finds out about his hyperdrive, added to his miniantigrav, they'll tear the solar system apart to get it."

"Fargo thinks Norby's ability to travel in hyperspace is related to his miniantigrav," Jeff said. "So it's all *one* secret talent of Norby's."

"What Fargo thinks doesn't mean a thing. The only way to keep the Inventors Union away from Norby is to arrange to have my own scientists...."

"Please, sir—"

"Cadet," thundered Yobo, "you know that eventually *someone* has to examine Norby, and it might as well be *my* scientists. He's too valuable to be just the pet robot of a boy."

Jeff stared at the admiral in horror. *He's* the enemy, too, he thought to himself. What do I do?

There was no time to wonder if any answer to that question existed because at that moment there was a loud thump in the bedroom.

"Norby?" asked Jeff, getting up from his chair. He felt a wash of relief sweep over him at the thought that his robot might be back. Yet a feeling of fear came almost immediately afterward at the thought of what Yobo might do.

Following the thump, however, there was a more complicated noise, a very strange one. Strange, that is, to be heard in an apartment in the sovereign nation of Manhattan, USA sector of the Terran Federation.

"Jeff, that was a rather disturbing growl," Yobo said. "Have you got an animal in there? It sounded like a large one."

"Not that I know of, sir . . . Norby!"

A small barrel shot out of the bedroom into Jeff's outstretched arms. Norby's hat tilted back and a pair of wide-open eyes looked up.

"It's not my fault!" said Norby.

Jeff's lips tightened. Norby said that frequently, and usually, it wasn't true.

Something followed Norby into the living room. It was sandcolored. It looked hungry. And it had the beginnings of a mane.

"Space and time!" said Yobo, in a husky whisper, "it's a lion. I've been meaning to get around to visiting the Africa of my ancestors, but I have no great desire to have this portion of it visit me."

"Norby, what have you done?" Jeff asked, scarcely able to force the words out.

The lion advanced slowly into the room.

2

Getting Away

"It's only a small lion," said Norby plaintively. "Just a cub."

"A cub, my foot!" said Jeff, who was clutching Norby and backing toward the kitchen door. "It's almost full-grown and you know it. Where did you get it?"

"In a sort of zoo," said Norby. "It jumped on me and came with me when I went into hyperspace to get home. It wasn't my fault. It *followed* me."

Admiral Yobo grunted and stood up. Slowly, majestically, he picked up the chair on which he had been sitting and held it in front of him, the legs pointing at the advancing lion. He moved around the table until he was standing in front of Jeff, shielding him.

The lion roared, and Yobo brandished the chair menacingly. The lion snarled and lifted one broad paw.

Norby's hat slammed down until his head had disappeared inside the barrel. His arms and legs sucked inward as well, so that only the metal barrel remained in view.

"Coward," muttered Jeff, but he might have been talking to himself. He was ashamed that he was not defending his own admiral as a space cadet should, instead of vice versa.

The lion's uplifted paw showed its claws as he hit out at the chair leg.

"Get back, you fatuous feline," shouted Yobo, stamping his foot as he pushed the chair forward.

"What zoo?" Jeff asked Norby as the lion began to alternately growl and roar.

"Not a nice one," came the words through the hat. "Very bad."

"I can see that," said Jeff. "The lion looks underfed."

"Cadet!" roared Yobo, louder and deeper than the lion. "Stop practicing the fine art of conversation by making diagnostic comments. *Do* something. Get into the kitchen and send for help. My ancestors might have battled lions, but not while wearing dress uniforms. I don't plan to get down to hand-to-paw wrestling with this beast. It looks as though it might have fleas."

The lion sprang and Yobo met it with the chair and forced it back. It snarled again and the muscles in its haunches bunched as if it were about to spring again, possibly over the chair.

Jeff put Norby down and ran to the table. The lion, possibly surprised at the sudden movement, stopped snarling at the admiral and turned its menacing yellow eyes on Jeff, who snatched up what was left of the roast chicken and threw it at the lion.

"A dubious accomplishment," said Yobo, as the lion retreated to a corner and began to devour the chicken, bones and all. "You've bought a little time, at the cost of feeding my dinner to that underfed, oversized cat. Now get to the phone and. . . ."

The door speaker interrupted. "Fargo and Albany are here," it announced.

Since Fargo's thumbprints were keyed to the lock, Jeff didn't have to let him in.

As she entered the apartment, Albany gasped, reached automatically for her gun, and stopped the motion midway. "Drat! No gun," she said turning to Fargo, "Well, you loquacious lout, you're the one who tells me it isn't dainty to wear a gun on a date. You say smooth talk is all one needs. Well, smooth-talk that oversized tomcat."

Fargo's eyes had lit up when he saw the lion. They always did at the sight of danger. But then they fell. "Is that my dinner that lion is eating, after I've saved up an appetite just for the occasion?"

"It's *my* dinner the lion is eating," said Yobo, still holding the chair in the direction of the animal. "I came here to explain to Jeff that the Inventors Union appears to be planning to confiscate Norby as an alien device possessing great technological secrets, and Norby seems to have retaliated by bringing us a wild pet from a bad zoo."

"Jeff always wanted a kitten," said Fargo, "but this is ridiculous. That lion has finished the chicken and I'm pretty sure he considers it only an appetizer with ourselves as the main course."

The lion gave a cursory lick to its paws, licked its lips on either side with a huge, pink tongue, and then growled. It eyed the four human beings with what seemed to be unsatisfied hunger and aggressive ideas. It rose to its feet and snarled.

Jeff said, "Fargo, do we still have those sedative pills you bought when the family shipping business went bankrupt and you thought you wouldn't sleep well? You never took them, but maybe the lion. . . ."

Fargo lifted his finger. "Good idea. They should still be in the kitchen behind the matchbox we never used till you got a pet robot that plays with kitchen computers."

Jeff kicked Norby. "Stick out your head and legs and go find those pills or I'll tell the admiral to take away your honorary cadethood."

"You wouldn't," said Norby.

"Oh, wouldn't I? Try me—and bring the meatloaf, too."

Norby's appendages and head popped out of his barrel and he ran into the kitchen in the kind of partial antigrav mode that allowed him to take long strides. He came back almost at once with the pills and with the meatloaf in its glass container.

Jeff stuffed the pills into the meatloaf while Yobo made small lunges with the chairlegs at the advancing lion, who growled louder. Albany was speaking softly into her wrist phone.

She said, "The Central Park Greater Zoo says it has no room for another lion and it's against the law for us to have one in an apartment in the first place. We could get into a lot of trouble."

"The lion's been telling us that for quite a while," said Yobo, shoving the lion back a step.

"The Bronx Zoo will take one, if we can present a certificate of ownership. I don't suppose Jeff has one," she finished.

"Not lately," said Jeff, swinging the meatloaf.

"But I've called for an antigrav squad car to come up to the windows here."

"Better than nothing," said Jeff, and let go of the meatloaf, which hit the lion in the muzzle.

Fargo said indignantly, "Must I start my vacation by letting you throw the only other dinner we possess to the lions?"

Yobo said, "That doesn't matter. I don't eat red meat. Cadet, did you put the sedative pills into that meatloaf?"

"All of them, Admiral," said Jeff.

"Good. Then it shouldn't be long."

Yobo sat down and began to eat vegetables while the lion

finished the meatloaf. "Vegetarianism is good for you," he announced. "Have some."

"Have some what, honored Admiral?" asked Fargo, with exaggerated politeness. "You're eating it all. Besides, I don't believe that the lion will be put to sleep. Those were pretty old pills and I never tested them."

"There's the squad car," said Albany. "Fully automated. Nobody in the precinct was keen on riding with a lion."

The lion yawned, displaying all of its large, efficient-looking teeth.

Four humans, an automated police car, and a guilty robot waited impatiently for the lion to decide to go to sleep.

"I'm sorry, Jeff," said Norby after awhile. "I suppose it *is* my fault. I got mixed up."

"That's apparently his specialty, little brother," said Fargo. "When McGillicuddy mixed up his insides, he mixed up Norby." Fargo turned to the robot. "How did you come to think it was a good idea to bring a lion home from the zoo, Norby?"

"It jumped on me, Fargo, and tossed me around as if I were a beach ball! Then it took a grip on me with its paws and I thought that if I went back into hyperspace that would scare it loose, but it didn't. It was too stupid to be scared and it must have held on to me because when I was back in the apartment, it was here, too."

"But where was this zoo, and why did you go there?" asked Fargo.

"It's a long story," said Norby.

The robot turned to Jeff, who came to his defense immediately. "He's too upset to explain clearly, Fargo. It was just some zoo in Europe or somewhere."

"In Europe," said Norby at once. "That's right."

The lion's head sank to its paws. It snored loudly and distracted Fargo, who shook both fists in the air and said, "See? You don't need a gun; just a few pills."

"And someone to think of the pills," grumbled Jeff under his breath.

Yobo had finished the vegetables and began on the large cake Jeff had bought for dessert. "I trust, Cadet, that you will think of a way to get the beast over to the police car, because I do not intend to help lift it. I'm wearing my dress uniform and I'm convinced that animal has fleas."

Albany marched toward the lion with a determined look on her face, but Fargo stopped her. He said, "You have your dress uniform on, too, and that beast must weigh 300 kilograms. It's a man's job. Jeff and I. . . ."

Albany was promptly offended. "What do you mean 'a man's job?' I'm as strong as you are, and Jeff is a boy."

"Jeff may be a boy," Jeff said, "but he believes in thinking out a problem and not just slam-banging into it. That's what Fargo always said I should do. So it's up to Norby."

"I don't want to pick him up," Norby said.

"I don't care whether you want to or not. You just follow orders. Put your arms under that lion and intensify your antigrav and put him into the police car."

"But Jeff, the lion is smelly and it has fleas."

"Fleas aren't going to bother you, and I never heard you complain about smells before."

"It may be sleeping lightly. It may wake up."

"Norby, all this is your fault in the first place, and you're the one who's equipped to deal with the problem. I'm giving you a logical order, and I order you to obey it."

"Oh, very well," said Norby, going to the lion.

"I'll never get used to your robot," said Yobo. "There isn't another one like it in the Federation."

"You mean sassy and rebellious?" asked Fargo.

"I mean intelligent and emotional," said Yobo. There was no smile on his broad, high cheek-boned face. "It's amazing that only the Inventors Union is after him. We should all be. I imagine that if we can find out how he works, everyone will want a Norby instead of the stupid, dutiful machines the Federation allows."

"Nobody would want a mixed-up robot," said Fargo with a shrug.

"I don't know about that," said Albany. "I think he's cute."

Norby winked one of his back eyes at her, wrapped his arms around the lion, and elevated. The lion opened one eye, growled, and began to struggle.

"Hold him!" shouted Jeff, running to help.

"I'm managing," said Norby. "You wanted me to do it myself and I'm going to do it. I'll show you. . . ." He was balancing the sleepily struggling lion on the window sill. "This stupid life form is scratching my barrel."

"Don't drop him to the sidewalk!" yelled Jeff. "Stupid or not, it *is* a life form. Put him in the car safely."

"All done," said Norby, stepping back from the window. The door of the police car shut, and Jeff could see the astonished and groggy lion inside.

Albany spoke into her wrist radio and the car flew off. "Okay. The car will take the lion to the Bronx Zoo, where keepers are ready to take it into temporary custody pending determination of ownership."

"Are we going to get fined?" asked Jeff.

"Not likely," said Albany. "They haven't forgotten how we rescued Manhattan from Ing the Ingrate, so it will be easy to fix things up. Besides, the admiral can use his influence."

"No, I won't," said Yobo. "You leave me out of your report. I don't want your Manhattan authorities to know I'm here. My problem is with Norby, not with the lion."

Norby jiggled up and down on his legs. "I'm Jeff's problem, no one else's.

"Unfortunately," said Yobo. "You're everyone's problem. The Inventors Union wants to investigate you scientifically."

"You mean, tear me apart?" squeaked Norby at the highest pitch of his voice range. "Eviscerate my insides? Tangle my circuits? Electrocute my electronics? Spoil my beautiful appearance? I'll disappear and never come back, that's what I'll do."

"No, you won't," said Jeff, "because I'm not going to let anyone do anything to you."

"It's a family matter," said Fargo. "I'm Jeff's guardian and legally responsible for anything he owns. We'll sue. . . ."

"Don't bet on getting the chance," said Yobo, drily. "I think it would make sense to have a serious discussion on how to handle the obvious necessity of doing something about Norby."

"I'm hungry," said Albany, tossing back her long, blond hair.

"Unfortunately," said Fargo, "there's nothing to eat. What the lion didn't devour, the admiral did, so we'll have to go to one of the neighborhood restaurants. If you'll cover up that uniform of yours, Admiral, you can come disguised as an ordinary citizen. If we can get a shielded booth, we can talk privately there, out of reach of the Inventors Union."

The admiral had no chance to respond because there was

a thunderous knocking on the apartment door and a loud call that drowned out any announcement the door computer might have tried to make.

"Open up! Federation security officers!"

Fargo went to the door and leaned nonchalantly against it. "My lady love and I are here and we don't want company. Go away!"

"We have a Federation warrant to confiscate your robot on behalf of the Inventors Union. Open up, or we'll break down the door."

There was another violent knock.

"Go to the bedroom," whispered Yobo to Jeff, "and I suggest you both go on a little trip *now*."

"Yes, sir," said Jeff. He added quickly, "If I don't get back right away, Fargo, please go on vacation in our scoutship. We can join you because Norby can tune into your ship with his space-location sense."

"Sure I can," said Norby. There was a short pause while Norby's eyes blinked. "I think."

"We'll be sunk if we have to depend on Norby," Fargo said.

Norby squawked incoherently at that, but the admiral pointed imperiously toward the bedroom as the banging on the door grew more forceful.

Jeff and Norby dashed into the bedroom. Norby grabbed Jeff's hand, "Ready?"

Jeff nodded. He was thinking. It's a good thing they don't know Norby's secret that he can vanish into hyperspace without special equipment, or they wouldn't have announced what they were here for.

Just before they disappeared, Jeff and Norby heard Albany say, "Oh, hello, men. Do have this small left-over piece of cake."

The grayness of hyperspace swallowed Jeff and Norby.

3

JAMYA

Norby's personal protective field came on automatically to save them from lethal stress of hyperspace, so Jeff was aware only of gray nothingness. And, since time does not exist in hyperspace, he was no sooner aware of it when he was out of it again, with only a vague memory that Norby had been trying to explain—telepathically—how he had got into the bad zoo.

"Where are we?" asked Jeff. They were sitting on a grassy lawn, facing interesting treelike plants that seemed familiar.

"You again!"

The voice was not speaking in Terran Basic, but Jeff understood, and Norby was already answering in the alien language. Nobody had the advantage of having eyes in the back of his head (except there wasn't any real back to his head; all sides were front).

Jeff turned around. In the other direction was a landscaped hill with a large castlelike structure on it. At the foot of the hill, quite near to Jeff, was a miniature castle with a female dragon standing in the doorway. She was green, her large eyes fringed by eyelashes, and she held a smaller version of herself. Both wore thin gold collars.

Jeff said softly, "You've brought us back to Jamya, Norby. I thought you didn't know how to get here."

"I don't," Norby answered in a low voice. "It's some instinct or something. I just came. Part of me *knows* the planet of the dragons."

"Well, then, *please* don't insult the Jamyns this time." He rose and bowed politely. "How do you do, ma'am? And how is your pretty daughter, Zargl, whom I see in your arms?"

"I'm fine," said the young dragon, as she spread her wings and flew to Jeff's shoulder. "I'm glad you came back. You didn't stay long last time. I'm also glad you've learned our language."

Jeff hoped his smile would seem a pleasant expression to the dragons. A gentle dragon bite had established telepathic communication with him when he and Norby had come here once before, and the bite had made it possible for him to learn the Jamyn language telepathically, almost at once. Perhaps the dragons could learn Terran Basic through telepathy.

"I detect your thought," said the mother dragon in Terran Basic. "If you speak your language carefully and think more clearly, then I will learn more quickly." She switched to Jamyn. "It is more important, however, for you to continue to improve your knowledge of *our* language, which is clearly the more civilized of the two."

Jeff did not think it would be wise to dispute that. He said, "Yes, ma'am," in careful Jamyn.

"I discussed your earlier arrival with the Grand Dragon, and she said you must know the secret of hyperspace travel, which we Jamyn have never been given. We were meant to stay on our own planet."

"Do you have many visitors?" Jeff asked.

"We have had none at all. You were the first. That's why the matter had to be discussed. It was decided that if visitors are approved by the Mentors, they will be permitted to stay for a short period. Do you intend to remain?"

"Do we intend to remain, Norby?" asked Jeff.

"Not exactly." Norby blinked several times in that exasperating way he had when he was debating whether or not to confess that he'd gotten mixed up again. "Part of me seems to want to be here, and *knows* the way even though the rest of me doesn't. And I *do* know the language. I just can't quite remember what a Mentor is."

"In Terran Basic, it means 'wise teacher,'" said Jeff.

"It means the same in Jamyn," said the mother dragon. "They are our teachers. We were once a wild and primitive species, but the Others came and left Mentors to help us, as our legends say; and, of course, our legends are inspired and therefore true. By the way, you mustn't think of me as mother dragon. That is quite belittling. My name is Ziphyzggtmtizm."

Jeff knew only so much could be expected of telepathic learning. "May I call you Zi?" he asked.

Ziphyzggtmtizm whispered it several times softly to herself, then said, "Yes. I like it."

"Who are the Others?"

"That is difficult to say. There are no descriptions of them in our legends, and the Mentors have never told us anything about them. . . . Zargl! Stop clawing at the alien's top scales! Mind your manners! Besides all that long, soft tangle may not be clean."

Zargl took her claws out of Jeff's hair and said, "What's your name, alien?"

"I'm Jeff and this is my robot, Norby."

"Odd," said Zi. "Robots are small devices for mechanical labor, controlled by household computers, and are without personality or intelligence. Naturally, they belong to thinking Jamyns, as any machine might. This Norby that you call a robot, however, seems to have personality and intelligence. How can he be owned?"

"That is a good question, come to think of it," said Norby.

"Norby and I are *partners*," Jeff said before Norby could work over the question.

The baby dragon left Jeff's shoulder and flew down to perch on Norby's hat.

"Get off, get off," shouted Norby, waving his arms.

"Won't," said Zargl. "You're not a Mentor."

"I am, too," said Norby. "I am a teacher. I've been teaching that human boy languages, history, and—uh—galactic travel."

Jeff sighed. Could you call it galactic travel when you were never sure where you were going, or how you would get away, or if you would return home when you did get away?

"Would you care to have something to eat in my house?" asked Zi, courteously. "It was rude of me to chase you away last time and I would like to make amends. The Mentors know you are here by now, but they may not get round to you for a while because, as far as we know, they spend most of their time meditating. They are trying to tune in to all parts of the universe so they can find the Others. We will have time to eat."

"I'm not sure I can eat your food," said Jeff, trying to sound apologetic so as not to give offense.

"I'll test it first," said Norby.

"You being so accurate?"

"Yes, indeed," said Norby, extending his legs to their longest and putting his hands on the sides of his barrel. "Testing the structure of foodstuffs is absurdly simple for a genius robot like me." Norby stalked into the dragon's home and Jeff followed.

Norby passed the food as safe. "Good protein," he said.
"High in fiber, lower in cholesterol. It will do you good, Jeff."

Except for something blue and mushy that he decided not
to try, Jeff thought it was delicious.

The dragons' furniture was another thing. It was not built
for human dimensions and angles and almost nothing looked
the least bit comfortable. The exception was something in one
corner that looked like a battered old green hassock.

"May I sit on this, Zi?" Jeff asked.

"Certainly. It's an antique tail rest that has been in our family
for generations. It's still quite useful. Of course, you don't
have a tail, you poor thing, but you are certainly welcome to
rest the place where the tail ought to be."

Jeff sat down and found it comfortable enough. It had a
small design on top that resembled a diamond-shaped figure
on the dragons' collars. A more interesting design of complicated wiggly patterns circled the sides of the hassock.

Jeff said, "Where is your husband, Zi?"

"What is a husband?"

"Well, the male of the species who—that is. . . ."

"Male? Oh, you mean a different variety of a life form?
I've read that such a phenomenon occurs on other planets. We
don't travel, as I told you, but the Mentors have provided us
with good galactographies. When I read about the peculiar
customs and habits of other worlds I can only be grateful that
we Jamyns live on a civilized planet."

"But if you don't have males, how do you have children?"

"Ah—you need males for that on other worlds, don't you?
I've never really understood that. We bud, you know, and I
don't see how it can be done conveniently any other way. Zargl
was such a *cute* bud, right here under my wing. You should
have seen her. But actually," she brought one wing forward
and covered her eyes with it briefly, "we don't really talk about
budding among ourselves. It's private. You're not Jamyn, of
course, so you don't matter."

"But if you bud," said Jeff, a little argumentatively, "there's
very little alteration of inherited characteristics, and you can't
evolve. In our species, the genes always get mixed up so that
children aren't exactly like their parents and we evolve quickly."

"See," whispered Norby to Jeff, "it's good to be mixed up."
Jeff glared at him, and Norby closed his eyes and pretended
he hadn't said anything.

"According to our traditions, the Others helped us to stay the same. I suppose, since the universe itself is changing, that there should be creatures that change. I wish you and your species well, for while we Jamyn contribute stability, perhaps you Terrans contribute exciting change."

"Exciting, indeed," said Norby, bouncing up and down slightly. "You have no idea how *mixed-up* all the Terran life forms are"—he glanced quickly at Jeff as he emphasized the word—"especially human beings. Their history has all the ex-citement of nasty wars and wicked persecutions and foolish plots and. . . ."

"Norby! How can you say such things about your own world?" Jeff asked. "You're just ashamed of being mixed up yourself."

"I told you I couldn't help the lion. I explained it all to you while we were in hyperspace and you're not helping me in the least with my *new* secret. It scares me."

What new secret? thought Jeff. He tried to remember and failed.

Just then the dragons' computer made a chiming noise.

"Oh," said Zi. "What an honor! It's a direct signal from the Mentors' castle. I've never been worthy of a direct signal be-fore. How my friends will envy me." She spread out both her wings as far as they would go and bowed deeply in the direction of the chime.

The computer said, "The aliens are summoned for an au-dience. Only the aliens. They must come at once, and alone."

Norby ran over to Jeff, his hat so low that you could barely see his eyes. "I don't want to go. I'm afraid."

"Why? You think part of you may be from here, don't you? Jamya may be where your alien portions were formed."

"I don't care. Let's go back to Earth and find Fargo. . . . Or maybe we could disguise ourselves and join a circus traveling through the solar system."

"The Inventors Union will find us if we do," said Jeff. "Do you want to be taken apart?"

Suddenly the dragons' computer screen swirled with an eerie color. When it cleared, a cold light shone on a monstrous shape standing in a cavernous space on two thick lower limbs. The figure had four arms, a head that bulged on top, with a slit below the bulge that could have been a mouth, and three iri-descent patches on the bulge that could have been eyes.

"Mama! I'm scared!" wailed Zargl, leaping into her mother's arms and folding her wings.

Jeff realized, a bit uneasily, that he felt the same way. And yet he was larger than Zi and, for all he knew, he might be larger than the creature on the computer screen. He flexed his arm muscles to reassure himself that he still had them, and wished he knew as much about karate as Albany Jones did. He grabbed Norby and stood up straight.

"Ouch!" Jeff had forgotten that the dragons' ceiling was low, and, in the process of rubbing his sore head and trying to stoop, he dropped Norby, who fell with a clunk.

"Ouch!" Norby said. "You keep dropping me, Jeff! What kind of an owner are you?"

"Why don't you turn on your antigrav when you feel yourself falling? You would if you weren't so busy retracting." Looking around for allies, Jeff saw with discouragement that Norby was not completely withdrawn into his barrel and muttering ominously. Zargl was cowering in Zi's arms, and Zi had backed as far from her own computer screen as possible.

Zi said with clear embarrassment, "Of course, there's nothing to be afraid of, but I never saw a Mentor before. We only receive verbal messages and there are no pictures of them in our books. This is most unusual . . . and a gr—reat honor, I think."

"But Zi," said Jeff, "how can *you* be afraid? We humans have always imagined dragons to be completely brave. It was dragons who terrified others. Dragons could even breathe fire."

"Oh, we can do *that*," said Zi, not taking her eyes off the apparition on the screen. She breathed out a small blue flame. "That's one of our old, primitive defenses, but it takes a lot of energy to separate the hydrogen from the. . . ."

Jeff had backed away from her. "There! You see! Even though you're small, you shouldn't be afraid."

Zi said, indignantly, "I am not small! Only the Grand Dragonship is larger than I am, and she's my aunt. And I'm *not* afraid of the Mentor—if that's a Mentor. I'm just overcome by respect and awe."

But she *acted* afraid.

Jeff shrugged and turned back to the screen. The strange figure was staring at them, if those patches of shimmering color were indeed eyes.

"What do you want?" Jeff demanded, determined that *he*

wasn't going to show fear, whatever the others did.

"Courtesy and respect," said the figure in a kind of creaky voice, as though it were something that was not often used. "I've summoned you to the presence, and you have not hurried. See to it that you come immediately to the Mentor castle on the hill. Alone!" The screen went blank.

Norby's head popped up. "Not without me."

"I thought you were too scared," Jeff said.

"I am, but I'm less scared when I'm with you. Besides, if we're together we can both escape through hyperspace. If we were separated," he added virtuously, "I wouldn't dream of escaping on my own and leaving you in danger here."

"We'll think about escape later," Jeff said, *after* we find out what the Mentors want. Come on, partner!"

4

MENTORS AND HASSOCKS

Jeff wanted to pretend that Norby didn't have antigrav but this had disadvantages. The path up the hill to the large castle was steep, and the paving was ravaged by age. It was rough and uneven, and rank weeds grew in the cracks.

Jeff sighed inwardly at the discomforts of their progress, while Norby, walking on his two-way feet, complained loudly and repetitiously until Jeff finally decided that carrying him was easier than listening to his grumbling.

Halfway up, Jeff was forced to say, "You're no pleasure to carry uphill full weight, Norby, so could I persuade you to turn on your antigrav a little?"

Norby complied with his usual mixed-up judgment of intensity, so that Jeff had to shout, "Not that much," as his feet began to leave the ground. "You'll reveal the ability."

Norby added a bit of weight and they continued to climb.

It soon became quite apparent that the paving was not the only imperfection. What had appeared to be lovely landscaping turned out to be full of flaws, although here and there it seemed as if someone had tried, halfheartedly, to prune trees and weed flower beds.

"The Mentors don't seem to care how things look," said Jeff.

"What's that?" Norby asked, jiggling so much that Jeff lost his balance and let go of him. Whit his own full weight suddenly restored, Jeff sat down hard. Fortunately, he sat on a patch of weeds growing where a paving stone should have been.

Norby came down much more gently. "You keep letting go of me. What's the matter with you?"

"Why were you jiggling? What's the matter with *you?*" Jeff got up and rubbed himself where he had made contact with the ground.

"I was looking at that. It startled me."

Among the flowers off to the side was an odd little metal creature, much smaller than Norby. It had a long arm with pincers at one end, another arm ending in a scoop, and yet another that looked like coiled wire. Underneath were lots of little legs, and the whole thing slightly resembled a Terran crab.

The creature uncoiled its wire, touched Jeff with it, and immediately backed off, waving its other arms furiously.

"We aren't going to hurt anything," said Jeff.

The creature made no sound but turned away and began to weed the garden.

"I think it's just a gardening robot," Jeff said. "It looks very old—all dented and discolored. No wonder the castle grounds aren't in good shape."

"It's not intelligent," Norby said and sailed into Jeff's arms again. "It was nothing for you to be afraid of."

"*I'm* not the one who. . . ." began Jeff, and then gave it up as a bad job.

They climbed on to the castle until its gigantic metallic door loomed ahead of them. It had hinges, but no doorknob.

"Do we knock?" asked Jeff, "I don't see signs of a computer scan."

"You might not recognize one on this planet," Norby said.

"Well, do *you?*"

"No," said Norby. "I keep feeling I know this place, but the memory is so faint, it doesn't seem to help me. The diamond design on the door seems familiar."

"That's because it's also on the dragons' collars and on the top of their hassock. Didn't you notice?"

"Come to think of it, I did."

"I'll bet. But now that you do, what does it mean?"

Norby paused. Then he said in a hurt tone, "I wish I weren't so mixed up with Terran parts. If *all* of me were alien, or Jamyn, I'd probably understand everything."

"I doubt that, somehow, but try to think. Does the design tell us what to do, or is it just the mark of the Others?"

"That's it," Norby cried out triumphantly. "It just came to me like a flash. It's the mark of the Others. Now why didn't *you* think of that? That's how the Others marked their special property. And if you use the right computer technique, the diamond plus that squiggly border design around the door. . . ."

"It was around the hassock, too," said Jeff.

"I'm glad you noticed," said Norby. "Well, the diamond

plus the squiggly border design tells you how. . . ."

"Tells us how to *what?*"

"I'm sorry, Jeff, but that's the part I can't remember."

And just as Jeff was going to express his opinion of *that*, the massive door began to creak slowly open. Jeff could see nothing inside but a long, dark hallway.

"Well, let's go in, Norby."

Norby took a step backward. "Do we have to?"

"Certainly. That's what we came for." Jeff strode boldly through the door and down the hall, looking for an opening into a room. Norby ran behind him, mumbling.

"What are you talking about?" asked Jeff.

"I'm not talking. At least, not words. I'm going over equations that keep popping into my head. I think the squiggly design is a set of mathematical relationships. I've got to figure it out. I want to understand myself so I don't keep getting into trouble, like landing in the Coliseum by mistake."

"The old building on Columbus Circle in Manhattan? Why did you land there?"

"No! The one in Rome," said Norby impatiently. I told you all about it in hyperspace."

There didn't seem to be any doors, and the corridor began to wind.

"I couldn't understand you in hyperspace. When were you in Rome?"

"When I got the lion. Don't you remember the lion? It was all very unpleasant in the Coliseum. People were fighting in armor and other people were being eaten by lions. Then guards picked me up because I was in the way and threw *me* into the lion's cage. . . ."

"Norby! Was the Coliseum—intact?"

"Sure. Not at all like the ruin in the pictures of Rome."

Jeff stopped short before another sharp curve in the corridor. "Are you telling me the truth, Norby? We were studying Roman history and you were working with Shakespeare's *Julius Caesar*. So when you left. . . . Norby! You *couldn't* have."

Norby said, "Well, where *did* the lion come from? I was thinking how nice it would be to see old Julius himself, and maybe I didn't quite make it and was a century short—a century later in time than Julius—with Christians being thrown to the lions, and one of the lions came with me."

Jeff, feeling stunned, said "That means you actually traveled through time; but scientists say that's impossible."

"Well, I did it anyway. I just don't know how."

"You don't know how you do *anything*."

"I'm sorry," said Norby. "I guess time travel is my *other* secret."

"Can you go back into time again?"

"I don't know."

Jeff shook his head. He walked around the bend in the hall and saw an archway leading to a vast auditorium. High, thin slivers of windows shed a feeble light into the murkiness. In the shadows were formidable figures like the one they had seen on the computer screen, all standing very still.

"The Mentors," said Jeff.

"Hundreds of them," agreed Norby, "but they're inactivated."

"Inacti . . . do you mean they are *robots?* Dead robots?"

"I can always tell a robot . . . almost always."

Jeff walked into the enormous room, moving from one figure to another. They were all about a meter taller than he, each with the bulge on its head and the slit and three patches. There was no color or light in the patches. Their black, metallic surfaces were discolored and, in some places, cracked. They certainly seemed inactive—and very old.

Norby sidled in ahead of Jeff and began rapping the Mentors' surfaces with his knuckles, now that he was sure they weren't alive. He stopped so suddenly that Jeff almost tripped over him.

"Something's alive in here," whispered Norby. "One of *them* is still alive. And the building—it's alive, too. There's a big computer inside the walls. I should have tuned in to it before. I think it's time to go home, Jeff."

Jeff squared his shoulders and looked around, but he saw nothing moving in the shadows.

"What do you want?" he called out loudly. "You sent for us. What do you want?"

There was no answer, but Jeff became conscious of a faint vibration in the soles of his feet. Norby was right—the building was alive. Had the castle itself sent for him?

"What do you want of me?" he called again.

"Jeff!" yelled Norby. "Help!" Four scurrying little machines, similar to the gardener robot outside, plunged out of the darkness and hurtled toward Norby. They grabbed and held him by his arms and legs.

As Jeff started toward Norby, one of the large Mentor robots suddenly moved. Its eyepatches began to gleam with an iridescence that was like shining quivering worms. Its four arms rose.

"Jeff—don't let it near you!" Norby cried out as he struggled to shake off the little machines.

It was too late. The robot's arms extended and caught Jeff in a tight grip he could not break.

"Norby," Jeff yelled, "go into hyperspace. Try to leave the machines behind, but take them with you if you have to."

"What about you, Jeff?"

"I'll be all right—until you get back. I know you'll remember how to get back," said Jeff, not at all sure that Norby would.

Norby pulled in his head, and with the small attack robots hanging onto his arms and legs, disappeared.

"Good riddance!" The big robot that was holding Jeff spoke now in a coarse grinding voice. He spoke in Jamyn. "I do not approve of alien machines. Or alien life forms, either."

"Now wait," said Jeff, trying vainly to twist an arm out of the robotic grip. "I'm here on a friendly visit."

"If you are friendly, prove it by staying and performing a task for us."

As he spoke, the Mentor lifted Jeff and carried him to the back of the room, where he pressed a depression in the wall with one of his feet. The wall split in two and slid aside, revealing machinery that glittered and flickered with shifting lights, although nothing else moved. In the center of the machinery, there was a space big enough for ten human beings to stand upright. The Mentor placed Jeff in the space and stood back.

Jeff tried to leave, but found himself encased in walls of force that he could not see but that stung him badly when he touched them. He sat down in the center and waited.

The lights around him began to turn and focus, as if they were concentrating on him.

I'm being scanned, he thought.

——Yes, you are, a telepathic voice replied——Think

slowly and clearly so that the scanning of your thoughts will be done correctly.

"No, I won't," said Jeff, aloud. "I'm not going to let you find out where I come from."

——You will stay here until everything is found out and you have completed your task.

"I'm not a machine." Jeff was shouting now, trying to let feelings of indignation drown out his thoughts. "I'm proto-plasmic. Organic. I need food. What about that?"

——The Jamyn will provide. Now stop talking so that your mind can be explored, or you will be punished.

"I won't stop. Ow!" He'd been given a rather unpleasant electric shock.

He stopped talking and began to think furiously, "Friends, Romans, countrymen, lend me your ears. . . ."

——Where is your planet?

——Never heard of it. 'I come to bury Caesar, not to praise him.' Ow! If you give me more electric shocks, I'll fall un-conscious and you'll have only mixed-up gibberish in my thoughts to read instead of good Shakespeare.

——Why are you here? What do you call yourself these days?

——The best species in the universe, that's what we call ourselves. And what do you mean these days? 'To be or not to be, that is the question. Whether 'tis nobler in the mind to suffer. . . .'

It went on for some time. Fortunately for Jeff, there was no need to get the Shakespearian speeches word-perfect, or even to think of different ones. After a while, he just kept repeating 'To be or not to be' over and over again. He had two more electric shocks, but after the second, he pretended to stagger and began to think nonsense syllables with all his might. After that there were no more shocks. Outside the walls of force, the figure of the Mentor seemed still, as if it had run down.

And then there was another telepathic voice in his mind.

——Jeff! I'll get you out of here.

Jeff saw Norby beside him, inside the scanner. ——Norby! I thought you weren't coming back from hyperspace after all.

——After I refueled I left my attackers in hyperspace and hyperjumped into your prison. I'm going to try to get us out of here and into the dragon's house.

——No! Take us home!

——What if the Mentors' computer can detect where I head for?

——That's smart, Norby! I should have thought of that. But why Zi's house?

——Because I've decided we want her hassock. I don't know what it is, but it's from the Others, and I think it's supposed to be opened. I'm sure Zi doesn't know that.

But the Mentor did. Its thoughts suddenly seemed to thunder out, overriding those of Norby.

——It is I who must have that hassock. I see a picture of it in your mind.

"Hurry," said Jeff, aloud, taking Norby's hand. "Hyperjump!"

It was as if they only dipped in and out of the grayness and there was Zi's little castle ahead.

"Tiddledewinks," said Norby. "I meant to land in her living room. ——And here come more of the Mentors' attack force," he added, pointing to the small crablike machines which could be seen as little dots beginning to scurry down the hill from the castle. Jeff and Norby ran.

Zi came out to meet them, along with Zargl who began to squeal with delight at seeing Jeff again. "What is it?" Zi asked. "How are the Mentors? How important you must be to be granted audience by them."

"Later," said Jeff. "May we have your hassock? I mean the thing you rest your tail on. It may be a device from the Others."

"Then please take it. I am afraid to own such things. Do come again for dinner." She stepped into her little castle, and then emerged with the hassock, which she handed to Jeff.

Jeff held the hassock to his chest. It was smaller than Norby, and much lighter in weight. The cover, which felt like leather, was a faded green, much scuffed by years of having scaly dragon tails rubbing about on it.

Norby said, "I'm sure, somehow, that this hassock opens up if you figure out the mental key encoded in the squiggles around its sides. Something's inside."

"What?"

"I don't know. But don't keep talking, Jeff. Those little attack robots are almost down the hill."

Norby activated his antigrav and sailed under Jeff's other

arm, the one that wasn't holding the hassock. "Ready?" he asked.

The oncoming crablike robots scurried faster. "Put down what you are holding and surrender yourselves. You are our prisoners," they cried out in chorus, their squeaky voices painfully shrill.

"No," said Jeff. "You have a nice planet but you don't know how to make visitors feel at home. Now, good-bye."

"Wait, don't go," they all squeaked.

Jeff said, "Straight back to our apartment, Norby. The security police will be gone by now. Make sure your protective shield reaches around the hassock while we're in hyperspace, and don't think about our home coordinates very hard. I don't want the Mentor to know."

"Don't worry," said Norby. "I don't think he's strong enough to use telepathy without the help of his main computer, or without touching us."

The attack robots were almost upon them. "Let's go, Norby!"

The grayness came and went—and they were falling.

"Norby," shouted Jeff, "turn on your antigrav before we hit!"

They zoomed upward and Jeff, trembling a little, looked down. He was still holding the hassock under his left arm, and Norby under his right, and they were no longer on Jamya. That was clear.

But they weren't in the Wells' apartment either. There was no apartment, no building, no Manhattan. Only a vast whiteness stretched below them.

"Snow?" said Norby. "It's summer. What's snow doing here?"

"That's not just snow," Jeff said. "That's a glacier."

5

TIME and OTHER TROUBLES

"You've brought us to Alaska!" Jeff was shivering. "Or some such place far north! Or someplace far south, like Antarctica. Or maybe even to some other planet."

"This is Earth. I'm certain of it," Norby said as they skimmed above the ice. "The coordinates check, and I'm sure that's Earth's sun. I guess it's Antarctica."

"No, it isn't," Jeff said. "If that's Earth's sun, it's quite high in the sky, so it can't be Antarctica. Or Alaska, either. I'd say it was the Tibetan plateau, except we'd be able to see mountains, and we don't."

"Don't get all excited, Jeff. Here come some horses, and maybe we can ask the riders. . . ."

Jeff squinted in the direction Norby was pointing. "There aren't any riders, and those are camels. Big, shaggy camels, and they're walking over snow! Uh, oh!"

Norby's pair of eyes facing Jeff closed suddenly and then popped open "You think. . . ."

"Yes, I think! Which you don't." Jeff studied the circle of the horizon. What had seemed to be solid whiteness resolved itself into a slope, and in the south—if it was south—there was a valley with stunted pine trees beginning where the glacier ended. The valley went on and on, deeper and deeper, and way out was the Atlantic. Or was it the Pacific?

"Norby! There's another herd of animals over there by those pine trees. Take us closer!"

It was worse than Jeff had imagined. "Do you know what those animals are?" he demanded.

"Elephants," quavered Norby, "and they shouldn't be up in the snow country, should they?"

"It's worse than elephants. Those elephants are *extinct* elephants."

"But they're alive."

"They're alive *now*, but they're going to be extinct some day. Look at them, Norby! Elephants don't have long blond hair. They're mastodons, and we're seeing them with our own eyes, which no one else of our generation has ever done."

"Maybe they're woolly mammoths. Aren't woolly mammoths supposed to live in cold climates?"

"Not any more. Not since the last Ice Age—which is where you've taken us to."

"I'm sorry, Jeff. I really am. I was thinking so much about time travel that I automatically did it when I was just trying to get us home."

"You said you didn't know how."

"*I* don't, but something inside me. . . ."

"Oh, never mind," Jeff said. "Anyway, mammoths had large round bulges on top of their heads and mastodons didn't. Mastodon bones were found up the Hudson River Valley in the eighteenth century."

Jeff paused. Then he said thoughtfully, "Well, then, this *is* the Hudson River Valley, or what will become the Hudson River Valley once the glacier retreats. Over there is the prehistoric Hudson canyon with a river carrying melted glacier water to the sea, and it will be covered by ocean in our own time. This could even be before the Indians entered the Americas. Norby, you've got to take us to our own century." The hassock was getting awkward to hold in the cold, and Jeff tried to balance it on his hip. He wished he could put his hands in his pockets because it was so cold.

"Jeff," Norby said, "I'm too scared to try. I muddle things. Maybe we should just stay here."

"In this Ice Age? We'll surely freeze to death. And if we go south to where it's warm, we'll still have nothing to eat, no weapons for catching game, and nobody to talk to but each other. Besides, I want to be back in my own time."

"But I don't know how to get back!"

"You got back from the Roman Coliseum."

"Well, when the lion jumped on me, I got so scared that I stopped thinking. I just time jumped."

"Then do it again now."

"I can't stop thinking."

It's my responsibility, thought Jeff. Norby is just a mixed-up little robot with talents he doesn't understand or know how to use very well. It's no use blaming him or trying to make him solve the problem. *I've* got to do it. Fargo always says "Don't think a lot, little brother, just think smart, and when you decide to act, do it with all your heart." He was still having trouble with the awkwardly shaped hassock. He couldn't get a comfortable grip on it with his chilled fingers. ——How do I think smart? he wondered.

——I don't understand you, Norby interjected. Then he remembered. Ever since the dragon bite, he and Norby had been able to telepathize when they were in contact and thinking hard. He said, "I was just trying to think, Norby, and you're reading my mind."

"I wish you could read *my* mind and tell me how to get back to our own time. I *can* do it, but I can't seem to make myself. Maybe it isn't part of either the alien me or the Terran me, but from the two being mixed together."

There was silence for a while, during which Jeff could feel himself shivering and hear his teeth chattering. Finally he said, "All I can hear in your mind is 'Oh, my, Jeff will sell me if I keep being so mixed up.' Now, just stop that, because I'm not going to sell you. You're my robot forever, mixed up or not."

"Thank you, Jeff," said Norby. "And all I can hear in your brain is 'I'm so cold. I'm so cold.' I feel terrible about that, Jeff."

"Well," said Jeff miserably, "at least it's summer here, or the sun wouldn't be so high in the sky, and it's a clear afternoon, with no wind blowing. It's cold enough, but it could be lots colder another day or another season. Let's try together, Norby. I'll think hard about our apartment. You tune into that image in my head and then perhaps you'll find the time coordinates maybe by reflex."

They tried and failed.

"It doesn't work!" Norby wailed.

Jeff bit his lip and tried not to feel despair. There had to be some way out. "Norby," he said, "maybe we're not trying hard enough because we don't really want to go back to the apartment, and it might not be safe. If we could go to our family scoutship, the *Hopeful*, that might make more sense, only. . . ."

"Only what?"

"Well, I'm not sure where it is. It could be at the big dock that orbits Mars along with Space Command—now that Fargo is part of Admiral Yobo's team. but there are thousands of berths there, and I don't know which one would be *Hopeful*'s.

In fact, I can't be absolutely sure the scoutship is even there."

"We can try," said Norby. "Try to visualize the Space Command dock. You've seen it, haven't you?"

"Yes, but I can't visualize the *Hopeful* there." Jeff clumsily managed to shift the hassock under his arm to a new position and tried to grip it comfortably. "I can imagine the control room of the *Hopeful* clearly, however. Maybe we can tune into it regardless of where she is." He winced with pain. "I'm so cold that the arm holding this hassock hurts. My muscles are cramping."

At that very moment, the hassock fell out of Jeff's numbed arm and tumbled over and over in the air—down, down to the snow.

"Oh, no," he shouted, and beat his arm against his chest to get circulation back into it. He didn't have a chance to make much noise or do much beating because the wind was knocked out of him by the force of Norby's dive.

Zoom! Norby plunged through the cold air, holding onto Jeff, and he managed to get under the hassock. He caught it just before it hit the ground. In the process, however, he let go of Jeff.

Fortunately, Norby was just starting his upswing again so that Jeff fell without the added velocity of the dive—and the top layer of the snow was soft. He landed spread eagle on his back and was half-buried. He struggled clumsily to his feet.

Contritely, Norby swept down again, holding the hassock in one arm, while the other arm stretched out to take Jeff's hand.

Up in the air again, Jeff writhed in his efforts to knock off the snow that clung to him.

"Hold still," said Norby.

"I can't. If the snow stays on me it will melt from what little body heat I have and I'll get wet. And one thing that's much worse than being this cold is being this cold and wet, too."

"Think about the control room."

Jeff tried. Fargo had taught him concentration and meditation techniques years ago, and now he needed them to save his life.

——The *Hopeful*. Small. Neat. Useful.

——Don't think in words, Jeff. Just pictures.

The pictures came and slowly Jeff immersed himself in

them, relaxing and trusting Norby to hang on to him, and to the hassock, too, and at the same time to keep them in air with his antigrav.

As Jeff relaxed, the pictures came more vividly until he forgot he was cold and cramped and desperate—or even that he was himself. He was he-and-Norby, looking at the control room of the *Hopeful* seeing it clearly in their joined minds, so clearly that it was real, located in space and time.

And suddenly they were *there!*

"Oh!" said Albany, who was much too cool a policewoman to scream.

Jeff smiled at them weakly and shivered uncontrollably as he brushed at his hair to remove the melting snow.

"It was all ice," Norby shouted. "Jeff nearly froze. It was all my fault, but I couldn't help it."

Fargo waved him to be quiet and had his hands on Jeff quickly. "Explain later. Get those clothes off."

"But Albany. . . ." protested Jeff.

Albany turned around. "I won't look," she said.

"Get them off, I say," Fargo said. "It doesn't matter whether she looks or not. And get me a blanket, Norby." In a few minutes, Jeff relaxed in the warmth of the blanket while Fargo rubbed a towel vigorously over his head and face. "Now tell me," Fargo said, "Where were you?"

"On a trip," Norby put in brightly.

"With a hassock?" asked Albany.

"Listen!" Jeff interrupted. "Is it safe here? No security police?"

"Just our own devoted Manhattan police," Fargo said, putting his arm about Albany's trim waist, "whom I was trying to persuade to go off on a little search expedition with me. She says she can't because a fiscal crisis in Manhattan has forced the lay-off of so many police that she dare not stay off the job for any length of time. Did you ever hear anything so crazy?"

"You mean we're still in Manhattan?" Jeff asked. "I thought the ship would be at the Space Command dock."

"It was, earlier, but after you left our apartment, I let the security police search it. Naturally, they found nothing and left, breathing fire and slaughter. Then I sat around and waited for you. But days passed, and you didn't come back, so I decided I'd look for you in the ship. But I brought it back to Earth first because I wanted Albany along. After all, she's a good person in a fray, and at other times, too."

"What do you mean 'the days passed'?" demanded Jeff. "How long do you think I've been gone?"

"I don't think, Jeff, I *know*. You've been gone thirteen days."

"What!"

"Why be surprised? Don't *you* know how long you've been gone?"

Jeff shook his head. "I guess I'm going to have to tell you Norby's other secret."

"Are you going to tell it while a non-family person is in our midst?" said Norby sounding outraged. His head popped in and out of his barrel.

Albany smiled—as beautifully as she did everything. "That's all right. Since I can't go with you on this trip, I had better not hear any secrets just yet. And now I must go back to my precinct."

She headed for the airlock.

"Do you mean we're in Manhattan?" asked Jeff again.

"On the Great Lawn of Central Park," said Fargo, "which isn't quite according to regulations for a craft of this kind, but I have an official paper from Admiral Yobo, and a police officer I know pulled a few strings," he smiled at Albany, "so here I am."

He went to the airlock and looked back at Jeff. "While I'm escorting my exasperating lass—who would rather be on her job than with me because of her civic spirit—why don't you have a cup of hot chocolate? You might as well get warm inside as well as out. And eat something if you're hungry."

Fargo and Albany went out.

Jeff said to Norby, "I hope you realize you got us back nearly two weeks late."

Norby said, "You really expect *everything*, don't you? Didn't I get you back right on the button—right in the control room? So I was a few minutes off."

"A few *minutes*. . . ."

Fargo came back into the *Hopeful* in a hurry. He sealed the lock behind him. "Prepare for takeoff, mates. The security police have discovered that my ship is in Central Park and they want to search it. We either leave *now* while Albany tries to hold them off, or you two will have to disappear again."

"Where shall I take you, Jeff?" Norby asked cheerfully.

"Not again," Jeff said. "Take off, Fargo. I'll stay in the *Hopeful*. I can't stand the thought of getting lost in time and space again."

Fargo's eyebrows shot upward, but he said nothing as he handled the controls. The *Hopeful* lifted.

The computer outlet spoke. "Security police in antigrav car outside, Captain. You are under arrest and ordered to surrender your ship. If you try to leave, you will be brought back by force grapple."

"So they say," said Fargo, "but they'll have to catch us first."

"But they will," said Jeff.

"No, they won't. I will lose them in the cloud layer, and while they're looking for us, we'll get into hyperspace if Norby can manage it. We'll go in and never come out, so far as they are concerned."

"Then they'll know we have hyperdrive."

"No, they won't. They'll only know we've disappeared, and presumably crashed. They'll spend days looking for the smashed torso of our scoutship." Fargo turned to Norby. "Can you turn this ship's engine to hyperdrive as soon as we're into the cloud?" he asked.

"I can channel my hyperspace entry system into the ship's computer. She's a stupid computer but maybe she'll be able to follow my instructions. If she were as intelligent as I am. . . ."

"Just *do* it, Norby," Fargo said.

Jeff, at the thought of facing another jaunt through hyperspace, buried his head in his hands.

6

Opening the Hassock

"That was a piece of cake," Fargo said.

"Thank you," Norby said, "but you can say that because you're not the one who had to do it. I had to work myself to death to get that stupid computer to do the right thing. Are you all right, Jeff?"

Jeff peered out from his blanket. "Well, I *am* tired," he said, "and hungry, too. Do you mind if I'm tired and hungry? Is there a law against that?"

"That's just like a boy," said Norby. "Always tired and hungry, and always getting short-tempered about it."

Fargo turned around in his captain's chair and fiddled with the computer. "A meal will be served shortly, Jeff, but it will be food and water in the brig if you don't tell me what's happened to you, and what Norby's other secret is; although after you talked about being lost in space and time, I guess I can guess the latter."

"We don't have a brig," Jeff grumbled, "and *first* I want to eat." He watched the glass door where the food would make its appearance. He didn't care what kind of synthomeal the *Hopeful* would manage to provide, so long as she did it quickly.

With a slight sound like a burp, the *Hopeful* served up synthoburger, synthofries, and real, if reconstituted, applesauce.

Fargo's blue eyes were amused as Jeff dove into the food, "I see I'll have to wait a long time to hear the story."

Through a mouthful of fries, Jeff said thickly, "Get it from Norby—not that you'll get an unbiased story."

"He's communing with the ship's computer."

"And I can't be interrupted right now," Norby said importantly. "I'm making some very delicate adjustments on the computer so that maybe you'll be able to put the ship into hyperdrive even if I'm not with you. I've altered the antigrav engine slightly to fit, because you can't get into hyperspace unless your hyperdrive is based on antigrav."

"How do you know?"

"It's just a feeling I have. This universe is all tied up with gravity, and I don't think you can get out of normal space unless you get rid of gravity for a while. Or it could be vice-versa. Maybe antigrav works by tying ordinary space to a little hyperspace."

"Where are we now?" Jeff asked some minutes later, his mouth still full of food.

"I don't know," said Fargo. . . ."Norby! Unplug yourself and tell us where you've brought us. That's a pretty planet out there, but it sure isn't Earth."

"Jamya," mumbled Norby.

"Oh, no! Not again!" Jeff suspended his labors over the applesauce and said, "Fargo, you'd better have the whole story."

Fargo listened quietly while Jeff recounted his and Norby's experiences on Jamya. "In summary," Fargo said, "we are faced with friendly dragons and villainous robots."

"Yes," said Jeff, "and the only mode of escape is a small robot who not only can't handle hyperspace with accuracy, but who also gets you to the right place at the wrong time and nearly freezes you to death."

"Well, I like that!" said Norby, leaving the computer. "And here I worked my circuits to the bone for you!"

"It seems to me," said Fargo, "that there's unfinished business on Jamya. I vote for landing."

"So do I," said Norby. "I keep yearning for that planet."

"I'm against it," said Jeff. "Never trouble trouble till. . . ."

"Two against one," Fargo and Norby said simultaneously.

"The only trouble is," Fargo said, a couple of hours later, "that the computer informs me there's some sort of force barrier around the planet."

"Right," said Jeff with sudden satisfaction. "Zi told me the Jamyns weren't allowed to travel to other planets, and I presume people from other planets aren't allowed to travel to Jamya. She said we were the first visitors ever. So let's go somewhere else."

Norby said, "We got to Jamya before because we used hyperdrive and went past the barrier by going out of normal space. All we have to do is to use hyperdrive now."

"Wait," Jeff said. He knew Fargo and he knew Norby, and

there wasn't much use trying to talk sense to either of them. The only thing to do was to place another problem before them and then, maybe, he could get some sleep. With his eyelids drooping on their own, what he needed very badly was a little unconsciousness. After that, he might be able to face Jamya. "Don't you think you ought to find out why the Mentors want that hassock?" he asked.

"Isn't the best way of finding that out simply to ask the Mentors?" Fargo asked.

"No," Jeff said earnestly. "They never thought about the hassock till Norby mentioned it. Maybe they don't know what's in it. And it's Norby who thinks he can open it if he can work out the meaning of all that stuff around the sides."

"You're right. Sensible boy! Norby, make a note—your young owner has the makings of a brilliant adult."

"Yes, Fargo," Norby said, "I have always suspected that. It isn't easy to decipher the designs on the hassock, though."

Jeff heaved a sigh of relief. "I'm sure it isn't, so just take your time Norby, and don't hurry it. And while you're working I'll catch up on some much-needed sleep. Fargo, *please*, don't do *anything* while I'm sleeping!"

Fargo yawned. "I won't," he said. "I could use a little nap myself." He leaned back in his chair, pushed his pilot's cap over his eyes and was, in fact, asleep almost before Jeff was.

Eight hours later Fargo and Jeff were eating breakfast while Norby was trying to explain that the Others' code was extremely difficult.

"But why?" asked Jeff. "You understand the Jamyn language, so why can't you read their writing?"

"Because it's not just writing. It's *code!*" said Norby, a bit shrilly. "And it may not be Jamyn. This is probably a code used by the Others—whoever they are—and it may not be coded from the Jamyn language. Anyway, I've got part of it. The first half says 'All-purpose.' At least, I think it does."

"All-purpose what?" asked Jeff.

"I don't know. I can't make out the second half."

Fargo grinned and took the last synthobiscuit. "All-purpose flour? All-purpose weapon?"

"It probably just means all-purpose cushion," said Jeff, discouraged. "That's what the hassock was used as. The dragons used it to rest their tails on. It was apparently very good for that. And I suppose you're no nearer to opening it now than you were at the start."

"No." The little robot's eyelids lowered halfway, and Jeff almost expected a teardrop of oil to come out.

"Any hints?" asked Fargo. "I mean, as far as opening it is concerned."

"Well, besides the words calling the hassock an all-purpose something, there are numbers. They come in batches in an odd pattern."

"Show me," said Fargo.

He and Norby huddled over the print-out from the computer, which represented Norby's attempts to solve the riddle of the hassock.

As for Jeff, he stared at the viewscreen while the other two muttered to each other. The planet, Jamya, seemed to swing in the black ocean of space, wreathed with clouds. He thought he could see blue ocean and green-brown landmasses beneath the clouds—or was it just one large landmass? Were the dragons the only intelligent creatures on Jamya? Jeff thought they probably were, because Zi had not mentioned any other civilized creatures besides the Mentors.

And what of the Mentors? Why did they want the hassock? And what task had they wanted Jeff to perform? They had never gotten around to describing that. What could one boy do that the Mentors and their powerful computer could not?

Jeff shook his head. He couldn't figure it out. He hoped Norby was doing better with the hassock.

Meanwhile Fargo said, "If that part of the code stands for numbers, it may be a double code with the numbers standing for words."

"If so, Fargo, it's too much for me," Norby said. "I'm just a small stupid robot and you mustn't expect too much of me."

Jeff realized that things were pretty bad for Norby to whine along those lines.

"Let up for a while, Fargo. Why don't we just sit and sing for a while until our brains clear."

There was a long pause while Fargo simply stared at his younger brother. Then he pounded his right fist into his left palm. "My brother is a genius."

"Why? What did I do?"

Fargo was too busy laughing to answer, so Norby answered for him.

"I think," he said, "that Fargo's decided that the numbers on the hassock stand for musical notes. I think he's right. As soon as you mentioned music, Jeff, my brain told me it was the solution. I'm surprised Fargo saw it, too. You both have your moments—for human beings."

It took another hour, but, with the help of Norby and the *Hopeful*'s computer, Fargo decided he had the song.

"Shall I sing it?"

"Yes!" said Norby.

"No!" said Jeff. "Let me get a stun gun first, in case the hassock turns out to be a lethal robot machine of the Others."

"We don't have any stun guns," Fargo said cheerfully. "You know my motto 'clever words are all you need.'"

"Albany uses karate," said Jeff.

"Well," said Fargo, shrugging, "beautiful women have their ways. If there's a nasty little machine inside that hassock, we'll make it Norby's responsibility to deal with it."

"Why me?" asked Norby.

"Because you have your moments—for a robot."

Jeff laughed. "Well, then, go ahead, Fargo. Sing."

Fargo sang the coded notes. After the last note rang out, they watched the hassock. Nothing happened.

"Wrong rhythm, do you suppose?" Fargo asked.

"I think it should be in a minor key," said Norby, "now that I come to think of it."

"If you didn't have your thought processes mixed up," said Jeff, "you'd come to think of it beforehand instead of afterward."

"Better afterward than not at all," said Norby loftily. "My alien machinery has been a big help to you. How far would you have gotten on this hassock without me?"

"True enough," said Jeff.

Fargo sang again, a sad song this time, slow and melancholy, and Jeff wondered what the hassock might contain that had to be released in this sorrowful fashion.

The song ended. The three in the control room, and the ship's computer, too, were all silent. Outside, the planet Jamya was also silent.

But something began to happen. The hassock cover seemed

to be getting thinner, lighter—and suddenly it cracked in two, the halves falling apart like a neatly struck eggshell.

"By all the satellites of Jupiter," said Fargo, "what is *that?*"

It was green and fuzzy—or maybe they were fuzzy scales, or scales so small and neat as to look like fuzz. Whatever it was, it looked like another dragon, all curled up with its head hidden.

The creature uncurled, shook itself, and the scales became much fuzzier. It was a small animal about the size of a cat, with a round head and tiny pointed ears, a thin gold collar, and an odd snout with fangs.

Fargo backed away. "Norby, do you think we ought to be protected from that fanged thing?"

Norby did nothing but stare at the creature.

"Is it familiar to you, Norby?" Jeff asked in Jamyn, hoping the creature would understand.

Its small ears pricked up, but the animal only yawned. It shook itself once more, stretched, and began to circumnavigate the control room—sniffing at everything and waving its long, very fuzzy tail.

"When cats wave their tails, it means they're angry," said Fargo.

"But when dogs do, they're happy," said Jeff. "If this is like the dragons, it ought to be able to understand when we speak Jamyn."

"As a matter of fact," said Norby, "it's a 'she,' and she doesn't talk. She's not very bright, you see, but she's not dangerous, either. I remember now."

"Why was she hidden away like that in the hassock?"

"I can't quite figure that out."

"How do you know it's a 'she'?" asked Fargo.

"They all are. Like the dragons. Only this type lays eggs."

The fuzzy green creature got as far as Jeff and stood on her hind legs to sniff him. He put out his hand and let her sniff that, too. She didn't bite, but bumped her head under his palm as if she wanted him to stroke her. Automatically, he did so, thinking that she acted just like a cat, even if she didn't feel like one. She felt both soft and bristly, a combination that Jeff couldn't find words to describe.

"I always wanted a cat," he said.

Under his hand, the creature began to change—the snout

receding, the ears and tail lengthening, the fangs disappearing.
"Meow!" it said softly.

"It *is* a cat," said Fargo. "Come here, kitty!"

The creature ran to Fargo.

"Nice kitty," he said as he stroked her, "Can you be a dog?"

It was even more amazing. She changed her body contours
until she looked very much like a dog. "Woof!" she said.

"Now I remember," said Norby. "That's an All-Purpose
Pet."

Jeff said, "The Others may not be so bad after all. I like
their taste in pets."

"Let's hope she continues to like *us*," said Fargo, cuddling
the All-Purpose Pet, who now resembled a very green beagle
(Fargo had always been partial to beagles). She licked his ear
and purred.

"Beagles aren't supposed to purr," said Jeff, somewhat annoyed. He couldn't understand why females seemed to like
Fargo best. He was glad he had Norby, who wasn't at all cuddly,
but was *his* robot and never showed any signs of wanting to
like anyone else instead.

Fargo said, "Let her purr. I'm going to name her Oola!"

"Why Oola?" Jeff asked.

"Because it seems to fit her," Fargo said.

The All-Purpose Pet pricked up her ears, now long and
drooping, and whined a little.

Fargo chucked her under the chin and said, "How about
that? Do you like your name—Oola?"

She patted Fargo's face with her paw—more like a cat than
a dog—and grinned, with her tongue hanging out.

"See," said Fargo. "It's her name. She admits it."

"You've got a pet that's half beagle and half Cheshire cat,"
said Jeff, "and she'll probably change to fit everyone's mental
wish and you'll never know *what* you've got." He still felt a
bit jealous. "I wonder where the Others got her?"

"Made her, probably," said Norby. "Some day on our travels
we'll find the animals the Others took genes from to do the
biosynthesis of this one. And don't ask me how I know this!"

"We won't," said Jeff, while Fargo continued to play with
Oola. "But I do think, Norby, it's time for you to tell us why
you brought us back to Jamya—before we go down there to
risk life and limb."

There was a long silence. Finally Norby spoke very softly.

"Because I think it's home," he said. "More and more, I think it's home—*my* home. and I don't want to be afraid of home."

7

More Time and Trouble

A cold apprehension gripped Jeff. It had nothing to do with the Mentors. Was Norby going to begin to feel as though he were a Jamyn? Wasn't part of him Terran? Was he going to choose between his two parts and turn his back on Jeff?

"Hey, Norby," Jeff said, sounding as jovial as he could, to conceal his feelings. "Don't get upset. We'll help you discover all about Jamya and you'll find there's nothing to fear."

The trouble was, Jeff thought inwardly, that he had been making entirely too many caustic remarks about Norby's being mixed up.

"The Mentors are after you, Jeff," Norby said. "I don't know why they think they can use you, but I don't think you ought to take the chance. I'd better go down to the planet without you. I can always escape them by moving into hyperspace."

"Oh, no," Jeff said. "You're not getting away from me—I mean, I can't let you take any chances without me. You and I are a team, an inseparable team, now and always. Right, Norby?"

"If I may interrupt this dialog," said Fargo with a grin on his face, "I'd like to point out that I am the senior member of this expedition, so I have to be consulted when decisions are made. I say that we're all going. Together. You don't think, do you, that I'm going to sit here and spend my time wondering what's happening to my little brother and his robot?"

"Well," said Norby, "that would be three of us against the villains—providing I don't have to spend all my time rescuing you two."

"There'll be some spare time for you to hide behind us, Norby," said Fargo, stroking Oola, who was lying in his lap.

"Leave Norby alone, Fargo," Jeff said. "He never hides behind anybody."

"I don't?" Norby said in a surprised tone.

"Besides," Jeff hurried on, "I have an idea. Those Mentors down there seemed very dangerous and not likely to listen to reason. But they are all very old and lots of them are dead and maybe they've deteriorated with time. After all, they were put on Jamya by the Others to teach the Jamyn how to be civilized. Why don't we go backward in time to when Jamya was first found by the Others and before they put up the force barrier? Maybe we'll speak to the young Mentors when they were healthy and reasonable."

"Hmm," murmured Fargo, "and then we'd know what the Others were like. Not a bad idea."

"I don't like it," Norby said. "The Others were probably more dangerous than the Mentors."

"Do you remember that they were?" Jeff asked.

"Well, no. I feel as though no part of me came into existence until long after the Others left, so I guess I wouldn't know anything about them."

"Are you telling us," Fargo asked, "that some of your parts are the creation of the Mentors?"

"That could be," Norby said. "I don't really know. I can't even remember what I used to be. Maybe I wasn't really a robot. Maybe I was a computer on that spaceship that McGillicuddy found. Anyway, I'm scared of the Others."

"Then we won't go back that far in time," Jeff said. "Do you think you can take us back the right amount if all of us concentrate on young Mentors?"

"Well," said Norby, "Fargo can't help, but you and I can join telepathically, and I'll try to link myself with the *Hopeful*, too, and we'll go back to soon after the Mentors arrived—I hope."

"Good! I'm sure the young Mentors will be reasonable," said Jeff. "Come here, Norby. Sit at the ship's computer, and I'll hold your hand."

A little wire pushed out of Norby's hat and inserted itself into the ship's computer. His hand grabbed Jeff's and held tight.

"Okay?" Norby asked.

"I'm not afraid," said Jeff. "In fact, I'm completely confident in you, Norby. If we could get back from the Ice Age smack into the *Hopeful*'s control room, we ought to be able to move the *Hopeful* back into time with pinpoint accuracy."

Jeff closed his eyes so he could concentrate better—also to shut out the doubting expression on his brother's face. So what if Norby got things wrong now and then? Think of all the things he got right! Norby kept saying that, and he was right, too!

Now . . . concentrate on Jamya . . . move back . . . back . . . to a much earlier time. . . . think of Mentors, with shiny metal, moving easily, resonant, pleasant voices. . . . .

"Jeff!" Fargo's voice was urgent. "Norby! The two of you— come out of it!"

"What . . . what. . . ." Jeff came to, blearily. "What's wrong?"

"I'm not sure. You two have been still and silent for half an hour. You didn't tell me how this works, either of you. Does it take you that long to do it?"

"I don't know. Didn't anything happen?"

"Nothing at all. I had a momentary sensation of dizziness at the start, but it passed, and here we still are and there Jamya still is."

Norby was quite conscious, too, for he made a snorting noise and pulled his wire out of the computer. "Of course, we're still here and Jamya is still there, but the position of its sun is different. It's now spring in the continent where the dragons live—a long ago spring."

"You mean we've moved back in time?"

"Of course!"

"In that case," said Fargo. "Get out of my chair, little robot, and let me take us down to this planet of yours."

He put Oola on the control room floor, where she sat placidly, and licked herself like a cat while still looking like a beagle.

Down they went, skimming across the Jamyn continent.

Jeff said, "Can you find Zi's castle, Norby? You did that two times before without trouble."

"In *our* time, Jeff. The castle doesn't exist at this time in the past."

"I mean. . . . Locate the place where the castle will some day exist?"

"I get no feel for it," said Norby, sounding worried.

The *Hopeful* skimmed low over the planetary ocean and headed back over the continent again.

"Trees. Lots of trees," Fargo said. "Those sea creatures that looked up at us might be interesting."

"No," said Norby sharply. "The Mentors chose land creatures to civilize. Maybe we went back too far. Maybe there's no animal life on land at all."

"Not likely," Fargo said, "when it's so richly forested and vegetated. See, there's a group of animals below in the grassland." He sent the *Hopeful* downward in a sharply banked curve for a closer view. "They look something like bipedal dinosaurs, but I don't see any sign of wings."

"That's odd," said Jeff. "They don't even have them furled. I think they don't have any wings."

The *Hopeful* came in for a quiet landing and rested upon the grass at some distance from the herd. Fargo moved to open the airlock.

"Hey," said the ever cautious Jeff, "aren't you going to analyze the air outside?"

Fargo paused. "You've been here, haven't you? And you breathed. And you're alive."

"That was at a different time. Why don't you ask the computer?"

"Oh, well." Fargo looked pained. "What's the air like?"

The computer said, "Breathable. There are plant seeds and spores to which allergies might exist, but I can't test for that without more information."

"We'll chance it," Fargo said, as he picked up Oola.

They moved out on the grass, which was waving in the wind. It was rather cool, but Jeff remembered the glacier and decided that he could get along easily with *this* kind of coolness.

Jeff said, "I'll just step over there and speak to the dragons. I can speak Jamyn, you know."

"Look out!" yelled Norby, tugging at Jeff's pant legs.

The dragons were approaching *en masse*, and at a run. They were also speaking, but not in Jamyn. Their language, if it could be called that, consisted entirely of loud roars, screeches, and hisses, punctuated by little puffs of smoke from their nostrils.

"Jeff, old boy," said Fargo, trying to control Oola, who was snarling and barking alternately. "These are *not* friends of yours. It's my opinion we had better get back into the ship at once."

Without arguing the matter, they did so, shutting the airlock behind them.

"I thought you told me that the dragons were smaller than human beings," Fargo said.

These were as big as the *Hopeful*. In the viewscreen, they could see the dragons swarming over the ship, trying to find a place to bite. Their fangs sounded like jackhammers upon the hull.

"Fargo," Jeff said, "I don't think their teeth are made of ivory. They look shiny, as if they were made of metal, or of diamonds."

"You're right, Jeff, and they may damage us." He moved to the controls. "We'll have to get away."

"They aren't speaking Jamyn," said Norby unnecessarily. "I don't think they've ever been civilized."

Fargo moved the *Hopeful* slowly upward on antigrav so that the dragons clutching at the hull gradually peeled off. The huge animals were now spouting flames in their frustration. Fargo seemed fascinated.

"From a whiff I got outside," he said, "I think they make their flames by splitting hydrogen sulfide...."

"The computer says the hull is heating under those flames," said Norby. "We should get back into orbit."

Again there was no attempt to argue the matter, and the ship rose precipitously. When it was safely in orbit, the three had another conclave, while Oola chased her tail round and round in the control room.

"My feeling is," Fargo said, "that we *did* get back to a time before the Others, even before the Mentors created a civilization on this planet. We went backward in time too far."

"I think that's my fault," Jeff said. "Not Norby's. He did very well. It's just that when Norby and I were linked and trying to move backward in time, I felt some kind of fear, and perhaps that threw us off."

"You weren't feeling *my* fear," said Norby, sounding outraged. "I was certainly not afraid."

"No, no," said Jeff. "You don't understand. You see, I was thinking of the Mentors very hard. And I felt something about them that I must have felt when I was in their scanning room, but didn't realize I'd felt because I was too full of my own fears. Do you understand what I mean?" He looked at Fargo helplessly.

Fargo said, "Sure, but what was it you felt without knowing you felt it?"

"It was the *Mentor* who was afraid. I was feeling *its* fear when we were trying to move in time."

"Was the Mentor afraid of you, do you suppose?"

"No."

"Of the Others?" Norby asked.

"I don't think so," said Jeff. "The Mentor was awfully afraid, though, and he *needed* me. I don't know what for, but it had something to do with his fear."

"If he is afraid of something and needs your help," Fargo said, "it doesn't seem to me he can afford to do us any harm."

Sounding doubtful, Jeff asked, "Should we go forward, then, and see if we can find the young Mentors?"

"Can we?" said Fargo with a grin. "It's up to you two."

"Let's try again, Jeff," Norby said. "Maybe there's nothing to fear. Maybe it was only Mentors' fear that made you afraid."

Jeff almost said, 'You were more afraid than I was,' but he pressed his lips together and didn't say it. Instead, he held out his hand. "Sure," he said, "let's try again."

Half an hour later they gave up.

"No dizziness, no nothing," said Fargo. "I guess we're still in the same time."

"Well," said Norby, "it seems to be very different to go into a time I've already existed in. It's easier to move to a time earlier or later than when I've been there. Do you know what I mean? I tried to push us all forward until we were well past where the Mentors showed up, but I couldn't seem to do it."

"In that case," said Jeff, with a sinking feeling, "that would mean that you, or parts of you, were present on Jamya sometime after the Mentors appeared, just as you thought you might be. I guess you're really Jamyn."

"I suppose so," said Norby. "It's exciting, isn't it?"

Jeff didn't think so. But all he said was, "Can you slide forward only a little into the future, before the time when you were constructed?"

"I can try."

"I can see where it's difficult to move to a time where you've already existed," Fargo said, "because one of the big paradoxes of time-travel involves the possibility of meeting yourself. Still, why don't we go really far into the future and find out what happened to us in the Jamyn historical records of the future, so that we'll know what to do to fix everything up? That would be exciting!"

"That sounds like another paradox to me," Jeff said, sounding unhappy. "I don't think we can do that. The future isn't all written out. Suppose we find out that we were killed when we went back to Jamya. Then we would be in despair and give up and that might be *why* we were killed."

"I don't understand that," said Norby, "but I don't want to be killed."

"Don't worry, little robot," Fargo said, "we won't let that happen, but I see Jeff's point. All right, Norby, just move us up into the nearest part of the future you can manage, shortly after the Mentors begin to work."

Jeff and Norby tried again. This time Jeff visualized a young Mentor and tried to feel full of confidence. He was distracted because Oola suddenly began to howl like a lost hound.

"Hush, hush, my beauty," said Fargo, stroking her long ears as she sat quivering, pressed against his leg. She stopped howling, but she whimpered instead.

Jeff was about to say, "Let's try it again, Norby," when Fargo cried out without any trace of his usual humor. "Wait! She's gone. Oola's gone."

8

NOT DANGEROUS ENOUGH?

Jeff looked about in astonishment, and the viewscreen caught his eye. Jamya was much closer. Norby must have been clever enough to move them nearer to the planet as they moved in time, presumably to put them inside the force screen once it was set up. But what about Oola? She certainly was not in the control room.

Jeff said, "Maybe she's in the sleeping quarters. Maybe we all blacked out."

But Fargo was already out of the room searching. A few minutes later he was back, his face deeply troubled. "She's not inside the ship."

"Oh, my," said Norby. "I never thought of her."

"You mean you forgot to bring her forward with us?" Jeff asked. Then, when Norby failed to answer, Jeff shook him. "Well? Say something."

"Don't rattle my works," Norby said. "I'm trying to figure it out, and getting me all jarred inside doesn't help. It's not my fault. I suppose she exists in this time somewhere and it was, therefore, much more difficult for the Oola of the future, *our* Oola, to exist here than for us. And I didn't allow for that and she couldn't come along—I think."

"If that were so, we could find her *here*, in *this* time," said Fargo.

"What time is *this* time?" Jeff asked. "When are we?"

"I don't know," said Norby in a querulous tone. "I get all mixed up with all these crises and with getting shaken and everything."

Fargo and Jeff looked at each other. Jeff said, "It's my fault, Fargo. I should never have suggested time travel; at least not involving you and Oola and the *Hopeful*. Norby and I should have taken our chances alone."

"Don't be foolish," Fargo said. "You couldn't leave me out

of this. We'll just find Oola here and now."

"Yes, but that will be before she was put into suspended animation and before we released her from the hassock capsule, and she won't remember us."

"Then she'll learn about us all over again; or, rather, all over previously, for this time is long before the time we got her."

"We don't even know *how* long before," muttered Jeff.

"It's not my fault," shouted Norby.

"It doesn't matter," Fargo said. "We have to explore the planet, Oola or no Oola. Knowledge is better than ignorance, even if it's sometimes more uncomfortable, so down we go for a landing."

"There's the castle!" Jeff said, as the *Hopeful* skimmed along above the treetops after a number of passes over the continent, with Norby guiding them very uncertainly.

Norby said, "See! Didn't I tell you I could lead you there?"

"On the twenty-fifth pass," said Jeff.

"The tenth," countered Norby. "Maybe the ninth. You don't know how to count."

Jeff remembered that he wanted to be nicer to Norby. "That's true!" he said. "You did a very good job."

But Norby just said, "Huh!"

Jeff said, "I don't see any of the small buildings where dragons like Zi live; just the big castle."

"That's a good sign," said Fargo. "You can see a number of huge robots there, and they're all busy doing something or other. The small buildings haven't been built yet, I suppose. Maybe the small dragons haven't even evolved."

"Yes," said Norby. "Everything has just begun. All the Mentors are new."

"Oh?" said Jeff. "If you know that, why did you tell us you didn't know what time it is?"

"Because I didn't," said Norby indignantly, "but that doesn't mean I can't use my eyes. Look at those robots. Can't you see that they're shiny? They're nothing like those old wrecks you and I saw in the castle when we were there before—I mean *later*—I mean before in our lives but later in time."

"I know what you mean," said Jeff and Fargo, speaking together.

The robots were watching them as the *Hopeful* sank to rest

just before the castle. The biggest signaled to the rest, who went inside the castle. Then the one remaining robot walked up to the ship.

"Message from outside on my radio pickup," said the *Hopeful*'s computer.

"Let's hear it," said Fargo.

It came promptly in forceful, clearly enunciated words: "Strangers, you have entered our planetary space without permission. Speak and reveal yourselves and your purpose."

The language was, of course, Jamyn, and Norby translated for Fargo.

"I think it would be more polite to answer from the airlock, in person," said Fargo. "It shouldn't be too risky. The airlock door can be closed quickly if the Mentor makes a sudden move. And since you speak Jamyn, younger brother, you'll have to be the one to take the chance."

"Maybe I should be the one to do it," said Norby, "I speak Jamyn like a native."

"No," said Jeff, who didn't like Norby's reference to being a native. "I think it would confuse the Mentor if you appeared. He's probably never seen a robot like you, and if he can sense that you are part Jamyn, he'll wonder how you came to be on this spaceship. I don't think it's a good idea for them to find out we're from the future. In fact," Jeff frowned and shook his head, "suppose we do or say something that changes the future?"

"Just being here and being seen may have done *that*," said Fargo, "but what's the difference? Now that we are here, let's see it through. These robots may look like newer versions of the ones you met in our own time, but they don't give me the impression of being aggressive. They seem reasonable."

"I don't know what you base that on, Fargo," said Jeff, "but if you really think so. . . . Hey, look at that! There's Oola!"

Oola, or a creature exactly like the one who had originally emerged from the hassock, bounded out of the castle and stopped beside the Mentor who had spoken. She wagged her tail.

Jeff said, "She must have realized we're here."

"No," said Norby. "Don't be ridiculous. You two haven't been born yet. She can't possibly. . . ."

"And it might not be our own Oola," said Fargo, sounding a bit depressed at the thought. "There are probably lots of All-Purpose Pets on this world, just as there are lots of big robots.

Presumably, they've only just begun to unpack the little gardening robots and those police robots you saw running around the castle."

The computer said, "The message from outside has just been repeated a bit more forcibly."

"We'd better get going," said Jeff with a sigh. He opened the airlock and stood just inside the outer door. He smiled in what he hoped would seem like a friendly fashion, then he remembered that on Earth some animals thought baring the teeth was a sign of hostility. He looked serious at once and said, in Jamyn, "I greet you."

"Ah," said the Mentor in a deep voice. "You know our language."

"Yes," said Jeff. "We are friendly people who are interested in this world which we have come upon in our travels. We hope you will help us by explaining what your world is like, who you are, and what you are doing here." He spoke very slowly, trying not to make any unfortunate mistake in his Jamyn, and trying also not to give away too much about themselves. Behind him, he could hear Norby translating for Fargo.

The Mentor stared at Jeff as though it were uncertain what to say in response to the boy's bold statement. And while the silence held, the All-Purpose Pet suddenly changed her shape.

"What's she doing?" asked Fargo in a whisper from behind him.

Jeff whispered. "I was trying to concentrate on her because looking at the Mentor makes me a little nervous, and it just occurred to me that our Oola had never gotten round to looking like a bear and this one changed immediately."

The Mentor looked down at the All-Purpose Pet who might or might not have been Oola. The little bear was sitting on its haunches and waving its forepaws at Jeff.

"Interesting," said the Mentor. "According to data left in our main computer by those who made us, there were creatures in the form of this little one, but much larger, on an icy planet they visited. There were also creatures rather like you in appearance whom they took to another planet for a suitable civilizing procedure. Are you those specimens?"

"No," said Jeff. "We travel on our own. Did your makers take a cave bear, too—the creature that, in form, was like the one beside you, now?"

"They did indeed bring specimens of various animals for

us. We—I—bioengineered some creatures into this All-Purpose Pet. Some resembled the shape she had when she came out of the castle. The originals had large and undesirable fangs. I constructed something smaller and more affectionate; altogether more suitable as a pet."

"Fargo!" said Jeff, turning back to him. "I think Oola may have been bioengineered from a saber-toothed tiger—a smilodon—but there may have been some cave bear thrown in, along with other Ice Age...."

The Mentor interrupted him. "It is impolite to talk in another language that we do not know," he said in reproving tones.

"I'm sorry," said Jeff, and he tried to explain about Oola, but succeeded only in getting muddled in his attempt to avoid mention of time travel. That proved useless under the penetrating stare of the large robot.

"I think I understand," said the Mentor. "I doubt, though, that these animals you speak of, smilodons and cave bears, are your contemporaries. You do not speak of them as though that were true, and you are sufficiently different in behavior from the specimens taken by our makers to make it reasonable to suppose you are from the future of that planet. If you are, do not tell us anything about the future, because we do not want to know."

"Smart robot," muttered Fargo, when he heard the translation.

"We are in trouble," said Jeff, carefully refraining from comment on what the robot had said about the future. "We need to know who you are and what you are doing on Jamya."

"We Mentors," said the robot, "were activated by the main computer in the castle. It is our task to bioengineer the most promising species on this planet and to train them to become civilized and self-sufficient. You have met the Jamyn?"

"We've seen them. Large animals."

"*Too* large. And too stupid. We'll change that, though, for they have definite possibilities. For that, we need a simple planet like this with one landmass and one intelligent species. We are here to keep—to keep—a home going."

The big robot looked down at his feet, as if he were emotionally upset. Jeff thought it wasn't any wonder that Norby had emotive circuits.

"A home for the Others?" Jeff said.

The robot's huge head turned up to Jeff. "You know of the

Others? I referred to them only as our makers."

"Only that they exist. What are they like? When will they return here?"

"I am disappointed," said the Mentor. "I had hoped *you* would know. Before they left the castle and its computer on this planet, Jamya, they erased from the computer all knowledge of their appearance and former history. All that is left in the computer is the bare fact that they existed, and were here for a time. After they left, the computer activated us and we began our work, but we wonder about the Others. We would like to know the organic creatures who made us."

"How do you know they were organic? Perhaps they were robots, too."

"There is physical evidence that they were organic. There were the remains of food-preparing machines. There were cremation ashes which we analyzed and which seemed to show residues of proteins and nucleic acids such as those in the living creatures of this planet and, no doubt, in you."

"Could you deduce anything about the appearance of the Others?"

"They could not have looked like you because your bodies have the wrong shape to use their equipment, but that is about all we can say. It is a problem that bothers us considerably."

"Jeff," whispered Fargo with clear worry, "I think we've got to know. Ask him if the Others bioengineered the primitive human beings they found on Ice-Age Earth, and if that's what he meant by saying we were different from the people that were found there."

Jeff's hands went cold at the possibility that the human species was the product of interstellar meddling, but he put the question to the Mentor in carefully phrased Jamyn.

"You seem concerned at the possibility, small organic friend," said the Mentor, "if I may call you that. By now, I have sensed your friendship and good will. There is no record that the Others did anything to your people except remove a few specimens to educate and put on another planet—we don't know where. It is only Jamya that seems to be getting special treatment. We hope it is because the Others want it for their own home. For that, we Mentors get it ready."

Jeff felt intense relief that the difference the Mentor had detected had lain in their wearing textile material rather than furs—or something like that. And then he felt silly. The evolutionary record of mankind was too smooth to suppose there had been outside meddling.

He looked down at the All-Purpose Pet. "Did the Others want you to develop an All-Purpose Pet?"

The Mentor took a step backward. Its eye patches dimmed. "No, that was my idea. It seemed to me that a Mentor might enjoy a pet. I also thought that some of the offspring of such a pet might be useful as exchange items in dealing with visitors to this planet, but then I found instructions left by the Others forbidding trade. It turned out the Others had also placed a force barrier around the planet to keep outsiders from coming here. That was one of our concerns when your ship suddenly appeared. How did you jump the barrier?"

Jeff said, "We have a special ship that can come or go through hyperspace anywhere."

"I hope," added Norby in a small voice.

Fargo poked Jeff. "Ask if we can exchange something for the All-Purpose Pet. I want Oola back. I have this craving for that little thing. Funny, considering the short acquaintance."

"You spoke of using your pet for trade—exchange with outsiders. Is there anything *we* can exchange for the creature?" began Jeff. "We have. . . ."

But the Mentor's eye patches shone red, and Jeff stopped.

"No!" The Mentor snatched up his pet and held her in his lower two arms. The upper two arms were drawn up, fists clenched. "I said I would exchange some of her young. She has not had any yet and I do not yet know if she *can* have young. So I am going to keep her. She is my experiment. I am different from the rest of the Mentors. I am—innovative."

Jeff felt he had better change the subject. "Do you have a name?" he asked.

"I am First."

"Ask about me, Jeff!" said Norby.

"Mentor First, do you have any small robots?"

"Those you see—for gardening, for construction, for discipline with respect to organic creatures, and so on. They are not intelligent, but they obey our commands."

"Do you have any others we don't see?"

"No."

"Do you take commands from the main computer in the castle?"

"No. We are self-controlled under my general guidance, of

course. The castle computer does not have the consciousness
we do and it is merely our tool."

Jeff could not help thinking that the robot seemed very proud
of its own superiority to all the others, and that it was this that
led it on to giving information freely—information that might
turn out to be useful.

It was almost as though Mentor First caught a whiff of this
thought, for he said, "You ask too many questions. You disturb
my peace of mind, and your presence here and the thoughts
you have induced in me may change the future. I will ask the
castle computer to wipe out the memories of you from my
mind."

The Mentor's eyes flared red once more. Odd metal eyelids drew up from the bottom, covering the eye patches completely. "Go back to your own time, or we will take forceful
measures to destroy you."

There was the feel of danger, and to Jeff it seemed only
sensible to retreat into the ship and shut the airlock door. In
the viewscreen, he could see Mentor First standing there, waiting for the ship to leave, while Norby was translating to Fargo.

Jeff said, looking a little shamefaced, "I'm sorry, Norby.
We didn't find out about your origins, or about the Others—
except that they were organic and not robots—but it's getting
dangerous here, and I'm sure we might end by changing the
future."

Fargo hesitated, then he strode to the control room chair,
seated himself in it, and called out, "Norby! Come here and
plug yourself in. We can go back to our own solar system, in
our own time, and do some exploring for McGillicuddy's
asteroid, the one where he found your alien ship. That will
keep you out of the hands of the Inventors Union, and it might
be more exciting than this."

"Wasn't this exciting?" Jeff asked.

"What? A reasonable conversation? Very tame!"

"Isn't it exciting to learn things? When the Mentors were
new, they had no robot like Norby; that's why he can be here.
But Mentor First bioengineered Oola for himself and is emotional about her. And *she's* here, which is why our Oola couldn't
be here. But that still leaves the problem of why the Mentors
became so angry and villainous later in time, and we ought to
find out why."

Fargo said, "That Mentor First of yours seems to be getting

angry and villainous. He's ordering up some machinery and it may be some sort of weapon."

"Then let's leave," said Jeff, "but let's go back to our present time in Jamya."

"Yes!" Norby said, loudly. "I want to find out why I was made. The Mentors here don't know about me, but I'm sure part of me is Jamyn. I know I was never part of these gardening robots because they don't have emotive circuits or imagination. Jeff, take my hand, and I'll try to move the whole ship forward in time to when you and I left Jamya."

"Well," said Fargo, settling back in the chair with a shrug, "back to something old. Everything will continue to be tame."

"You wouldn't say that if you'd been inside the Mentors' computer scanner," Jeff said. "Go forward, Norby. I'll visualize the castle as we first saw it."

This time the ship itself seemed to shiver.

"There's a miniature dragon outside," Fargo said. "I tell you again. Everything will be tame."

9

NOT SO TAME

"Hello," said Zargl. "You're back. You shouldn't be."

Jeff waved at her as he left the *Hopeful,* followed by Norby and Fargo. Then he waved at Zi, who was coming out of her home rather hurriedly at the sight of the ship.

"This is my sibling, Fargo," he said to mother and daughter dragon, pronouncing the name carefully. He hesitated before choosing the Jamyn word to describe Fargo's relationship to him. There was no Jamyn word for "brother," of course.

Jeff then asked, with a fine air of casualness, "How long have we been gone?"

"Fourteen day/nights," said Zargl. "Ever since you left, the Jamyns have been arguing about what to do if you returned. The Mentors sent word that you are to be captured and taken to the castle if we ever see you again. Isn't that exciting? Of course, they didn't expect you to come with a ship and reinforcements."

"Which probably makes it even more exciting," muttered Fargo, as Norby translated softly for him. "Maybe things won't be so tame at that. Ask this Pseudoreptile to bite me so I'll be able to understand her language."

"Good idea," said Jeff. "Then if things don't live up to your notions of danger and adventure, you'll at least be able to tell Albany that you were bitten by a dragon. And you, Norby, you can tell her how you missed by a couple of weeks again."

Norby said haughtily, "Can you do better, Jeff?"

Jeff, still mindful of his manners, said, "No, I can't. True is true. Zargl, would you bite my sibling, just a little bit. Just a tiny little bit."

Zargl said, "Certainly." She came shyly up to Fargo, and nuzzled his arm. "Your sibling is very attractive," she said to Jeff.

"There you are," said Jeff. "The girls always fall for him."

Fargo smiled. "It's to be expected. No one can resist my devil-may-care attitude and my incredible charm."

"It's the way he shows his little teeth," she said, showing her own much larger ones. Then she nipped a bit of flesh on Fargo's forearm between an opposing pair of her sharp teeth.

Fargo said, "Ouch," and frowned at the tiny droplet of blood that seeped from each of two delicate puncture marks.

"There you are," said Jeff. "The knowledge is transmitted by the blood somehow. The bite is so neatly done, it won't even bruise. In a few minutes, you'll be able to catch the Jamyn words telepathically, and not long after that you will understand them spoken aloud, and be able to speak them yourself."

Fargo waved his arm. "I wish they could teach differential equations that way."

Zi, who had been looking at the *Hopeful* very carefully, now pointed her right front claw at it and said, "What's that?"

"That's our small scoutship," Jeff explained. "It's ours free and clear; in fact, it was all we had left when the family business failed a few years ago. . . ."

"Look at that!" said Fargo, with sudden energy. "Jeff, do you see what I see?"

Jeff turned to look at the *Hopeful* and there in the open airlock was a green creature peering up at the castle, and panting.

"Oola!" cried out Jeff in astonishment. "I'll bet she automatically joined us when we went forward in time past the point when we opened the hassock."

"She seems to know the castle," Fargo said. "Look at her reacting to it."

Zi said, "I have never seen a creature like that before. How can she know the castle if I have never seen her?"

"Oola was inside your hassock," said Jeff, "the one you let us have. She was bioengineered by a particular Mentor named First."

"First?" Zi scratched her tail. "He is an important part of our legends. The great Mentor named First organized the construction of the buildings on Jamyn, and carried out the instructions of the Others for the civilizing of the Jamyn and, as you see, did a very good job of it. All Jamyn are in awe of First and feel great respect for him."

"And where is First, now?"

"No one knows. Perhaps he is still at the castle. Perhaps he was the one that spoke to you on my computer screen."

"That can't be," said Jeff. "The Mentor who spoke to me, and who saw me in the castle, was malevolent."

A bell chimed in the dragons' house. "Excuse me," said Zi. "Zargl, come with me and begin the preparations of a meal for our guests, while I find out what the Grand Dragonship wants." In a lower-pitched version of her voice, she said to Jeff and Norby "It is a great honor for her to call upon a mere Congressperson such as myself." She seemed to breathe quickly at the thought of it.

Left to themselves for a moment, Jeff said in Terran Basic, "Fargo, things seem no different here than when we left. Zi remembers our previous visit just as we do. Doesn't that mean that our visit to the past of Jamya didn't change anything?"

"Let's hope so," Fargo said.

Norby, however, teetered nervously on his partly extended legs. "I can tell, Jeff, I can tell. I can sense that nothing important has changed. Mentor First must really have had his memories of us wiped out. And that means that the Mentors in the castle right now are still crazy and mean."

"Good," said Fargo. "Maybe that will mean a chance for us to be battling real nasties."

Zi came out of her house carrying a little table, and Zargl followed with dishes of food. "You'll have to sit on the lawn," she said. "Please accept my apologies for that, but I have no furniture in my home that will fit your peculiar bodies—no offense intended. Even my hassock, my tail rest, is gone, for you have changed it into an unknown green animal. Still, it's such a lovely day, I thought you might be willing to have a picnic before the Grand Dragonship arrives."

"A picnic would be very welcome," said Jeff. "And I'm looking forward to meeting such an exalted person."

"And she's my great-aunt, too," said Zargl, holding up her foreclaws and making them quiver. "Isn't she, Mother?"

"She certainly is, my dear child, and my own aunt."

Half an hour later, they were all, including Oola, finishing the meal. Oola kept looking up at the castle and twitching her tail when Norby suddenly shot up on antigrav, his foot catching Jeff's ear on the way.

"What are you doing?" asked Jeff, rubbing his ear hard.

"I want to hurry back to the *Hopeful*," said Norby. "I suggest you two bring Oola and join me. Look what's coming."

From over the trees at the left of the castle, came a strange airborne procession. Majestically, a retinue of Jamyn flew toward Zi's home, and from their jeweled claws hung a glittering hammock that supported a dragon considerably larger than Zi.

"It's my aunt," cried Zi, clacking her teeth in excitement and respect. "Please do not leave. I so want you to meet her."

The hammock came overhead and was let down in front of them, dragons hovering about with a great swirl of wings to insure that it landed safely.

"Make way for her Grand Dragonship," shouted all the dragons in a medley of squawks that was totally unmusical.

When the hammock was flat on the lawn, the Grand Dragon stepped off it. She unfurled her wings, each leathery portion brightly painted in contrasting colors, and shook them. A diamondlike jewel adorned each point of the projections that went down her back to the tip of her gilded tail.

"So, my niece," she said, holding herself high with her wings akimbo to make the colors show dramatically, "you make friends with the enemy when I instructed you not to!"

"I'm sorry, Aunt—Your Dragonship—but I do like these humans and their little robot. And Zargl and I had already made friends with them weeks ago, so it was already too late when your instructions came. And see, they have discovered this green creature that was inside my tail rest—which they call by the interesting nonsense word, 'hassock.'"

"You don't understand," said Her Dragonship. "This green creature, as you call it, is the Mentors' Pet. They have watched the situation through monitors and they have sent me to correct the theft. Otherwise *we* will be punished."

"Correct the *theft?*" asked Fargo. "What do you mean by that? The hassock was given us by your niece freely."

"Nevertheless," said the Grand Dragon, "you two strangers and your ugly robot and this pet will be brought to the Mentors."

Norby said to Jeff in a furious whisper, "Are you just going to stand there and let her call me ugly?"

Oola whined and became more like a beagle than ever.

Fargo said, "This pet is my pet. It belongs to me now."

"No, she doesn't," screamed the Grand Dragon, stamping her foot, which was large and had wicked claws on it. "My guards will prove that by overpowering you...."

"That would not be sporting, Your Dragonship," said Fargo.

He paused and bent down to Norby. "Have I got the right word? Jamyn is not an easy language to learn in a great hurry."

"Say it isn't *fair*," Norby said in Jamyn. "Dragons don't play sports the way you do, but they are fair."

"Surely, Your Dragonship, you have some more civilized way of settling a dispute than brainless force?" Fargo smiled his most charming smile.

The dragon guards began to move toward him, but the Grand Dragon gestured them back. "This stranger appeals to our civilized nature," she said, "and no one can appeal to that in vain. It would be an insult to the Mentors otherwise."

She smiled, too, her pointed teeth and front fangs showing to full advantage. She adjusted her jeweled gold collar and stepped forward until she was only a few centimeters from Fargo. She was a little taller than he was, and, counting the tail, considerably bigger.

"There! It will be I alone against two of you and a robot. It is three to one in your favor so it is you who will be uncivilized, yet I will personally bring all of you to the Mentors."

"Is that indeed so?" said Fargo, as he thrust out his chin.

"Fargo!" said Jeff, reverting to Terran Basic, "Let's just go with her. . . ."

"Never!" said Fargo, pushing up his sleeves.

"Listen, you're not going to try to punch her, are you?" asked Jeff. "Her fangs will tear into your knuckles."

"Fist fighting is crude," Fargo said, adjusting his stance. "I'm going to see if I can use any of the defensive arts that Albany has taught me. I wouldn't mind having a sword or rapier, though. Cold steel against hot fang, eh?"

"This isn't funny!" said Jeff. "You can't win!"

Norby was ascending and descending on his telescopic legs, forcing his way between Jeff and Fargo and shouting, "Listen to me, you human idiots! The Jamyn respect tradition and authority and they never use force among themselves!"

"Well?" asked Fargo, "Are you trying to spoil the fun?"

"Of course. Your kind of fun is no fun. But there is something else. . . ." He rose on antigrav and whispered in Fargo's ear.

Fargo nodded, but did not change his position, "En garde, sir, I mean, madam, Your Dragonship." He moved into the ready-to-attack position.

The Grand Dragon snorted and little puffs of smoke came

out of her nostrils. "There, you see! You have made me revert to the primitivism of my ancestors; you have forced me to be angry enough to breathe fire. You ought to be ashamed of yourself."

"It would not be fair for you to use fire," Fargo said.

"I do not intend to. I will cow you by the superior nature of my personality and take you all to the Mentors, who will imprison you."

The Grand Dragon and Fargo moved toward each other. They began circling, feinting, and reaching. Suddenly the Grand Dragon lunged and Fargo went head over heels. The Grand Dragon drew back in surprise. Clearly, she hadn't expected that to happen.

Fargo picked himself up with a groan. "She's quick."

Jeff watched the battle with sinking heart. Karate against slippery dragon scales was not working too well. Fargo managed to trip the Grand Dragon, who seemed more surprised than ever when *she* went down, but once she got back, she retaliated immediately, saying, "If you are going to be aggressive, so will I."

"The fight isn't fair, Your Highness-ship;" said Fargo gravely. "Your arms are much longer than mine. May I have a short stick?"

"Certainly, since that will make all the more plain your uncivilized nature and force you to abase yourself to my higher culture."

"Norby," said Fargo, "go get the skewer in the galley. You know the one that you were curious about the other day. That ought to be about the right length."

Jeff's eyebrows shot up. The object Norby had been curious about had been an apple picker that Fargo had bought at a tool sale, a sticklike device with a collapsible grasper at one end for plucking apples too high to reach by hand. Fargo would buy anything that was a bargain, however useless. It was one of the reasons the family business had done so badly after the deaths of their parents.

The battle began again with Fargo wielding the apple picker against the Grand Dragon's sharp foreclaws (which, however, she wielded so carefully that Fargo had not yet been scratched).

They again circled and circled, reaching out, feinting; but the Grand Dragon was obviously getting angry over the fact that Fargo had not yet admitted her superiority and given in.

She was puffing smoke in spite of herself and growing angrier still at this demonstration of her animal nature. Fargo took advantage of the manner in which her anger was disrupting her concentration. As she lunged forward, he leaped to one side, caught her arm, pulled her forward, and down she went.

"Bravo!" said Jeff.

"Stupid human being," muttered Norby. "Showing off, when I have told him how to conclude this ridiculous exercise in a perfectly simple way. . . ."

"I'm not sure I should fight a female," said Fargo, pushing back his hair, "but there are no males on this planet for me to fight."

He stopped talking because the Grand Dragon was up, fire spurting out of her nostrils.

"That's very animal," said Fargo, waggling his apple picker at the Grand Dragon's nose.

She stifled the flame, but as Fargo sprang forward, she unfurled her wings and elevated, then made a feint at him from the air.

"Unfair!" shouted Jeff.

"It certainly is," said Fargo, reaching up with the apple picker, activating the grasper at the end and seizing the golden collar which circled her scaly neck—just as such collars circled the necks of every other dragon they had seen. One twist, a pull, and the collar was off.

"Mine!" shouted Fargo, "spoils of war!" He put it around his own neck, where it hung loosely.

Jeff watched what followed in amazement. The Grand Dragon, instead of soaring majestically, began to flap her wings frantically. The enormous effort broke her fall, but did not prevent it. She landed on the lawn with a loud "plop" and in a most undignified posture.

Her guards gaped. Zi and Zargl hid their mouths with their claws. Norby tittered metallically.

"What happened?" asked Jeff.

"This is an antigrav device," said Fargo, touching the collar. "I've been thinking that the dragons must be too heavy to fly, especially with such comparatively small wings, and Norby confirmed that."

"That's right, come to think of it," said Jeff. "They didn't have wings at all in their prehistoric history. Remember?"

"I do. The Mentors must have added them as part of their

bioengineering program for esthetic reasons and perhaps to add stability in antigrav flight." Fargo elevated. "It's done mentally. One thinks 'up' and there one is. A great device. Probably Norby has one incorporated into his own works."

"Of course, I do," said Norby shrilly. "I keep telling you all the time I'm Jamyn in origin—in part."

"Now," said Fargo, "I think I'll pay a visit to the castle under my own steam and not as anyone's prisoner."

The the Grand Dragon had recovered from the mixture of shame and physical confusion that had beset her, and now she struggled to her feet. Her guards rushed to her side as she screamed, "Get that stranger! Bring him down!"

"No," said Fargo, skimming over her head. "I think not. I won the fight fairly and you cannot try to upset the result without showing yourself to be most uncivilized. You just sit there and recover, Your Majesty, while I. . . ."

"No you don't," said Jeff. "Not alone, you don't." He snatched up Norby under his left arm and scooped up Oola with his right. "We're *all* going. Up Norby—to the castle."

10

Villains?

As Jeff and Norby swept up and forward to follow Fargo, who was already approaching the castle door, Jeff saw that the Grand Dragon was vehemently ordering her guard back. Either she had taken seriously Fargo's stern comment about uncivilized behavior, or else she had decided it didn't matter how the strangers were brought to the castle as long as they got there.

Inside the castle, everything seemed the same as before. The four intruders, two humans, one small robot (now on his feet again), and one All-Purpose Pet, proceeded down the dark corridor. around the sharp curve and into the auditorium, which was still lined by the silent figures of dead Mentors. Oola was restless in Jeff's arms.

"Where's the villain?" asked Fargo. "I don't see any live robot."

His voice echoed in the vast room, and no one answered.

Jeff took Norby's hand, and then Fargo's. ——Let's talk telepathically. It will be safer, and perhaps private, but we have to touch each other, Jeff said to their minds.

——What's that? That was Fargo, startled.

——I'm sorry. I forgot you haven't experienced telepathy. Eerie, isn't it?

——Certainly not. That was Norby. His thoughts were loudest because he was designed for telepathy. It is a perfectly natural way of speaking to one another if one has the talent for it.

Jeff smiled to himself. ——Yes, but we human beings aren't used to it. Do you sense anything, robot or otherwise, that's alive in this building, Norby?

——I've been trying. I think there's a barrier field around this room at the moment. I can't sense beyond it. It comes from the scanning section of the computer, part of which must be on the back wall, though nothing shows there.

Fargo let go of Jeff's hand and walked quickly toward the back wall. Jeff ran after, pulling Norby with him. He caught up to Fargo, and grabbed him.

——Don't let go of us, Fargo, or we can't communicate privately. And don't touch that wall, or the computer may give our thoughts to the Mentor.

——Jeff, you are fourteen and I am twenty-four. As your much older brother....

——You can also be my stupid brother. I'm the natural leader here, age or not, because I've been here before....

——And you got yourself captured. I've been working with the giant computers at Space Command so I ought to....

While they argued (neither managing to finish a sentence), Norby withdrew his legs and arms into his body, elevated on his antigrav, and floated slowly to the featureless computer wall. Jeff and Fargo stopped their mental conversation and watched him as he sailed up and down the wall, over and back.

——What are you doing, Norby?

——He can't hear you now, Fargo, when you talk telepathically. You aren't touching him.

——I forgot. Maybe you should be leader for a while, Jeff.

"*I* am leader," said Norby out loud. "I can sometimes catch the telepathic drift, even when I'm not touching you. This is my planet, after all, even if I can't remember much, so let *me* try."

"Try what?" asked Jeff.

"Try using my intuition."

"Do you have one?"

"Not a human one. I seem to have a built-in imagination and the ability to make guesses and take chances. Or maybe being with human beings has taught me how to take chances, even though I certainly don't enjoy it. Still...."

Norby's feeler wire came out and entered a small crack in the surface. Minutes passed. Norby's back eyes closed. Suddenly the crack began to expand and the wall opened like sliding doors. Inside was an opening covered by a misty atmosphere and around the opening was the mechanism of something that might have been a computer, though it was certainly like no computer Jeff had ever seen.

Jeff said so and Fargo added, "Well I've seen a great many more computers than you have, Jeff, but it isn't like any I've seen, either. What is that place inside?"

"That's the scanning room, Fargo," said Jeff with distaste. "Don't go in. It doesn't feel good."

Norby fiddled with the computer and the mist began to clear.

Fargo said, "There's an old beat-up Mentor. What's it doing in the scanning room?"

Jeff stared at the huge figure within the computer. "I don't know. There was no Mentor there when I was inside."

Norby put out his legs and arms and walked back to Jeff. "I must go inside the scanning room. It is necessary."

"Aha," said Fargo, "your alien nature is coming out, Norby. You're not planning to turn us over to the Mentors, are you?" He did not sound as though he were entirely joking.

Jeff fired up at once. "Don't talk to my robot that way, Fargo. He's loyal to us."

"Are you sure?"

"He rescued me from Mentors before, and I would trust him even if he hadn't."

Norby came closer to Jeff and touched his hand. "Stay here with Fargo, Jeff." ——And thank you for trusting me, he added telepathically.

Norby inserted his wire into the computer once more. The mists began to swirl up as the protective field formed, but before it closed in entirely, Norby hopped inside, withdrawing his wire as he did so.

Jeff changed his mind at once, feeling oddly alone without Norby's funny barrel shape in his reach. "I shouldn't have let him go, Fargo. It was a mistake. We've got to get him out of there before he's destroyed."

"Why should he be destroyed? That's not a very brave robot. He wouldn't go in there in a million years if he thought there was danger."

"He's plenty brave in a crisis. Besides, he may have miscalculated. Norby's part Jamyn and if the Mentors made him, perhaps they will try to keep him, or change him or. . . . I don't want that! I want Norby back, just as he is, mixed up and all!"

"Patience, patience," muttered Fargo, studying the computer's complex surface. He touched a few spots. Nothing happened.

"On the other hand," Jeff said, "maybe we should wait and do nothing." He knew he wasn't thinking clearly. He wanted to believe that Norby knew what he was doing, but with Norby, one could never tell when his mixed-up nature might rise to the surface.

Fargo seemed totally absorbed in feeling the odd surface of the computer. He also put his hand out to the mist at the computer entrance and drew it back quickly. "No entry. Strong barrier field. The question is, Can we undo it somehow?" He went on trying.

Jeff finally managed to put it into words. "What if Norby doesn't want to come back with us, Fargo? What if he would rather be on his native Jamya than come back to Earth with me? What if—and what's happened to Oola? I put her down when Norby went inside and now I don't see her."

"Oola," called Fargo. "Here! Come to me!"

"Woof!" She was still beaglelike in appearance as she bounded out of the shadows, ears flapping. She sprang into Fargo's arms, licked his nose, and wriggled in her effort to get down again.

"All right," said Fargo. "You can get down, but don't run away. Stay right here."

She sniffed all over the floor, as if she were looking for something. Then she followed a trail up to the scanner entrance, was blocked by the barrier field, and sat down.

"Oooo-o-o-o."

Jeff's spine tingled at the sound. Oola howled more like a primeval wolf than a beagle. "She must miss Norby," he said, hoping it was that.

"I feel like howling in frustration, too." Fargo said. "I've fiddled with some things on the surface that seemed promising, and a few that didn't, and nothing happens. I can't figure out this computer. I just can't fit my mind into the alien mind that constructed it."

Oola stood on her hind legs and pressed her nose against one of the little panels marked irregularly over the surface. The mist began to clear at once.

"I touched that one," said Fargo indignantly.

"Maybe it had to be touched by something cold and damp," said Jeff.

Norby was facing them at the opening. "I'm so glad to see you," he said. "I couldn't seem to open the scanner again from inside, and I was afraid that you'd never manage to work the other side. I felt very scared at the thought of having to stay in here forever, because I was having trouble getting out through hyperspace. How did you remove the energy barrier?"

His legs were telescoped out as far as they could go, so that he seemed to be walking on stilts. Indeed, he *was* walking—moving round and round the immense hulking shape of the silent Mentor, who was sitting on the floor, with his eye patches covered.

"Oola did it," said Fargo. "And what were *you* doing in there?"

"I was trying to wake him up," Norby said, pointing to the large robot, "but I failed."

Oola bounded inside and, with one leap, landed on the Mentor's shoulder. She settled down and yowled in his ear, her fangs growing and her body altering to look more tigerish.

"She's reverting to her original shape!" Jeff said.

Abruptly the Mentor stood up. "She is mine!" he said. His voice was harsh as if the mechanism for producing it was seriously out of order. His body was covered with discolorations and dents. He seemed even older than the first time Jeff had encountered him.

"If she's yours," demanded Fargo, sounding angry, "what was she doing inside a hassock all these years? You didn't even know where she was. You didn't care for her one bit, and I do. I claim her. Oola, come to me."

Oola jumped down and stood between the Mentor and Fargo, looking anxiously from one to the other, her ears growing first longer and beaglelike, then shorter and tigerlike.

The Mentor's massive head turned to Jeff. "You were here intruding before. You refused scanning, and you would not help me. You will be scanned now, you and this other creature like you."

Fargo stepped between Jeff and the Mentor. "Now just a minute, sir. Not only are you wrong about the All-Purpose Pet, you are wrong about us. We mean no harm. We have come to find the origins of our own robot, part of whose mechanism may have come from Jamya. . . . Norby, where are you?"

Norby was inside his barrel completely up against the computer. Only his feeler wire was extended and it touched the computer.

Jeff ran to him, "Norby? Are you all right? Answer me!"

He bent to touch him and got an electric shock. "Fargo, something's wrong! Norby's tied in to the computer and I can't get him loose!"

"Release our robot, Mentor," said Fargo threateningly.

With that, the Mentor's eyes flashed red. His two right arms seized Fargo about the waist and held him up in the air.

"Monster!" shouted the Mentor. "You interrupted me at important work and I may never.... I will not endure this! You will be scanned until everything you know and are becomes part of the computer and your body will be left an empty shell incapable of harming or disturbing me."

Fargo stopped struggling because nothing could break the Mentor's grip. Instead, he laughed, and at that Jeff shook his head. It was Fargo's up-and-at-'em laugh, and it never failed to create trouble.

Jeff stepped up close to the Mentor to try to reason with him, as Fargo had so carefully taught him to do all his life— and as Fargo so infrequently did himself.

It was too late. Still wearing the antigrav collar taken from the Grand Dragon, Fargo rose in the air, carrying the Mentor with him. They swung out into the main auditorium, zooming up into the thick darkness of the high-ceilinged room.

"Fargo, don't!" Jeff called, but Fargo was out of sight in the gloom and did not answer.

"Norby, come out of it. Help me! I can't antigrav without you."

"Meow?" Oola pressed against Jeff's leg and he patted her, absently. As he did so, he became aware of the thin, expandable collar around her neck.

"Oola, can you antigrav?"

"Rowrr?" Oola's fangs disappeared and she looked very much like a Terran housecat, purring against Jeff's leg.

There were terrible noises coming from the darkness overhead, and Jeff, feeling frantic about Fargo, picked up Oola. Holding her close to his chest, he bent his head to hers and thought, very hard, picturing a small cat going up in the air.

Oola meowed once more, and Jeff began to rise. Linking himself telepathically with a not-to-bright All-Purpose Pet that had saber-tooth ancestors was an interesting experience, but difficult to manage. They went up and down, and finally sailed upward—a bit too quickly—toward the Mentor.

The darkness began to separate into distinct shapes, and Jeff could see that the Mentor was still holding Fargo.

Fargo's eyes were shut, his jaw grimly set.

Jeff somehow guided Oola that way. "Don't hurt my brother, Mentor! If you want me to help you. . . ."

Fargo opened one eye, "Shut up, kid. I'm under a strain, trying to do battle with this antiquated hulk, and I have no room to take care of you."

"Why don't you just threaten to let go of your antigrav?"

"Then I fall, too, don't I?"

"Just a little. Fall slowly and let him bang against the floor, then up, then down with another bang, and so on." Jeff had trouble getting the words out, so anxious was he that Fargo understand.

The Mentor understood. He made a sound like gears grinding horribly. "I will let you go, alien monster, if you get me down to the ground. Don't do as the other monster suggests. I am nearly dead and I will be quickly destroyed it there is hard contact with the ground."

Fargo looked at Jeff. Jeff looked at Fargo.

"Let's go down," said Jeff, "Nice and easy." Unfortunately, he didn't count on Oola's reaction. Without warning, she jumped from his arms to the Mentor's shoulder and Jeff found himself in midair without antigrav.

He cried, "Help! I'm falling!"

Fargo yelled, too, as he desperately dropped with the Mentor and tried to snatch at his falling brother.

Jeff was trying to shrink back from the rapidly approaching floor when he felt two hard hands grab him. They were not Fargo's, but the Mentor's. Jeff was hanging from the Mentor's left arms, facing Fargo, who was still wearing the antigrav collar, and was still clutched by the Mentor's two right arms.

Fargo cancelled the fall with such vigor that all three—four, counting Oola—shot upward again.

"Wow!" said Fargo, shaking his head to free his left ear from Oola's enthusiastic licking. "That was close!"

He slapped Jeff's arm and grinned. "Let's *all* go down slowly, now, and have a reasonable conversation about this. Haven't I always told you, Jeff, that logical argument is better than derring-do?"

"Sure," said Jeff. "You've always *told* me. What you don't do is *show* me." His feet reached the floor and the Mentor let go first of Jeff and then of Fargo.

The two brothers watched while the enormous robot, with Oola resting comfortably on his shoulder, clumped slowly back into the scanning room, where Norby still sat inside his barrel. The Mentor sat down and put his head in his hands.

"Suddenly, I'm sorry for him," said Fargo in Terran Basic. "He's such an old robot."

"I think he's Mentor First," said Jeff in Jamyn.

"Yes," said the Mentor, looking up. "How did you know that?"

"We came to see you, long ago, just after you had been activated to do your work here," said Jeff, gently. The Mentor First they'd met then had been so strong, so gleamingly new.

"Surely you could not be alive for so long; we were activated thirty thousand years ago. And I do not remember you," said the Mentor. He said this in Terran Basic.

"You have learned to *speak* our language!" said Jeff.

"Since you left two weeks ago, the computer analyzed your language and I have learned it—enough to know that you pity me. An alien such as yourself should not take the liberty of pitying me; it is not your place to do so. And yet—and yet I find it strangely comforting. Perhaps, now, you will help me remove this terrible fear I have."

"What is the fear?" Jeff asked softly.

"When you would not help, I scanned you, hoping the computer and I could find out how you got to Jamya." The Mentor's head hung lower, and his body seemed to quiver.

"What's the matter?" asked Fargo. "Are you afraid of us?"

"No, no. I am afraid of *myself*. I am so seriously out of order that, at times, I am not in a position of mental stability, and the moments—of insanity—have come more frequently. When my Pet came back to me so unexpectedly, I felt myself becoming sane once more, but I don't know how long that will last. If I become insane again, you must leave me here in the scanner. The computer is adjusted to deactivate me if I become too dangerous."

Jeff was horrified. Suddenly the thought of Mentor First as a villain seemed grotesque. He was a sad and suffering machine.

Jeff protested, "But you mustn't kill yourself."

"I must, if I cannot be cured. And I do not think a cure is possible. I am too old. All the other Mentors have died, and I am too much alone. Caring for the Jamyn by myself is more

than I can manage and even my Pet has been away from me
for too long. We have no means of entering hyperspace to
refuel ourselves, you see. The Others wanted to isolate this
planet, and they must have thought they would be back long
before our enormous supply of fuel would be consumed, but
they have not come back."

"And you thought I came from hyperspace," said Jeff, "and
could get you into hyperspace where you could refuel—and
perhaps find the Others."

"Yes. It is as though you read my mind. . . . But the dis-
turbance in my brain has progressed too far. It is too late. Go
away."

"Then have the computer release Norby. *He* can help.
Norby!" shouted Jeff.

"I heard," came Norby's voice, and his head popped up.
He elevated on antigrav and hung in the air before the Mentor.

"I was exploring the computer, Jeff," Norby said. "I'm sorry
you thought I was helpless in its grip and that you were upset
by that, but I could not allow anything to interrupt me. I'm
done now, though, and I'll be glad to help you, Mentor First.
I will take you into hyperspace so you can refuel."

The Mentor's eye patches flared in a blue iridescence, but
quickly dulled. "You? A small alien robot?"

"I am not alien. I'm yours. You made me. At least partly.
Can't you tell?"

"You don't look familiar," said Mentor First. "You are lying."

"Take my hand," said Norby. "Find the data in my mind.
It's available now that I've explored the data banks of your
computer. I remember—and you will, too."

They touched, and while Jeff watched, his heart thumping,
the Mentor's eye patches began to brighten and he reached out
his two lower arms to hold Norby's barrel. "You are the
Searcher," he said in Jamyn.

"Part of it," Norby said. "When you realized that the Others
might not be returning and that you could not go into hyperspace
to find them or to refuel, you finally worked out a device that
would go into hyperspace for you." Norby spread out his arms.
"Inside me is that device."

"You never returned," said Mentor First, softly, "and I thought
my attempt to build a hyperpenetrator had failed."

"Your attempt did *not* fail, and I found the ship the Others
had promised to send, but a collision with a small asteroid

ruined the ship and damaged me. I lay paralyzed for a long time until a human being named McGillicuddy, a creature like these two with me, explored the asteroid on which the ship and I were wrecked, and found me. He repaired a damaged robot of his own, using some of my parts. Since I have been in this new and beautiful shape, I have been drawn back to Jamya over and over. Now I remember everything and can help you and at the same time, fulfill my original function."

"It is too late, my son, I am dying."

"No! Come with me to hyperspace and refuel."

"I do not think I can. I am too weak to refuel now."

"I'll do it—and channel the energy to you." A wire extended from Norby's hat and touched Mentor First's chest. "Now, father, join minds with me. I will think of hyperspace, and together we will go. . . ." Norby and Mentor First vanished.

11

PIRATES!

Oola whined, her ears lengthening. She slunk on her belly over to Fargo.

Stroking her ears, Fargo muttered, "Poor Oola. I guess she's torn between Mentor First and me. And poor me, because I guess if Mentor First lives, I'll end up minus a pet."

"He'd better live," said Jeff, "even if it means you being petless. and he'd better come back with Norby intact, because without Norby, how are we going to get home? The *Hopeful* will be forever stuck within the energy barrier around Jamya if we can't make use of Norby's mixed-up abilities."

"You're right. But let's be optimistic. *When* Norby gets back, we'll go out in search of the Others, if they still exist."

"Or, if they don't, we must at least find that wrecked ship of theirs that McGillicuddy stumbled on. No telling what information it might have on it."

"Either way," said Fargo, "whether it's the Others, or their ship, we'd better do the finding before anybody else in the Federation does."

"Absolutely," said Jeff. "We could use that knowledge as ransom for Norby. It's Norby I worry about. Right now, and after we get back home!"

The two waited with increasing impatience. Then Fargo said, "This doesn't seem to be an appropriate time for it, but I'm getting hungry. How about you?"

Jeff said, "I'm a growing boy, superannuated brother. I'm more or less always hungry."

"Too bad. Part of the problem of being organic rather than metal is that one has to refuel so much more often. Do you suppose Zi will feed us if we go down there?"

"Sure, she's a great hostess, but her aunt, the Grand Dragon, will try to chew us up."

"Let me try my charm," Fargo said, sauntering out with Oola in his arms.

• • •

Charm or whatever, Jeff thought a while later, it certainly worked.

Fargo, collarless since he had restored her property to the Grand Dragon, had eaten and was now serenading Her Dragonship, who sat in royal splendor against the sunset light of Jamya. She reached out with one careful claw every now and then and ran it through Fargo's hair.

"These are such pleasant scales," she said. "Soft and fine. How did you come to get them?"

"I have noticed," said Fargo, "that they have grown softer and finer since I have had the good fortune to meet you, Your Dragonship."

At this, the Grand Dragon made a gargling sound that seemed to signify gratified pleasure. She was obviously infatuated with him.

With his melodic tenor, Fargo had no trouble acting the part of a troubadour, and was now well into a peculiar translation of "God Save the Queen" which seemed to delight the Grand Dragon.

Jeff lacked Fargo's ability to live in the passing moment, however. He did not enjoy either the food or the song, for he could think only of the absent Norby. Even Zargl, who sat next to him and made fearsome faces at him in an apparent design to make him laugh, failed to cheer him up.

As the sun sank below the trees, the Grand Dragon offered to fly Jeff and Fargo to her palace where they might spend the night. It seemed to the appalled Jeff that Fargo might actually accept the invitation, and he said, "I think we had better stay in the *Hopeful,* in case our small robot returns."

Fargo, looking guilty for a moment, agreed.

But Norby did not return. The night was very dark because Jamya had no satellite and seemed to be in a section of space rich in cosmic dust that dimmed most of the stars that might have been visible in the sky.

"Fargo," Jeff said, as he lay in the top bunk of their cabin. "I'm so worried I can't sleep."

Only snores answered him. Fargo could sleep through anything.

Jeff stared gloomily at the darkness above with increasingly dire visions passing through his mind, when he heard Oola's paws plunk against the floor and pad down the corridor to the control room. Apparently, she had leaped down from Fargo's stomach, where she had been curled up when the lights were put out.

Jeff slid over the edge of his bunk, dropped quietly to the cabin floor, and followed her.

"What is it, girl?" he said, scratching her behind the ears. She must have changed into a cattish phase now, for her eyes shone in the dim lights from the control panels.

Crash! A falling object struck the Captain's chair, bounced to the floor, and rolled.

Jeff put on the room light. Out of the falling object, half a head popped up and large eyes peered from under a metal derby hat.

"Norby!" Jeff cried out in sheer joy. The pleasantest sight in the world, it seemed to him, was the little robot appearing out of nowhere, even if he failed to make a good landing. What other robot would be as clumsy as delightful, wonderful, mixed-up Norby?

Norby said, "Sorry, Jeff. I was so upset I forgot to turn on my antigrav when I reappeared from hyperspace. Didn't you get my telepathic message warning you I was trying to get back?"

"No, but I think Oola did."

"That's very annoying," said Norby. "We're going to have to work on your long-distance telepathy . . . but that's for later. Right now, you've got to wake up Fargo, and both of you had better help me take the *Hopeful* back to the Terran solar system. After we refueled in hyperspace, the Mentor First and I tuned into the Others' supply ship and found it on an asteroid, but so have the pirates. I came back here to get help."

"What about Mentor First?"

"He's holding off the pirates, and I don't know how long he can do that, so we'd better get to him *fast.*"

"Did I hear you say pirates?" asked Fargo from the doorway.

"I'll say it again. Pirates! Pirates!" yelled Norby. "Let's get going." He grabbed both brothers and all three ran to the computer.

The *Hopeful* emerged in normal space next to the asteroid.

"Wow—from Jamya slam-bang through hyperspace to my own solar system! And right on target, Norby," said Fargo softly.

"Have you stopped being mixed up?" asked Jeff.

"I'm tuned to Mentor First. Getting us here was easy. Do you have any suggestions as to how to cope with those pirates who are trying to steal the Jamyn's supply ship? Look at the size of it!"

Following Norby's pointing finger, Jeff watched the viewscreen intently while Fargo was whispering rapidly to the little robot.

Another ship, tiny by comparison, but larger than the *Hopeful* was anchored to the small asteroid. Jeff could dimly see the huge outline of a strange wreck on the asteroid, partially hidden by its irregularities. On the asteroid, Mentor First was confronting three men in spacesuits who were holding weapons.

"But are they pirates?" asked Jeff, doubtful. "They could be Federation police."

"No chance," said Fargo. "Those are known pirates; I recognize their ship. They're renegades from the Inventors Union. Up and at 'em."

"With what?" asked Jeff. "The *Hopeful* doesn't carry weapons."

"You're not up-to-date, little brother. Admiral Yobo insisted that once I became one of Space Command's secret agents, my ship would have to be armed. You and I will go out in suits and distract the pirates, and Norby will plug into system G6YY of the computer. The computer will tell you what to do, Norby."

Norby was plugging in. "Right, Fargo. Are you sure you also want me to notify. . . ."

"Yes, those are my orders. I'm certain," said Fargo hastily, pulling Jeff to the airlock and throwing him a space suit from the three hanging there.

"Fortunately, we don't need antigrav in open space—or on an asteroid either," he added, readying the jet propulsion system of the suit. He and Jeff stepped into the airlock.

"I wish you'd tell me what we're planning to do," said Jeff in exasperation, over the suit's intercom.

"Just follow me."

Jeff followed, landing between the Mentor and the three pirates.

"Howdy," said Fargo. "How about cutting me in on the spoils, boys? If you've found anything, that is."

The pirates were clearly startled at the sudden and unexpected voice in their radio receivers. Apparently they had not been aware of a ship materializing silently out of hyperspace and into their vicinity.

One of the pirate guns turned on Fargo and Jeff, with the clumsiness that attended all movements in open space.

"Who are you?" demanded the pirate.

"Fargo Wells, descended from an ancestor who was tarred and feathered in North Dakota, American sector of the Terran Federation. My buddy here and I are interested in what you found. An old robot?"

"That robot's alive, mister," said the pirate leader, "and it's dangerous. If you want anything out of us besides destruction, you'd better get ready to help us. That thing is holding some gadget that repels our force guns and produces a nasty shock when you get near enough. If you two do something useful, maybe you'll get something in exchange."

Fargo said, "Sounds good, if you can really get something out of an old robot. Is *that* all you've got here?"

"The wreck of an alien ship, too, that the Inventors Union might pay a lot for."

"Why should they? Is there anything on the ship?"

"That's what we aim to find out, and we don't figure on delaying things with talk. Are you going to help us or do we poke holes in your suits and let out all that nice air?"

"As it happens," said Fargo, "we're attached to our air. My buddy here is a robotics expert, so let him approach that monster."

The three pirates touched fingers and conferred in sound, the waves being carried by the material of the suits. The first pirate, clearly the leader, switched back to radio.

"You have one chance," he said. "If you can handle the robot, fine! If not, say good-bye to each other real fast, because we're not going to wait for you to say your prayers."

Jeff used rocket microsurges to bring himself down to the asteroid surface and approached Mentor First in the slow, swaying steps enforced by a nearly gravitationless world. He touched Mentor First and said, telepathically and in Jamyn, ——Hold on, First, Fargo and I have come to. . . .

——I recognized your ship, said Mentor First telepathically. I am recharged and in much better health, but this weapon is nearly exhausted. I have very few options. I could tear off their suits and kill them, but I cannot bring myself to destroy living things. It is against my programming. And yet I must keep them from taking the ship.

The pirate leader said tensely to Fargo, "How did your pal get past the repulsion field? And is he talking to that thing? How can he talk to an alien robot?"

"Maybe it's not an alien robot," said Fargo. "It could be an advanced experimental gadget of Space Command. My pal would be able to speak to a Command robot. He knows Martian Swahili."

But while Fargo and Jeff had been engaging the attention of the pirates, the *Hopeful* had been edging closer to the pirate ship. Now the *Hopeful* plunged outward and away from the asteroid, dragging the pirate ship with it so the pirates would be stranded.

"A force grapple," shouted the pirate leader waving his weapons furiously. "You tell your friends to bring it back or you both die. You have one minute to convince me my ship is being brought back."

"It's mutiny," shouted Fargo, shaking his gloved fist at the *Hopeful*. "They've taken over our ship, stolen yours, and marooned us all. Killing us won't get you off the asteroid now. We've got to do something fast. If you don't have any ideas, I do."

"Like what?" asked the pirate. His gun lowered as the uselessness of killing Fargo penetrated.

"We persuade this robot, probably a Command robot, to join us and use *him*. . . ."

"You talk Martian Swahili, too?"

"A little."

Fargo, while still talking rapidly and ignoring the guns that were pointing at him, walked over to Jeff and the Mentor. He put his hands on Jeff's suit. ——It's a great thing to have linguistic ability, to say nothing of dragon bites. Try to look as though you're talking with Mentor First, and follow my lead.

He called back on radio to the pirates, and said, "My buddy knows how to push this big robot's obedience buttons, so that's no problem, and there's something on the wreck—I don't know what—that will help us get those ships back. My buddy has to get behind the wreck because there's one piece of equipment. . . ."

He pushed Jeff energetically in the direction of the wreck

and continued to talk smoothly and persuasively, while the pirates, unable to decide what to do, had no choice but to listen.

Hidden behind the alien ship, Jeff found Norby waiting for him with both small ships nearby. He took Norby's hand, and telepathically asked, ——What's going on?

Norby responded, ——You know Fargo. He's got it all figured out. He wants you to take the *Hopeful* and place it above the pirates.

——What about you?

——I'll rescue father, and then I have to readjust the *Hopeful* for some heavy duty lifting before we can lift the Jamyn ship, Norby said, moving off.

Inside the *Hopeful*, Jeff took off his space helmet and sat down at the controls. He did not have Fargo's touch at manipulating the *Hopeful*, but spaceships were all but foolproof, thanks to the computers they carried, and Jeff had had at least the preliminaries of an education in spacecraft control.

As the ship came over the pirates, Jeff saw Norby move up unnoticed behind Mentor First, seize one arm, and then lift upward with increasing speed, taking Mentor First with him, while Fargo was busily and energetically engaged in pointing in the other direction.

Norby slid into the *Hopeful* easily and then helped Mentor First get through the airlock. Fortunately the *Hopeful*'s control room was large.

With deep concern Jeff asked "What about Fargo?"

"He's next," Norby said.

The little robot ejected himself from the *Hopeful* and looking like a small metal barrel with a lid partly open, hurled himself at the pirates.

Jeff could not tell what the pirates were saying or doing, but they had clearly noticed that Mentor First was gone, and their guns were pointing at Fargo, when one of them noticed Norby speeding down upon them.

As the pirates scattered, Norby grabbed Fargo, zoomed away from the asteroid, and headed back to the *Hopeful*. And just then, Jeff saw five ships of the Command Fleet approaching, their lights blazing like bright stars in the sky.

12

HOSTAGE

When the airlock closed, Jeff quickly settled the *Hopeful* behind
the large alien ship while Mentor First watched.

"How was that for adventure and drama!" Fargo said ju-
bilantly as he and Norby came into the control room.

"Listen, Fargo, when did you send for the fleet?" asked
Jeff with a scowl.

"At the very start, little brother."

"And why didn't you tell me?"

"Because it was going to take time for the ships to get here.
They don't hypertravel, and I had to jolly the pirates along till
then. And you're no actor, kid. You'd have given it away and
they'd have shot us down and taken off in their ship."

Norby went immediately to the *Hopeful*'s computer and
began to work.

Mentor First shook his odd-shaped head ponderously and
made a sound like grinding gears. He said in Terran Basic, "It
is important that the wrecked ship be taken back to Jamya."

He was holding Oola, whose loud purr changed into a snarl.

"Doesn't *anyone* approve?" Fargo asked. "The pirates are
beaten and the Command ships will have prisoners."

Jeff said, "Yes, but you heard Mentor First. We have to go
back to Jamya with the Jamyn ship in tow. We can't allow the
fleet to take it. That ship is the supply ship the Others had
prepared for Jamya, and it has the material needed to rebuild
all the inoperative Mentors."

"My world," said Norby, "my people. We can't let the fleet
have it."

Fargo looked from one to the other and then shrugged, "I
suppose you're right. Jeff, if you and Norby want to link minds
with the *Hopeful*'s computer and hyperjump us with the Jamyn
ship, I'm willing."

Norby was holding out his hand to Jeff when Admiral Yobo,

encased in a regulation fleet spacesuit, opened the control room door and walked in. He stopped, stared at Mentor First, who was even larger than himself, and said, "Someone may have to leave and make room."

Fargo's jaw dropped. "How did you get in?"

"Sorry, Wells, but surely you're not surprised to know that I have the combination of every airlock in the fleet. You've brought us three of the worst renegades on our wanted list and it seemed only right that I thank you in person. . . ."

"That was not necessary, Admiral. . . ."

"And," Yobo went on severely, "I've come here *alone* to find out what kind of illegalities you're engaged in. You've got a large-sized alien robot, I see, and an alien wreck next to your ship."

Norby jiggled forward and backward on his two-way feet. "We've got to go home, Admiral!"

"Yes, home," said Mentor First.

Yobo looked at the large robot with interest. "It speaks our language, too, and I suspect it belongs to the wreck. Identify yourself, robot."

Jeff quickly stood between Mentor First and the admiral. "This large robot is Norby's father, and we have to take them both home."

"What are they talking about?" Yobo asked Fargo.

"Just what they said."

"Now see here. . . ." Yobo thundered.

Jeff sighed and closed his eyes, reaching for Norby's small hand, while Mentor First's large one came to rest upon his head. Norby must have been touching the control board, too, because Jeff could feel the ship's computer becoming part of the linkage. The augmented force grapple reached the alien ship.

Then, through the sense organs of the computer, Jeff could see the flagship of the fleet, hovering in space near the slowly turning asteroid on which the *Hopeful* rested.

The admiral was saying something in an indignant shout, but Jeff tuned it out, linking his mind to Norby and Mentor First, visualizing Jamya. The *Hopeful* trembled slightly and left the Terran solar system with the alien ship in tow.

"Ah, well," said Admiral Yobo, leaning forward to take the last cookie—after being assured that they *were* cookies—"one can't have everything. I was thinking only this morning that I need a vacation badly, and I suppose a picnic on this lawn can count as one."

Jeff grinned at Fargo with relief, but Fargo did not smile. Oola was reclining on Mentor First's lower arms while Zi talked animatedly to him. The Grand Dragon hovered near Admiral Yobo with a sparkling red smile because she had put ruby caps on her fangs in honor of the occasion. On the other side of Yobo, little Zargl nuzzled his chest under his medals.

"Oh, Admiral," gurgled Zargl, "you are the largest and most magnificent human being I've seen. Surely you are the leader of them all."

"Dragons or not," Fargo said, "that's women for you."

"You didn't mind when she switched from me to you," Jeff said.

"That was just good sense. This isn't. And look at Oola making up to Mentor First."

"Come on, Fargo. He designed her and he was her original master. Don't be so jealous."

"I'm not," said Fargo. "I'm devoted to Albany Jones and she's allergic to cats and that probably included modified smilodons."

"You're devoted when you remember to be," Jeff chided.

"I can't help distractions. I'm young, handsome, musical, brilliant—and, if we don't get the admiral back to Space Command soon—unemployed again."

Admiral Yobo rose splendidly from the cushions which had been brought hastily from the palace for the enjoyment of the Terran aliens. "Gentlemen! Ladies!" He bowed to the Grand Dragon, whose emotions caused her to breathe so hotly upon his uniform that Yobo was forced to move back a trifle.

He continued, "This has been a delightful repast and I am proud to be considered as acting ambassador from the Terran Federation, but I'm afraid that we Terrans must return to our own solar system. By now, our fleet must be convinced I have been somehow destroyed."

Mentor First, after some hesitation, held out his top right hand to the admiral, who, after an equal hesitation of his own, took it with his right hand.

"It is generous of you," said Mentor First, "to agree so readily to leave the wrecked supply ship with us after it became clear that you had no way of taking it with you."

"It's called practical politics," said Yobo, "and is much practiced in the Terran solar system."

Mentor First said, "Now that you three have consented to the Jamyn bite, and therefore understand our language, we make you honorary Jamyn, co-equal with the dragons and the Mentors, the two intelligent species on this planet."

"Thanks," said Yobo, "but. . . ."

"Furthermore, we will work on our wrecked ship, and when we understand its hyperdrive mechanism, we will bring it to the Federation as our gift for the start of trade between our two civilizations."

"And that means, Admiral," said Jeff eagerly, "that Norby would be able to stay with me. He won't be in danger from the Inventors Union once the Federation understands that we will be getting hyperdrive soon."

"We also want miniantigrav," said Yobo, his dark face solemn.

"Sir," said Jeff. "I don't want Norby to be put in danger of destruction. . . ."

"Cadet," said Yobo, "I don't either. In fact, you'll remember that I came to warn you against the aims of the Inventors Union. That, however, was before I traveled through hyperspace. It's a spectacular achievement, and the Federation should not be deprived of this technique simply because of one unimportant robot. We will do everything we can to inflict no permanent damage upon him, but Norby *must* be examined by our scientists."

"No," said Jeff, "I don't trust anybody with Norby!"

Mentor First put down Oola, whose strange fur was standing on end. He stood up, taller even than Yobo. The atmosphere of the party suddenly chilled.

"Norby is my son," said Mentor First. "He can trust only *me*. Jamya is his home, and I need him here to work on the wrecked ship."

"But Mentor. . . ." began Jeff, only to stop as the Mentor's eye patches flared red.

"Norby will stay here!"

The Grand Dragon, abandoned by Admiral Yobo, puffed out a cloud of smoke that set everyone to coughing except the two robots. Then she turned to lean heavily upon Fargo's shoulder and began to stroke her claws gently through his hair.

"You are silly, all of you," she said. "I have a plan."

"Ma'am?" said Jeff, hopefully.

"Have you all forgotten that none of you Terrans can go home unless Norby adjusts your ship to go through hyperspace? You *cannot* go to your own planet if you leave Norby here, so he *must* go with you. In that case, we Jamyns must take precautions to make sure that Norby is returned to us unharmed, and before very long."

"What do you suggest, madam?" asked Yobo with an impressive roll to his deep voice.

The Grand Dragon put her claws around Fargo and lifted him off the ground as she rose on her antigrav. "Fargo will stay here on Jamya as my hostage until Norby returns safely."

Before anyone, even Fargo, could object, the Grand Dragon flew rapidly over the trees and disappeared with Fargo in the direction of her palace.

"Norby!" said Jeff, "take me to the palace so I can get Fargo back."

"No," said Mentor First, holding Norby. "The Grand Dragon is quite correct. If Norby must leave, then Fargo must stay here till he returns."

Oola was acting strangely, her fangs lengthening and then getting shorter as she changed shape back and forth from tiger to beagle. Finally, she barked, whined and rose on her own antigrav. She licked Mentor First's bulbous head, and as he reached for her, evaded his grasp and flew off in the direction of the palace.

Mentor First folded all four of his arms. "So! Divided loyalty!"

"Father," said Norby. "Oola and I are both mixed up. She was made from animals that originated on Earth, but she was made by you, a Jamyn robot. And I am part Jamyn—and part a Terran robot. My loyalty is divided, too."

"Good," said Yobo, "then listen to your Terran part and come back to cooperate with our scientists, Norby."

"No," said Mentor First, "listen to your Jamyn part and, after you return these Terrans, come back to help me."

Norby closed all four of his eyes and withdrew into his barrel.

Jeff wanted to say, "Please stay with me, Norby," but could not. Norby had too many beings wanting him for their own purposes.

——You want him not for any purpose but your love for

him. The thought was that of Zi, who was touching Jeff's arm gently, and who had apparently sensed his thought.

Jeff smiled at her and nodded. He noticed that Mentor First's eye patches were still red, and that Admiral Yobo's chin was sticking out grimly.

——Zi, we were all so friendly for a while!

——The friendship is still there. As is my friendship for you.

——But Mentor First and Admiral Yobo seemed filled with hatred of each other. Look at them!

——Then do something about it, young Terran. Find a solution!

——That is so easy to say, Zi, but I can think of nothing.

Jeff felt very young and very unhappy. Admiral Yobo wants Norby's miniantigrav and hyperdrive, he thought. Mentor First wants his son, and to restore the other Mentors. Fargo wants the freedom to have adventures. And Norby?

Norby wants to be with a robot he considers his father, and that's worst of all. At least, for Jeff it was worst of all.

"Mentor First," said Jeff, "how is it that only Norby can fix things for you? He's not really good at it on Earth, and when you first realized who he was, you called him 'the Searcher.' He was designed to find the wrecked ship, and he has now found it. His job is over. Why can't *you* repair the hyperdrive and work out its mechanism without him?"

"I cannot do that."

"But you gave Norby *his* hyperdrive mechanism. How was that?"

Mentor First seemed to be trying to remember. "I installed Norby's device for refueling from hyperspace. I know that. It seems to me, though, that one of the other Mentors, just before he became totally deactivated, was the one who actually installed the search mechanism that enables Norby to travel through hyperspace."

"But you were the Mentor leader, with the best mind among them. If the other Mentor understood about hyperspatial drive, you must have, too."

"I cannot remember," said Mentor First.

Jeff tried again. "Well, then, what about the replacement mechanisms for all the Mentors? Now that you have them at last, and can bring them all back into existence, why not do so and have *them* help you?"

Mentor First said sadly, "Thinking is not easy for me—I have been half-demented for so many years. Perhaps you are correct, youug Terran, but Norby is my creation—like a son—and still belongs here."

Jeff bit his lip, while Norby stayed in his barrel. Zi's thought came again.

——Courage. We dragons will help the Mentors heal themselves. It is time for you Terrans to leave.

——But when we are back home, Norby will come here again and stay here. He will leave me.

——After all, that is his choice, is it not?

Norby's legs extended and he bobbed up and down. His arms came out and rested on his barrel. Apparently he had come to a decision.

"All right," he said as his head popped up, "I'll just take these Terrans home, and then return."

Already, thought Jeff, we are nothing but a bunch of Terrans to him and he doesn't care about being my partner. Aloud he said, "What about Fargo?"

"He must stay as hostage," said Mentor First. "I am sorry, but I cannot trust you, Admiral."

"Nor can I trust you," said Yobo, starting for the *Hopeful*, "On our way, Cadet. On the double!"

Jeff ran. Norby stumbled after, complaining loudly until he evidently remembered that he had antigrav, for he withdrew his legs and sailed past Jeff into the *Hopeful* just after Yobo.

He didn't even look at me as he passed, thought Jeff. He doesn't like me anymore.

"Good-bye, Jeff," said Zargl.

"Take care of yourselves," said Zi. "And take this as my gift."

She spread her wings, caught up with Jeff, and tossed him a gold collar.

"Don't try to keep Norby," said Mentor First, his four arms folded against his heavy body.

Jeff stopped at the airlock of the *Hopeful* and glared back at the Mentor. "Just you remember to tell the Grand Dragon that Fargo is my brother—and my best friend."

The airlock door closed behind Jeff, and he heard a small metallic voice say, "*I* used to be that."

Jeff gulped. Past tense. Could he change it?

13

Useful Time Trouble?

"I'm sorry, Cadet," said Yobo as Jeff sat down in Fargo's chair in the control room. "I was perhaps a bit undiplomatic in the matter of Norby, and I've alienated Mentor First needlessly."

"I would like to trust you, Admiral," said Jeff.

"I would rather you *understood* me, Cadet. My first duty is to the Terran solar system. I want the secret of hyperdrive and I must have it before anyone else gets it; in particular, before the Inventors Union does. The Union was founded for praiseworthy purposes, I suppose, but it has been increasingly taken over by militant radicals, who want to use their inventions for the establishment of power."

"Do you suppose they plan a revolution and to take over the Federation?"

"It's my job as head of Space Command to see to it that they don't. And if I'm to do that properly, Norby's talents can't be viewed as amusing toys anymore. They have become vital. We must have his secrets."

"You'll be killing the goose that lays the golden egg, sir. Norby, intact, would be far more useful to the Federation than any of his parts would be."

They both looked at Norby, who was plugged into the *Hopeful*'s computer.

"Ready to go back to the Terran solar system, Admiral?" asked Norby.

"Yes. Take me to Space Command Spome."

"Do you need my help in visualizing it?" asked Jeff.

"No," said Norby.

"Admiral," Jeff said, "please watch the monitor viewscreen closely so that you can tell us exactly where to go to drop you off."

Once the admiral was occupied in that fashion, Jeff leaned forward and touched Norby.

——You haven't taught me long-distance telepathy, so I've had to distract the admiral to keep him from watching us touch. I'm sorry that we can't trust him any more than we can trust Mentor First.

——My father is trustworthy!

——They both are, under ordinary conditions, Norby, but they both want something desperately, and that's you. They want to use your talents, find out your secrets, because for each of them, a world is at stake.

——That's true, Jeff. Mentor First wants hyperdrive before Terrans have it, because he is afraid of Terrans. I made the mistake of giving him a short telepathic course in human history. He was particularly appalled at my personal experience with the lions in the Roman Coliseum. I tried to explain that human beings have improved in behavior since then, but the fight with the pirates convinced him that you are all dangerous.

——That was thoughtless of you, Norby. What you told him of us made him suspicious and defensive, which encouraged Yobo to grow suspicious and defensive, and I just wonder if anyone will ever be friendly again.

——You won't have to be mad at me for long, Jeff. I'll take you home and then bring Fargo back, and then I'll go to Jamya where I'll be safe.

Jeff let go of Norby and put his hand over his eyes. I've messed things up even worse, he thought.

He was suddenly aware of something on his forearm. He looked down at it and discovered that the gold collar Zi had thrown to him circled it. He had put it on absently and promptly forgotten it.

"Admiral!" he said, awed. "See here. You won't have to use Norby! This collar is a powerful antigrav device. Take it to your scientists and let them use *it* to work out the mechanism for mini-antigrav. And from that they might get hyperdrive without trouble."

Yobo grunted and took the collar. "How does it work?"

Jeff said, "Imagine yourself moving up."

Yobo did, and his head hit the ceiling with an audible thump. He yelled and must have visualized dropping again, for he hit the floor with a considerably louder thump. He sat there, looking pained. "I accept the mini-antigrav part, but what makes you think that will lead us to hyperspatial travel?"

"Fargo thinks it will."

"Fargo is not a theoretical physicist, but an overgrown adolescent. I still must have Norby. My duty to the Federation. . . ."

"Ready?" asked Norby. "I can't keep my mind properly adjusted forever."

"Just a minute," said Jeff, thinking furiously. "I know you said you could hyperjump back to any solar system yourself, but I don't want you to. If you have to be taken over by the scientists of the Fleet or leave Earth for good, I must, either way, learn the technique of hyperspatial travel to the point where I can do it without you in a ship like this, adjusted for it."

Quickly, before Yobo or Norby could say anything, Jeff tuned into the controls of the computer and reached out to touch minds with Norby.

——You're up to something, Jeff.

——You bet I am, Norby. Take us into hyperspace, and then out of it to Earth, like this. Jeff visualized it for Norby, who chuckled.

As the *Hopeful* leaped out of the space-time of Jamya, Jeff felt the usual odd sensation inside himself. It was much worse than usual, almost as though something had turned over in his abdomen, but that might only have been because he was nervous about what he was doing.

The admiral said, "Very good, we're in the solar system. but where's Space Command? I don't see *any* spomes anywhere."

"Perhaps," said Jeff, "we missed the solar system. We may be in the planetary system of another star."

"Nonsense," said Yobo, "that's the moon over there. It's quite as usual. And directly ahead is Earth. Those are Terran cloud formations. I've studied them for decades. And if there's any question. . . . Can this visiscreen be adjusted for microwave emission and reception? Yes, I see it can."

He made the necessary adjustments. "We can look through the cloud cover and see the continents. Although clouds can be mistaken, continents cannot be."

Even as he spoke, the swirls of white clouds that hid the blueness of Earth's atmosphere thinned and disappeared, and the Earth's globe turned into a circle of ruddy artificial color in which red continents showed up against a black ocean.

Yobo's breath came out in a large whoosh, as though he

had been bashed in the abdomen. It was a minute or so before he could say in a strangled way, "There's no Atlantic Ocean. There's one big continent. If that's Earth—and it must be because the moon is still unmistakable—we're 250 million years ago."

Jeff stared at the viewscreen. "Interesting."

"Interesting?" Yobo didn't quite gnash his teeth, but if he had had fangs, he might have shown them. "You and that idiot robot of yours haven't just moved the *Hopeful* across hyperspace—you've moved it in time as well."

Jeff said, "I'm afraid that's part of Norby's mixed-upness, Admiral. Sometimes he takes you right where you want to go and sometimes. . . ."

"Sometimes he doesn't! That is horribly obvious, Cadet. Since when have you known that Norby gets mixed up in time as well?"

"Well, he was reading history. . . ."

The admiral waved Jeff to silence and shook his finger at Norby, whose back eyes were staring at Yobo with equal innocence. "Listen, you Jamyn robot. Did that sick Mentor make you capable of traveling through time as well as through hyperspace? Is this something that Mentor First planned?"

"No, sir." The domed hat slid down until only the tops of Norby's eyes were peering out at the admiral in his wrath. "I think that McGillicuddy did something that caused this talent of mine."

"Talent? It's a liability!"

"It's Norby's other secret," said Jeff. "The only trouble is that he can't seem to go to any time period when he existed— at least not easily—and he can't go into the future."

"You mean we can't get back to our own time?"

"Oh, no, sir. I mean he can't go into the future from our present—the present we used to be in. I mean. . . ."

"I know what you mean, Cadet. Don't confuse me. Is this— talent—controllable?"

"Not exactly, sir. Time traveling keeps getting mixed up with space traveling, and we hardly ever go directly where we want to."

The admiral sat down against the visiscreen, his huge shoulders slumped and an expression of dismay on his broad face.

"Tell me, you miserable robot and you ridiculous human being, is there any *slight* possibility of my being taken forward to a time when human beings exist on Earth?"

"Yes, *sir*," said Jeff. "Norby—let's try."

"Aye, aye, Captain," said Norby, overdoing it as usual.

The *Hopeful* shivered and shook, and so did Jeff. What if he and Norby got things so mixed up that they were all lost forever?

"I can't see a thing," said Yobo as he peered at the visiscreen. "You've brought us close enough to Earth to be inside the cloud cover. That's dangerous, a little closer and. . . ."

Jeff said hastily, "I'll bring the *Hopeful* closer through ordinary space. There'll be no danger."

The *Hopeful* poked her nose out of the cloud and the visiscreen magnified the ground. They were over a continent; in fact, they were over a city. In view were buildings and people.

Jeff said, "We're back to human beings and civilization, Admiral."

Norby said, "And the Coliseum. Jeff, it's Roman times again. We tied into where and when I was before, so maybe now I'll get to see how that gladiator came out in the fight. They took me to the lion cage just when the fight was starting. Big husky fellow, that gladiator. Reminds me of you, Admiral."

"You mean to say," said Yobo, apparently suppressing a snarl, "that your fascination with this period of history had caused what passes for a mind in that tin hat of yours to get mixed up and drag all of us into Roman times just so that you would have a chance to find out what happened to a gladiator?"

"I didn't exactly mean to do it, sir," said Norby. "I mean, even if I'd intended to do it, I couldn't always guarantee that I could. It's not my fault that I've got emotive circuits and imagination and special talents that get mixed up. I can't help being different from other robots."

Jeff manipulated the controls of the *Hopeful* and the little ship rose back into the clouds. Hiding a smile, he said, "I think we'd better go someplace else. We don't want to be seen and cause any changes in history."

"Changes in—*history?*" The admiral mopped his brow. "I suppose that if our scientists tried to copy talents such as this, we'd end up with the constant danger of messing up the past and changing history in such a way that none of us would exist?"

"I think you're right," said Jeff. "Maybe the whole human race wouldn't exist." He touched Norby.

——Mission accomplished, Norby.

——Right, Jeff. He's convinced I'm unreliable.

——Well, you *are,* aren't you?

——Not really. It's just that. . . .

——Never mind. Now let's really go home.

Only they didn't.

"Where are we now?" Yobo asked weakly.

"Norby," Jeff asked, "where are we?"

Norby was plugging himself into various parts of the computer rather frantically. "I don't know, Jeff. You got my emotive circuits stirred up and something's gone wrong."

"Can't see a thing in the visiscreen," said Yobo. "Everything is all shiny and vague."

"The screen's polarized," said Jeff in horror. "The light outside is so strong that the *Hopeful* is compensating for it by not letting it show on the visiscreen. And the instrument panel shows that the outside of the hull is getting hotter and hotter."

"I think we're stuck, Jeff," said Norby, his voice tinny.

"Unstick us," yelled Jeff. "We humans won't be able to live much longer if the heat goes any higher!"

"Neither will I," said Norby. "I have delicate brain mechanisms."

"Then put them to work on solving this problem," roared Yobo.

Jeff's head was pounding and he had never been so frightened in his life. "Have we come inside a star?"

"No, Cadet. Impossible! We'd be dead in a microsecond."

"Then where. . . . Look, Admiral, the readings show a gravitational pull on us. We're being dragged in, or down, *somewhere.*"

"I have deciphered the incoming data," said Norby importantly, "and this is the situation. We are quite close to a star much dimmer than Earth's sun, close enough so that it is heating us rapidly and is pulling at us strongly."

"And we are spiralling inward under that pull," said Jeff. "Norby—get us out of here quickly."

"But Jeff, my circuits are resonating improperly. I can't."

Jeff touched him.

——Norby, I bought and paid for you, and until you go back to Jamya, you are my robot. Join minds with me and we'll both try to move the *Hopeful* back into hyperspace.

——But Jeff, we're both mixed up when it comes to time travel.

——We tried to show how mixed up we were to fool the admiral. But now we're in trouble, and it serves us right. So let's try to move again and let's try not to be mixed up.

They touched each other and the control panel and suddenly Jeff felt as if he were the *Hopeful* herself.

He was not Jefferson Wells. He was not Norby. He was just the ship, fighting to save her life and the lives of three sentient beings she carried——and winning.

"Oof!" said Yobo, rubbing his bald head. "That was a rough trip."

"We're out!" Jeff picked up Norby and jumped around the control room. "We did it!"

"This is our own time exactly," said Norby proudly, his little arms waving triumphantly.

"Quiet!" roared Yobo. "I see Space Command ahead, and I have never before thought it to be the most beautiful object in the Universe, but I certainly think so now. Take me home."

The great artificial world of Space Command Spome, the circling wheel of the fleet's space home (for which "spome" was the universally used term), hung like a brilliant three-dimensional pattern in the blackness of space.

In the distance was Mars, around which the spome circled, and Jeff could see the lights of the small shuttle boats going back and forth. People took shuttles because the transmits were so expansive, but soon, with hyperdrive, human beings would be able to spread through the galaxy and establish a great empire of the stars.

——Maybe that's not such a great idea, Jeff.

Jeff was still holding Norby.

——The Mentors will be traveling, too, Norby. There will be room for both of us.

——And I'll be a sort of go-between, won't I. I'm part both, aren't I, Jeff?"

Jeff laughed.

——Well, let's assume an optimistic attitude, Norby. Or at least have a sense of humor about it. Everything might go well.

But Admiral Yobo shouted impatiently, "Let's get a move on, Cadet!"

14

FOREVER MIXED

Norby was gone!

Jeff waited disconsolately in the old Wells apartment on Manhattan Island, Earth. He stared out the window at Central Park, where the leaves were turning to gold and flame because it was now autumn. The dying of the year seemed to resonate inside his chest and he felt as though something were dying within him, too.

Admiral Yobo had sworn strict confidentiality concerning Norby's other secret. In fact, the admiral had shuddered and said, "I will never mention to anyone that your robot is capable of time travel. If he's the only being in the universe capable of it, I would be relieved. If even he were not capable of it, I would be still more relieved."

"I understand, sir."

"So we can forget about having our scientists go through him to dig up things too dangerous for anyone to have. In fact, if he weren't useful and your friend, I would be tempted to put him into a stasis chamber," he had said.

"No, sir. Please don't do that."

The admiral ignored the plea. "We can only wait and hope that the Mentors will consider being friends with the Federation and give us the secret of the Others' hyperdrive."

"I'm sure the fleet scientists will discover hyperdrive for themselves just as quickly."

"Probably. They've already expressed optimism over the matter of the gold collar, and that's the first step, I suppose. Just keep your robot out of their way so that there won't be any missteps!"

Norby and Jeff returned to Earth from Space Command. The admiral himself paid their transmit fees because he said he didn't want Jeff to risk going anywhere with Norby through hyperspace.

And now Norby was—Jeff hoped—back on Jamya, where Fargo was, presumably, in the Grand Dragon's castle dungeon. He pictured his older brother looking wan and emaciated and longing for Earth. If only Norby would be able to persuade the Grand Dragon and Mentor First to set Fargo free! Then if he could bring Fargo safely back, and not end up with him on some other planet or in some other time....

"Ouch!" It was a familiar voice.

"Fargo!" shouted Jeff in pure joy. "Norby got you out of Jamya!"

"Hi, Jeff," said Fargo, matter-of-factly, picking himself up from the floor and rubbing his rear end violently. "What was your hurry, Norby?" he asked. "I was just beginning dessert when you appeared out of nowhere and grabbed me into hyperspace."

Fargo was resplendent in a crimson garment with a full cape that was spangled with gold slivers. He wore a gold belt, crimson shoes, and a flashy diamond ring. He did not look at all emaciated. In fact, he might have gained a pound or two.

"Jeff was worried about you, I'm sure," said Norby through his hat as he rolled across the floor, all his limbs retracted. His head popped up and he righted himself with his feet out. "He probably thought that Her Dragonship had you imprisoned in the lowest dungeon under the castle moat."

"Imprisoned? I'd been serenading her in the most impressive room in her palace and we were well into another banquet, so couldn't you have waited till after dinner?"

"Another banquet?" wailed Jeff. At fourteen, one feels hungry much more often than a twenty-four-year-old brother can appreciate.

"Yes," said Fargo. "A special feast in honor of a song I wrote especially for her highness."

"Fargo, old pal," said Jeff, through his teeth, "I don't suppose you mind that *I* was concerned about you, but Albany hasn't been getting much attention from you lately."

Fargo had the grace to blush. He said, "Well, I'll go and see her just as soon as I wash up. You call her at the department and let her know I'm back. Oh, and I had time to grab a present for you before Norby dragged me away into hyperspace and home. Here!"

Fargo tossed Jeff something green and leathery that resembled a miniature hassock about the size of a baseball.

"Oola's egg!" said Jeff. "It couldn't be anything else."

"Right on," said Fargo. "This female pet will be yours."

"No beagles? Not that I dislike beagles," said Jeff hastily, because he didn't, "but I have wanted a kitten."

"You may get one with saberteeth, if you're not careful," said Norby sourly. "That hassock grows slowly until the All-Purpose Pet is ready, so you'd better keep it with you and influence it by thinking constantly of friendly kittens. You'll undoubtedly like it better than you do me."

Jeff felt a leap of hope in his mind, but he tried not to put pressure on Norby. He opened his mouth to reply but could think of nothing.

"Close your mouth, Jeff. I haven't finished telling you about All-Purpose Pets. When they're upset enough, they grow a leather shell around them, and then you can't get them out—perhaps for generations—until you sing the right song, and only they know what the right song is."

"Like the first Oola," said Jeff, turning the egg in his hands.

"Call this one Oola Two," said Fargo.

"I will."

"Huh," said Norby. "I suppose our apartment will soon be overrun with green critters."

"Oh?" said Jeff. "You said you were going home to Jamya."

"Where's home?" asked Norby, shutting his eyes that faced Jeff. He stomped noisily across the floor to the main computer terminal and tuned it to a particularly idiotic puzzle game.

Fargo looked at Jeff, who gulped again and pretended to be absorbed in Oola's egg. He could not beg Norby to stay, nor order him. Norby was no longer his possession, but his partner, and the decision had to be up to Norby alone.

"Maybe you've got two homes, Norby," said Fargo gently. "How about using both?"

Norby turned off the game and shut all four eyes. "Maybe nobody wants me."

There was something in Jeff's throat and, when he tried to speak, he croaked.

"Well, well," said Fargo, stretching. "I think I'll have to leave this to you two to settle. I'm going to wash and change my clothing. Albany believes in utilitarian clothing and disapproves of men wearing diamonds."

"How about gold belts?" said Jeff, getting his voice back.

Out of the corner of his eye he saw Norby's metal eyelids snap up. Jeff took a deep breath.

"Oh, that," said Fargo carelessly, unhooking the one he was wearing and tossing it to Jeff. "That's a special antigrav belt the grand dragon had ordered for me. We'll take turns at it until the fleet scientists design some of their own."

Norby snatched the belt from Jeff and handed it back to Fargo. "No," he said. "You keep it, Fargo, Jeff won't need this. He'll have me most of the time."

Jeff let out the breath and picked up Norby.

Fargo smiled and said, "I'm in charge of this family, Norby, and perhaps I should have doubts about you. It took you a long time to get the *Hopeful* back to Space Command. Didn't you almost lose my ship—and my brother and my admiral?"

"On purpose," said Jeff, holding Norby tightly, "So Yobo would see him as unreliable and not want him."

Norby jiggled his head up and down in assent. Then he grabbed onto Jeff's arm and said, "It gave me time to think, and I decided that I could visit Jamya and my father, but what I really wanted after all was to stay with Jeff. He is my *friend.*"

"I see," said Fargo, "but I suspect that you're just as mixed up as ever, Norby."

Norby said, "I'm afraid so," and one of his eyes that faced Jeff closed its metal eyelid in an exaggerated and tremendous wink.

"Norby," said Jeff. "You're *my* friend, too, and I want you just the way you are, forever mixed up."